A Rose for Beauty by Irene B. Brand
Beauty Bartlett's Virginia home has been sold to Grant Palmer, a man with scarred features, and her family has been displaced to Kansas. But Beauty returns to help pay off her father's debt to Grant. Can she help him with the internal scars that run much deeper than anything visible?

The Shoemaker's Daughter by Lynn A. Coleman
Cameron Flynn's shoe repair business is dwindling, as he is physically unable to keep up with orders. Marissa Jones, the old owner's daughter, decides to secretly help out. But if Cameron finds out, will he resent her help, since she caused part of his problem?

Lily's Plight by Yvonne Lehman
Lily White goes to work for Grant Harmen's advertising agency and is immediately attracted to him. But he is involved with a witchy lady client. Can her seven new male friends help her fit into the challenging job?

Better to See You by Gail Gaymer Martin
Visiting her ailing grandmother in Germany, Lucy Blake, or "Red" for her hair, meets and rekindles an old flame with Ron Woodson. He is also from the States and learning woodcrafting in Germany. Can Ron help Lucy when a criminal tries to take advantage of her kindly grandmother's savings?

Fairy-Tale Brides

A Rose for Beauty © 2000 by Irene B. Brand
The Shoemaker's Daughter © 2000 by Lynn A. Coleman
Lily's Plight © 2000 by Yvonne Lehman
Better to See You © 2000 by Gail Gaymer Martin

ISBN 1-59310-830-3

Cover image by Dan Yaccarino

Illustrations by Mari Goering

Published by Barbour Publishing, Inc., P.O. Box 719, Uhrichsville, Ohio 44683, www.barbourbooks.com

Our mission is to publish and distribute inspirational products offering exceptional value and biblical encouragement to the masses.

 Member of the
Evangelical Christian
Publishers Association

Printed in the United States of America.

Fairy-Tale Brides

Four Modern-Day Love Stories
with All the Enchantment of Legendary Romance

Irene B. Brand
Lynn A. Coleman
Yvonne Lehman
Gail Gaymer Martin

BARBOUR
PUBLISHING

A Rose for Beauty

by Irene B. Brand

Chapter 1

The taxi turned off the highway onto a secluded lane lined with blooming dogwood trees. With hands clenched tightly in her lap, Beauty Bartlett's gray eyes eagerly surveyed the red brick Georgian structure that had been her home until a year ago. She had longed for months to see Barwood Estate again, but she anticipated a bittersweet homecoming. The taxi stopped beside the six curved marble steps that led to the front portico.

"Which door, Miss?" the driver asked.

"The service entrance, please," Beauty answered around the knot in her throat.

He revved the motor and sped to the rear of the house. After she paid the driver, he deposited her two suitcases at the foot of the back steps and drove away. Beauty paused to look at the boxwood-enclosed terrace that separated the house from the spacious lawn, sweeping toward a small tributary of the Elizabeth River flowing toward Chesapeake Bay. Taking a deep breath and straightening her shoulders, she rang the doorbell.

Who would answer? Would it be Grant Palmer himself? Would it be Mrs. Fillmore, the housekeeper who'd stayed on when the Bartletts moved away?

Beauty's speculation ended when the door was opened by a young woman in a light green uniform, a stranger to Beauty.

"I'm Annabelle Bartlett. I have an appointment to see Mr. Palmer."

"This way, please," the maid said, motioning toward a hallway that connected the service quarters to the main section of the fifteen-room house. Beauty had lived here most of her life, and it was awkward to be treated as a visitor.

Don't look at his face. Don't look at his face, she mentally repeated over and over. To serve as her father's representative, she could not antagonize Grant Palmer. *Do not look at his face!* she reminded herself one last time as the maid knocked on a door and a deep, pleasing voice said, "Come in."

Beauty's face blanched as she entered the office and saw a tall stranger standing at her father's desk. Her eyes focused on the thick, blond hair curling around his ears, his deep blue eyes, and the broad shoulders that tapered to a slender waist. She did not look at his face.

"I'm Annabelle Bartlett," she said, praying that the emotional strain she experienced wasn't evident on her face.

"Sit down, Miss Bartlett," he said in his pleasant voice. "How is your father's health?"

"His speech has returned to normal, and he's slowly regaining use of the left side of his body."

"He's had many problems during the past few years. No wonder he had a stroke."

"Yes," she answered, unwilling to discuss her father's downfall.

"Am I to understand that you came here of your own

free will to finish the work your father started?" His blue eyes searched her face intently.

"That's right. I appreciate the opportunity you've given Father to settle his debts. After he became ill and could no longer fulfill his commitment to you, he said you were willing for one of his children to work in his place. My brothers have taken jobs in other parts of the country, and my two sisters are ill-suited for this work, so I came."

She didn't add that her sisters had refused. Frances had told her father, "You needn't think I'm going to work for that beast and have to look at his scarred face." And Etta had said, "Let him lose the money he loaned you. Nobody but a beast would have taken our home."

"You said your name is Annabelle. Are you the one called Beauty? I heard your father use that name in speaking of one of his daughters."

She smiled. "My father started calling me that when I was a child. My family and close friends still use the nickname."

"I prefer to call you Beauty," he said.

"As you wish, Sir," Beauty replied, coloring slightly. This wasn't a liberty she granted easily, but her father's reputation was in Mr. Palmer's hands.

He pushed a button on his desk. "I'll have Mrs. Fillmore show you to your quarters. Since you must be tired from your trip today, we'll meet in the morning at eight o'clock to discuss your duties."

Beauty glanced quickly around the oak-paneled office. With the exception of the elaborate computer station in one corner, the room was as her father had left it. The walls, lined with paintings of ancient seacraft, expressed the shipping interest of the Bartlett family.

The door opened and a short, scrawny woman entered. Mrs. Fillmore stopped to look at Beauty, she shook her graying head, and her eyes filled with compassion. With a contentious glance at her employer, the housekeeper moved quickly to wrap Beauty in a bearlike hug.

"You poor child!" she said, sniffing loudly. "Come along. I'll get you settled."

"I'll be ready in the morning, Mr. Palmer," Beauty said as Mrs. Fillmore tugged on her hand and led her from the room. He nodded, and Beauty's eyes had a glimpse of his face, but she looked away quickly before he could see the horror in her eyes.

Beauty. Grant couldn't imagine a more appropriate name. She had silver-flecked gray eyes and long black hair that fell around her shoulders in soft waves. She stood at medium height and her body was well formed. She had even, regular features, a firm chin, and teeth that flashed pearly white when she smiled.

"That insufferable man is putting you in a maid's room on the third floor," Mrs. Fillmore said when the office door was closed behind them, and Beauty understood the housekeeper's belligerent attitude toward her employer. Mrs. Fillmore had always been Beauty's champion.

"Where else would he put me?" Beauty said, not wanting Mrs. Fillmore to guess her own dismay as she trudged up the back stairs.

When she entered the small room furnished only with a single bed, a dresser, a table, and one chair, Beauty thought longingly of the luxurious bedroom and adjoining bath she'd once occupied on the second floor. Blinking her eyelids rapidly, she looked out the dormer window at the lawn and its raised brick terrace edged with perennial borders.

Perhaps sensing that Beauty needed time to compose herself, Mrs. Fillmore said, "There won't be anybody sleeping on the third floor except you, so you can have the bathroom to yourself. Anna, the girl you saw, sleeps in the room next to the kitchen. I'm still in my apartment in the left wing. We're the only live-in help. Most of Mr. Palmer's helpers are daytime employees hired through an agency in Norfolk. I don't know whether he liked it or not, but I told Mr. Palmer you'd be eating with me. I won't have you eating at the same table with the servants."

Mrs. Fillmore's brown eyes snapped with anger, and Beauty laid her hand on the housekeeper's rigid right arm. "Don't forget what we Bartletts owe Mr. Palmer. Without his intervention, Father might have ended up in prison. After the hurricane destroyed the Bartlett shipyards and the insurance company went bankrupt and defaulted, none of Father's friends would help him. Grant Palmer bought our home so Father could pay off his creditors, and he personally took up the notes on that shipwreck salvaging venture."

"Which also turned into a disaster!" Mrs. Fillmore said.

"That wasn't Mr. Palmer's fault either. The salvaging venture was Father's last asset, and when the crew didn't recover enough artifacts to pay for the expenses, he lost everything."

"And I'll admit Mr. Palmer did pay for an ambulance to take your father to Kansas when he got sick. Luckily, that farm your mother inherited in Kansas wasn't included in the Bartlett holdings, so you at least had a place to live." She patted Beauty's shoulder. "Here I am chattering at you when you need to rest. Come down to my rooms in an hour, and we'll catch up on family news while we eat."

Determined not to dwell on the bad luck that had ruined her father, Beauty unpacked the luggage and put her belongings in the closet and dresser. She couldn't get that one brief look at Grant's face out of her mind. The right side of his face bloomed with health, but shiny red and white charred patches marred his features on the left. Between the splotches, the skin was stretched and scaly, causing his lips to curve upward into a lopsided grimace.

Beauty had seen a few pictures of Grant before his face had been marred, when he'd been a handsome, young man. The heir to one of Virginia's vast fortunes, Grant had become the CEO of one of Norfolk's banks when he was in his early thirties, and he had the reputation of a shrewd, but honest, businessman. Since money wouldn't have been an issue, she wondered why Grant hadn't had his blemishes altered by skin grafting.

Unpacking didn't take long. She hadn't brought many clothes, for she anticipated a brief stay at Barwood. The long train trip from Kansas, combined with the trauma of returning to her home under such circumstances, had drained Beauty's strength. She stretched out on the bed for a few minutes' rest before she went to have dinner with Mrs. Fillmore.

"God," Beauty prayed, "give me courage to handle this difficult situation, and help me to have the right attitude."

In spite of her placating words to Mrs. Fillmore, Beauty was sometimes resentful of the circumstances that had forced her into such a position. The problem was, she didn't have anyone to blame. A natural disaster had destroyed the Bartlett shipyards. She supposed she could blame the insurance company for going bankrupt or her father for overextending his finances to indulge his hobby of collecting rare nautical treasures. Remembering Simon Bartlett's poor health, she couldn't blame him either.

Certainly, she couldn't blame Grant Palmer, who'd been more than generous with her father. He could have taken Simon's nautical collection and made a large profit on it, but he'd given Simon sanctuary at Barwood until he could catalog the vast assortment of items and find a buyer for them. With the proceeds from that sale, Simon would have enough to pay off his debt to Palmer, with perhaps some money left over. Even if her father was still penniless, at least his reputation for honesty would be intact.

Simon had tried to persuade her not to come to Barwood, and when she'd demanded why, he'd said he didn't want her working so closely with Mr. Palmer. When she pressed for a reason, he wouldn't give one, latently assuring her that the present owner of Barwood would be kind to her.

She hoped she'd been successful in hiding, from both Mrs. Fillmore and Grant, her humiliation to be sleeping in a maid's room when she'd once been hostess of the Barwood estate. After her mother's death, six years ago, Beauty had taken over the household management and the supervision of her two younger sisters. Although she still missed her mother very much, Beauty was glad that Idelle Bartlett hadn't lived to see the disintegration of her family.

But Beauty knew Mrs. Bartlett would have met the situation with her head up. "Pride goes before destruction, a haughty spirit before a fall," Mrs. Bartlett often admonished her children, but except for Beauty, Mrs. Bartlett's words had fallen on deaf ears. Her sisters had railed at their father when he lost his fortune, although before that, they'd enjoyed the largesse of his money.

Beauty believed the reality of one's Christian faith wasn't tried when all was going well. The true test of a Christian was when she was down-and-out, struggling under difficult conditions without any hope of improvement, yet still trusting in God's providence. She was at that place now. Beauty left the bed and reached for the Bible she'd placed on the table. She searched until she found encouragement from God's Word to fortify her during the next few months.

In his letter to the Colossians, the apostle Paul had written, "As God's chosen people, holy and dearly loved, clothe yourselves with compassion, kindness, humility, gentleness and patience." She would exemplify those virtues in her relationship with Grant Palmer. She wasn't aware of his spiritual beliefs, but she intended to set a Christian example before him while she fulfilled Simon's obligations.

Determined to hide her unhappiness from Mrs. Fillmore, Beauty talked about the farm in Kansas during the meal and how they'd managed to live there for a year.

"The farm consists of a thousand acres of prime crop land, and my brothers could have made money for all of us if they'd tried. They didn't like the hard work needed to be farmers, so they went off to seek their fortunes elsewhere," Beauty said. "Father accepted the situation and was doing his best to learn to farm until he heard the salvage ship had returned to Norfolk. He thought his fortune would be restored, so he turned the farm over to renters and hurried to Norfolk to find out what treasures had been recovered. He was so sure he was rich again that he promised us lots of presents. Frances and Etta asked for lavish gifts. Somehow, I suspected that salvage operation wouldn't recoup our fortunes, so I didn't ask for anything except a rose from Mother's grave."

"He asked Mr. Palmer for a rose to take to you."

Beauty smiled sadly. "It was wilted by the time he got home, but I pressed the rose in my Bible."

"To give Mr. Palmer his due—he's taken care of Mrs. Bartlett's grave as if his own mother were buried there. He planted a boxwood fence around it and made it into an attractive rose garden."

"Before he restricts my activities, I'm going to visit my mother's grave. Surely he won't mind."

"I don't think so," Mrs. Fillmore assured her. "At times, he growls like a bear and he can be a hard man, but I suspect his anger breaks out when he thinks about his disfigurement."

When Idelle Bartlett died, Simon hadn't buried her in the family cemetery; instead, he'd chosen a spot near the house visible from his office window. Beauty walked toward the formal gardens through the honeysuckle-covered pergola near the house. She took a pathway that wound along the clematis-covered fences, the extensive perennial borders, and flowering trees and shrubs. Wooden carvings, garden seats, fountains, and statuary gave a touch of elegance to the vast expanse of lawn. Bluebirds flitted back and forth, preparing their nests in strategically located boxes; and robins, with twigs of grass in their beaks, streaked into dense shrubbery. Spring had come to Virginia!

Dozens of rosebushes circled the neatly mown plot

around Idelle's grave. Only a few of the roses were blooming, but Beauty bent to sniff one of the fragrant flowers. She sat on a white marble bench and listened to a mockingbird's song.

"God, thank You for Grant Palmer and his kindness. Give me the courage to repay his goodness with loyalty and compassion. In spite of his wealth, he seems to be lonely. Help me look beyond his scars and find the real man."

Chapter 2

Grant stood at the window and watched Beauty's slow progress to her mother's grave. He wondered how difficult it had been for her to return to Barwood, knowing that the ancestral home was hers no longer. He'd heard of Beauty Bartlett long before he'd come into possession of her family's estate. She had the reputation of being a gracious, compassionate woman whose beauty was more than skin deep. He'd bought the Bartlett estate "lock, stock, and barrel," with the family removing only clothing and personal items.

Bartlett ancestry meant nothing to him, and he'd sometimes wondered why he kept personal mementos of Beauty's family. He'd hardly changed anything in the house. Often he'd paused in the drawing room and studied the portrait of Beauty hanging over the mantel. The likeness must have been painted when she was in her late teens. Grant thought that the vivid gray eyes in the portrait didn't notice the scars on his face, and he sometimes wondered what effect his disfigurement would have on Beauty Bartlett if he should ever meet her in the flesh.

After a year of looking at Beauty's picture, he felt as if he knew her, often wishing she would step out of the picture and talk to him. Why else had he suggested that Simon send one of his children to inventory his nautical collection when he could have gotten dozens of authorities on naval history closer at home? Had he hoped that Beauty might take over for her father?

Eager to know if she'd come of her own free will, he had watched her expression carefully. If she'd noticed his scars, she hadn't reacted as most people did. In the past five years, he'd gotten used to two reactions when people saw him for the first time. Either they registered horror and disgust, or their eyes filled with pity. All looked away immediately. Beauty's gaze, though fleeting, had remained serene and cordial.

Grant picked up the binoculars laying on the window ledge and focused on Beauty where she sat on the marble bench. Her face wasn't serene now, and he felt her pain as she mourned a lost mother and the breakup of her family. Had he contributed to her sorrow by treating her like a servant?

"And what do you find interesting from that window?"

The words jolted Grant out of his reverie, and he whirled to face his best friend, Dallas Winthrop, leaning against the doorjamb, a lazy smile on his strong, lean features, his unruly dark hair drooping over his forehead.

Returning to his desk, Grant said, "There's no law against looking out a window."

Dallas sauntered over to the window. "Well, well!" Dallas picked up the binoculars and looked at the rose garden. "Well!" he said again after a few minutes. He sat in a leather lounge chair near Grant's desk.

"So that's the famed Beauty Bartlett! When did she get here?"

"A few hours ago," Grant said shortly, toying with some papers on his desk, reluctant to look at Dallas. "What have you been doing today?" he asked his friend.

"Same old thing. I spent the morning playing golf and tennis, and this afternoon, I hung out at the club with my friends."

Dallas had inherited a fortune, too, but unlike Grant, he admitted he was too lazy to work. He'd invested his money and let it work for him while he loafed his life away. Grant, who didn't approve of laziness in anyone, wondered how he and Dallas could be such good friends. But Dallas was Grant's only confidant, and in spite of his other faults, Dallas would never betray a confidence.

"What do you think of her?" Dallas asked.

"It's too soon to tell, and I doubt I'll see much of her. She came here to do a job. When that's finished, she'll go back to Kansas."

"She might be willing to stay on indefinitely if you gave her the right encouragement."

This wasn't the first time Dallas had played the matchmaker for Grant. "I don't see you in any hurry to take a wife. I'm happy as I am."

"Ah! You lie," Dallas said with the candor of an old friend. "You're lonely. You need a wife. Why do you keep punishing yourself just because Callie broke your engagement after your accident? Not all women are like her."

"Show me a woman who loves me instead of my money, and I might consider matrimony. I don't doubt there are women who'd marry me, scars and all, and then divorce me in a few months, expecting a generous stipend."

"I don't know why I continue to argue with you, but I've told you before—you don't have to have those scars.

You could have had surgery on your face when the accident occurred, and now with the rapid advances of laser surgery, your face could be scar-free in no time. Why don't you do it?"

Grant walked to the window again and picked up the binoculars. Beauty was slowly returning to the house, walking with head down, so he couldn't see her expression. He wanted to comfort her and restore her to the former position as daughter of this house. When Beauty passed from view at the rear of the house, he laid down the binoculars.

"No! I was the same person after I had the accident as I was before. Callie threw me over because my face was scarred, which proved to me that she didn't want *me* but what marriage to me would give her. Having to live with my disfigurement is daunting enough, but I have a lot of scars on the inside, too. My heart is too vulnerable to be hurt again. Besides, I haven't met any woman I want to marry."

"Until now," Dallas said softly.

"Don't be foolish! Beauty Bartlett is a stranger to me."

Promptly at eight o'clock the next morning, Beauty knocked on the office door. Despite the trauma of her homecoming, she'd slept well, and she'd taken special care with her makeup to erase any sign of fatigue around her eyes. She'd twisted her long hair into a roll on the back of her head and secured it with two jeweled combs she'd inherited from her grandmother. She wore a pair of dark brown slacks, a plaid, long-sleeved shirt, and comfortable shoes.

Be cheerful and don't look at his face! she mentally admonished herself before she opened the door at his word.

"Good morning, Mr. Palmer," she said brightly. "I'm ready to start working."

Grant stared at her, his blue eyes dull and guarded. "You apparently slept well," he said grumpily.

What had she done to irritate him already?

"Yes, I did. I was tired after the long train ride."

"You didn't fly?"

"No, by bus into Kansas City, and a train from there."

Apparently, she couldn't afford a plane ticket. He should have thought of that. Grant motioned her to sit down.

"Your father may have told you what he was doing. Although I bought Barwood as it stood, I didn't feel justified in taking your father's vast nautical collection. He thought he could pay his debts with the income from the salvage ship, and when that venture was unprofitable, I gave him the opportunity to sell the nautical collection to pay off the remainder of his debts. He took inventory during the daytime, and I entered the items on the computer at night, categorizing the collection into equipment, paintings, photographs, and miscellaneous items."

"Before he had the stroke, Father had written several letters to me, discussing his work. He indicated it would take several more weeks to finish the inventory, but since I won't be as efficient as he, it may take me longer."

"There's no hurry. I purchased several nautical memorabilia books, and if there's something you can't identify, you'll probably find it listed in one of those books. I'm filing a description of everything, and when you're finished, I'll advertise the collection. I expect the sale to not only provide funds to pay off your father's remaining indebtedness, but perhaps something also left over to provide a new start for him."

"I've had computer experience, and if it will be any help to you, I can take care of entering the items on the computer, too. I'm sure you're busy with your other work."

Grant readily agreed.

"I'll provide a computer for you in the warehouse, so you can list the items as you go along." He took a key from the desk drawer. "I assume you know where your father stored his collection, but I'll walk to the warehouse with you before I go to work, in case you have any questions."

The warehouse had been a barn and stable when Beauty's great-grandfather had established the estate. Several years ago, when Simon rented the farming rights to his neighbors and no longer needed storage buildings, he started depositing his artifact collection in the barn. When Grant opened the door, Beauty was overwhelmed with the conglomeration before her. She'd forgotten how many things her father had collected.

"My, what a mess!" she said. "Apparently, Father never sorted anything. He just kept buying!" She shook her head. "I'm afraid Father didn't always exercise good judgment."

Grant apparently was of the same opinion, but he only said, "He did purchase some rare items, and that will be a benefit for him now. Anything that's too heavy for you to move, I'll take care of it at night."

"Thank you. Today, I'll try to get oriented."

The first week passed quickly as Beauty cataloged posters, passenger lists, china, menus, souvenir logs, and other items used during the great days of transatlantic liners, and she had hardly touched the surface of the collection. She took a cursory inventory of the rest of the things Simon had gathered. Hundreds of prints and paintings of steamboats and schooners. He had models of famous ships, including the *Mayflower,* one of Columbus's ships, and an American gunboat used in the War of 1812. There were replicas of the Civil War ironclads, the *Monitor* and the *Merrimack.* He had books and hardware from a ship captured by American privateers in 1778. A birchbark canoe, whaling harpoons, and a vast array of nautical instruments attested to the wide range of Simon's interests.

In spite of Mrs. Fillmore's scoldings, Beauty worked long hours, and although Grant admonished her to pace her work, he joined her in the warehouse in the evenings. They worked companionably, admiring the unusual items and recording the information on the computer. When they closed the warehouse for the night, they walked to the house side by side, often stopping by the rose garden where Mrs. Bartlett was buried.

"Thanks for caring for Mama's grave," Beauty said one evening. "It concerned me to leave my mother's final resting place in the hands of strangers."

He acknowledged her appreciation with a nod and dared to sit beside her on the marble bench, their shoulders touching. It had been more than a week since Beauty had come into his life, and he was yet to find any dent in her friendly attitude toward him. If there was any resentment in this woman, it hadn't surfaced.

"And I also appreciate your kindness to Father. His downfall wasn't his fault, but it would have shamed him to declare bankruptcy and have his creditors lose what he owed them. I'm sure you paid more than this estate is worth and more than anyone else would have paid. Thank you for that, too."

Grant squirmed uncomfortably. "Not many people would thank me for taking their home away from them."

"You didn't take it away. We lost it. I'm happy that you've kept Barwood in such good condition."

"If I hadn't liked the property, I wouldn't have bought it."

"Then you've been happy here?" She glanced toward him and had a full view of the scarred side of his face, for he stared straight ahead.

"I haven't been happy for a long time, but Barwood has served as a sanctuary at the end of the day."

Without asking permission, Beauty picked a red rose from the rambler on the trellis behind them. She laid it on her mother's headstone. Grant picked a bud and placed it beside the one she'd chosen.

Walking on toward the house, he said, "You've worked night and day since you've been here. Tomorrow is Sunday. I want you to take the day off." He hesitated. "We can go for a drive if you like."

"I want to go to church, if you don't mind. Our family held membership in a large church in Norfolk, but I wouldn't go there even if I had a way to travel. We were affluent when we worshiped with that congregation, and I'm not quite ready to meet my friends yet. I don't think any of them would shun me, but I don't want to experience their pity."

Grant could understand that well enough. "I'd be glad to take you to any church you want to attend."

"There's a small church a few miles away, and if I cut across the estate, it's only a half-hour walk. I'll feel more comfortable there, and I'd enjoy walking over our former property—if you don't mind."

"What kind of monster do you think I am?" he demanded angrily. "Go where you want to. I haven't placed any restrictions on you."

"That's true, and I apologize. I've tried not to overstep my position. I know very well why I'm here."

Why did she turn down my offer to go for a drive? Grant wondered. *Doesn't she want to be seen with me?* Fearing that might be true, he didn't insist on taking her to church.

Chapter 3

Three weeks later, as Grant entered the rear door of the house after his day's work, a florist delivery truck drove up to the steps. He couldn't imagine who would be sending flowers to his house, so he waited until the driver opened the rear of her van and started toward him with a crystal vase containing three red roses.

"Does Beauty Bartlett live here?" she asked.

"Yes," Grant said, and his heart plummeted. Who would be sending roses to Beauty?

"Will you see that she gets these?"

"Yes."

"I hope she has a happy birthday," the woman said as she slid into the driver's seat of the van and drove off.

Grant carried the vase inside and, without a prick of conscience, pulled the card from the small envelope.

"Happy twenty-seventh birthday, Beauty. Father."

The message brought elation and dismay to Grant. He was relieved the flowers were from Simon Bartlett, but he was unhappy to know he was almost thirteen years older than Beauty. Grant placed the vase on a hall table where Beauty would see it when she came from the warehouse. He strode purposefully down the hall and entered Mrs. Fillmore's office.

"Why didn't you tell me about Beauty's birthday?" he demanded.

Surprise overspread Mrs. Fillmore's face. "I had no idea it would concern you," she said.

"It does. Please tell Beauty that I want her to have dinner with me at seven o'clock, and tell the cook to prepare her favorite foods. Perhaps you can think of a special treat she's always had for her birthday."

Mrs. Fillmore glanced at the clock. "That only gives the staff three hours," she said to his back as he left her office.

After several telephone calls, Grant located Dallas at the country club.

"I want you to do me a favor," he said when his friend answered. "There's a lapel pin in the jewelry store next door to our bank. I want you to buy the pin and bring it to me. By the time I drive back into town, the store will be closed."

"Why didn't you buy it before you went home?"

"I didn't know I wanted it then. Will you do it?"

"Sure. How much do you want to pay for the pin?"

"Whatever it takes to buy it. If they won't charge it to me, pay for it and I'll reimburse you. I need it before seven o'clock."

"Describe it. There may be more than one pin in that window."

"The pin is shaped like a rose stem, with a ruby rosebud attached. Have it gift-wrapped."

"Will you tell me why you want it?"

"Later on, but not now. I'm busy."

"If I go to all of this trouble, may I stay for dinner?"

"No."

Dallas laughed. "You owe me, buddy."

Smiling, Grant said, "I don't doubt I'll have to pay for this favor. Hurry!"

Beauty's birthday gave Grant a reason to make a move that he'd been contemplating for days. He'd lain awake too many nights since Beauty had arrived at Barwood, fretting because she was sleeping in the servants' quarters rather than in her own bedroom a few doors away from his room. He'd watched her carefully for signs of resentment or for any indication that she was attempting to attract his attention. Or that his scarred face was revolting to her. His close scrutiny had revealed that she regarded him serenely as if his face was as untouched as a baby's skin.

She was friendly and easy to talk to, but she'd never flirted with him. In a few weeks she'd been able to do what no one else had done in five years. She'd given him back his self-esteem. Since his accident, he hadn't sought anyone's company. If he had friends, they'd made the overtures. He met people on a business basis, but he had no social life. When he finished work, he came home. The weeks that Beauty had been at Barwood, he'd hurried home in the evening to spend time with her. And she seemed to enjoy his company! Even after he went to his room at night, her presence stayed with him. How much did he want from Beauty Bartlett?

Grant didn't blame God for the accident that had maimed him, but he'd been so full of bitterness, he couldn't worship God. Being with Beauty had kindled a rebirth of his spirit. She didn't talk to him about God, but he'd never known anyone to set a better Christian example. Life hadn't been easy for Beauty. Her mother had died, her father had lost his fortune, and she'd had to leave her ancestral home. How had she attained such spiritual maturity in twenty-seven years? He remembered a Bible verse that said, "Set an example for the believers in speech, in life, in love, in faith, and in purity." Beauty exemplified those words.

The day had been long for Beauty. She'd never spent a birthday away from her father, and stopping by her mother's grave didn't boost her spirits. Her steps lagged as she walked to the house. The floral arrangement was like a ray of sunshine. Tears pricked her eyes as she looked at the card. Her father couldn't afford to send her roses, which made the gift even more precious.

She picked up the vase and walked down the hall to Mrs. Fillmore's office. The housekeeper cradled the house phone as Beauty entered.

"Look, Mrs. Fillmore. Father sent roses. I knew he wouldn't forget me if he was able. I'd like to telephone and talk to him, but I don't want to reverse the charges, and I certainly can't make a call from here."

"Sit down," Mrs. Fillmore said, and she got up from the desk to close the door. "I have a feeling conditions are going to improve. You have an invitation for dinner."

Beauty listened in wonder as Mrs. Fillmore repeated Grant's words. "How did he know?" she asked.

"He's the one who received the bouquet when the florist brought it."

"But you and I were going to celebrate my birthday!"

"Makes no difference. We've been eating together every day since you got here. If Mr. Palmer wants to start treating you as a guest rather than his hired help, I won't throw a hitch in the plan," Mrs. Fillmore said, a scheming glint in her eyes. "I'll send in that Italian creme cake I made for dessert, and he won't need to know that I'd already prepared it."

Looking down at her soiled slacks, Beauty said, "But my clothes! I only brought a couple of casual dresses to wear to church."

"Have you forgotten that box of clothes you left behind when you moved to Kansas?"

"Oh, yes. I hardly thought I'd have much use for dinner garments on the farm. That's the reason I asked you to donate them to charity."

Mrs. Fillmore laughed. "I didn't do it. I stashed that box away in my bedroom closet." Bouncing with energy, the housekeeper entered her private rooms.

When she produced the box, Beauty thought of the sadness she felt when she'd packed those clothes—expensive silk, linen, cotton, and knit garments she'd never expected to need again. Appraising Beauty, Mrs. Fillmore said, "You've lost some weight, but these should still fit you."

Not wanting to overdress for the occasion, Beauty chose a sleeveless black imported crepe dress with a scoop neck style and a flowing, full, calf-length skirt.

"That's the right choice," Mrs. Fillmore approved. "I can freshen the dress by running it through the fluff cycle of the dryer. You put that on with your mother's pearls, and we'll see if that won't open up Grant Palmer's eyes."

"Mrs. Fillmore! He's only being kind because it's my birthday."

"No. Mr. Palmer's lonely, and if you play your cards right, you might not have to return to Kansas."

"Stop that kind of scheming," Beauty said coldly, "or I won't even go to the dinner. I'll be ill at ease anyway without you talking like that."

❖

Beauty brushed her hair and let it flow freely over her shoulders, enhanced her pearl-like skin with makeup, and sprayed on a faint fragrance of French perfume out of a bottle that she hadn't used since she'd moved to the farm. She wore the black dress without jewelry.

A few minutes before seven, she went downstairs and presented herself to Mrs. Fillmore for inspection. The housekeeper's eyes gleamed with satisfaction.

"Mr. Palmer asked me to bring you to the dining room."

Located across the gallery from the formal drawing room, the dining room was furnished with two tables, and the smallest table was set with the Bartlett crystal, china, and silver used only on special occasions. With a shy smile, Beauty stood on the threshold as Grant approached her.

"Happy Birthday!" he said, his blue eyes glowing. She'd never seen him in this mood before. Did he enjoy making others happy? "You should have told me, so I could have laid more elaborate plans."

He wore a white suit with a blue knit shirt that reflected the shade of his eyes. He had his smooth profile turned toward her, and he looked very handsome.

"I hadn't given much thought to my birthday," she said, "but it's thoughtful of you to take notice of it."

He seated her at the table, saying, "I asked Mrs. Fillmore to provide your favorite food."

He sat to her right, so that each time she looked at him, she saw his scarred face. Had he done this deliberately?

With Mrs. Fillmore hovering in the background, they were served a salad of fresh fruits, but before he started eating, Grant said hesitantly, "Do you want to say grace before we eat?"

"Yes, please." She bowed her head, wondering if she could pray without crying. The last time she'd offered thanks to God at this table was the day they'd vacated the house and moved to Kansas.

"God, I thank You for Your goodness to our family since we left Barwood. Thank You for the food and the kind and loving hands that prepared it. If it's Your will, please restore my father's health. And bless Mr. Palmer for his kindness toward me. Amen."

"My name is Grant," he said.

Beauty lifted her fork and took a bite of the fruit laced with a light honey syrup. Stifling a smile, she said, "Yes, I know."

"I looked at the florist card and learned that you're twenty-seven today. I'm almost forty, so I suppose I must seem ancient to you, but I'd like for you to call me by my given name."

"Certainly, if you prefer that."

The salad plates were removed and the main entrée of grilled pork chops, curried rice, fresh green peas, stewed apples, and buttermilk biscuits was served.

"I wish you wouldn't treat me as if I were your employer," he said, a bit testily.

Beauty lifted her eyebrows. "How else can I treat you? Our relationship is a bit difficult to define. Theoretically, I suppose I'm working for my father, but when the items I'm cataloging will be sold to pay his debt to you, I feel as though I'm in your employ."

"I don't like your servile attitude," he said harshly. "I've done nothing to make you think you're indebted to me."

"Of course you haven't," she said earnestly, "but since Barwood was once my home, it would be easy to overstep my position. I never forget this is your home now, and I'm a visitor. I appreciate what you've done for our family, and I've tried to be circumspect."

He didn't comment, but asked about her day's work.

"I'm not progressing as rapidly as I expected to. I promised my sisters that I'd return within two months, and I hope I can meet that deadline. There are a few items I've laid aside to get your opinion in which category they belong. Perhaps we can go to the warehouse after dinner and you can advise me."

He shook his head. "No. This is your birthday, and you shouldn't have to work tonight."

"This has been a delightful dinner," she said, "and all of the foods are favorites of mine."

When dessert was served, Beauty exclaimed over the three-layer pecan cake, topped with coconut frosting. After they'd each been served a generous slice of the cake, Beauty said to Mrs. Fillmore, "Please take the rest of the cake to the workers in the kitchen and thank them for the delicious meal. I've enjoyed it."

She lowered her eyes, realizing that she'd overstepped her position after all. Grant was the one to have sent congratulations to the kitchen staff. And what should she do now? The meal was finished. Should she excuse herself and go to her room?

"Mrs. Fillmore, please bring coffee to the garden room," Grant said as he stood behind Beauty's chair. "Or do you prefer tea?"

"Tea, if you please," she said, trying not to sound servile, but his closeness made her a little breathless. He put his hand under her elbow and walked beside her into the garden room. Furnished with wicker sofas and chairs, enhanced with brightly flowered cushions, the room had always been one of Beauty's favorite places. Sliding glass doors on three sides gave access to the brick and stone terraced garden planted with perennials, herbs, and flowering plants in shades of pink and gray.

Grant guided her to a sofa and sat beside her. Again, she was facing the scarred side of his face. Anna soon appeared with a silver tray that held a coffee urn and teapot.

"We'll serve ourselves when we're ready, Anna," Grant said.

He took a small gift-wrapped box from his pocket and handed it to Beauty. "I could have done better if I'd had more notice."

Flustered, Beauty said, "I don't know how you were able to buy anything in such a short time."

His lips curved upward in a crooked smile—the first time she'd seen him smile.

"I contacted my friend Dallas and asked him to make the purchase. He doesn't do anything else, so he might as well do a favor for me once in a while."

Beauty's hands moistened as she held the gift. How should she deal with the change in Grant? During the past three weeks, she was conscious that their relationship had altered gradually. They had worked well together at the warehouse—sometimes in silence, other times discussing the value of the items Simon had collected. She'd enjoyed the walk from the warehouse each evening and always experienced a sense of loss when she had turned toward the back stairs and he'd walked toward the main section of the house. She'd almost come to look upon him as a friend, but tonight was different. Should she accept his gift?

"Open it," he said, and she shook her head.

"The dinner was gift enough. I can't take anything else from you."

Grant took the box from her hands, unwrapped it, opened the box, and removed the lapel pin. She gasped at the dazzling jewelry. She'd always been partial to roses. She knew it was expensive, for the name on the box indicated the pin had been purchased from the jewelry store where the Bartletts had shopped in their affluent days.

He leaned forward and attached the pin to her dress.

"Perfect," he said. "I'm glad you wore black tonight."

She stood up and moved to the mirror hanging over the fireplace. "It's a beautiful pin, and it does look exquisite on the black dress, but I wish you hadn't done it. I don't want the Bartletts to be any further in your debt."

"A gift is not a debt," he said grimly. "Sit down. I'm not finished yet."

Uneasily, she moved back to the couch, sitting as far away from him as possible.

"And as long as you remain here, I want you to consider this house your home just as it always was." He handed her a set of keys. "Here's a key to the front door and to my sedan. It's yours to use wherever you want to go. I use the van most of the time."

"No, really," Beauty protested. "It isn't necessary. I don't expect this."

"And you're invited to share my evening meal every

night, not just tonight. It's a trite expression, but make yourself at home."

She continued to shake her head, and he took her hand. The soft glow in his eyes took the sting from his words. "You've indicated we have an employer-employee relationship. I'm giving an order—you're to do as I say."

She wouldn't look at him.

"And I took the liberty of asking Mrs. Fillmore to move your possessions into your former bedroom. You're not going back to the third floor."

Beauty raised startled eyes to his. She assumed he slept in the master bedroom, just a short distance from her bedroom door.

"To observe the proprieties, Mrs. Fillmore will sleep in one of the rooms on the opposite side of the hallway." He lifted her chin until he could look into her eyes. "Do this for me, Beauty. It will make me feel much better. I've never felt right about taking away your home."

Her gray eyes dimmed with sorrow. "If I get adjusted to my former surroundings, it will be like losing my home all over again when I go back to my father and sisters. I'm not sure I can bear such a parting another time."

"I hadn't thought of it that way," Grant said in a contrite voice. "I don't want to cause you any further distress."

"But because I appreciate your kindness, I'll do as you request." She touched the pin on her shoulder. "Thank you—for everything."

"Is there anything else I can do to make your birthday complete?"

"I shouldn't ask since you've been so generous, but I want to telephone my father. I won't reverse the charges because he can't afford any extra expenses, but I didn't want to use your phones, and I don't have any way to get to a pay phone."

"You have a car now, and you can go anywhere you want to. But it isn't necessary. Telephone from here. There's a phone jack in every room, so call your father when you want to."

He walked with her to the front hallway, where they crossed the Italian marble floor to the staircase. She extended her hand, and he held it briefly before she started slowly up the stairs. When the staircase curved, she paused beneath the crystal chandelier with shaped hurricane shades that had been imported from Ireland and turned to look at him where he stood in the center of the hallway. Their gazes held for a long moment.

"Good night, Grant," she said before she moved to the second floor.

Chapter 4

Beauty easily resumed the role of mistress of the house, for Grant's attitude kept the situation from being awkward. At dinner, they visited much as she'd always done with her father. After the meal, he joined her when she went to the pergola or to the garden room to read. He brought his paper and read, and sometimes they watched television. If she strolled along the river, he went with her, and she saw the estate through his eyes, learning to appreciate it all over again. Every morning, a fresh rose appeared beside her breakfast plate. Obviously, he'd meant what he said when he told her to make herself at home.

Why was he doing this? Did he have some ulterior motive? Why was her father reluctant to approve her return to Barwood? Was there a side to Grant that she hadn't seen?

Contented to be at Barwood again, Beauty had no desire to go anyplace except to church, and she would have preferred to walk, but she didn't want to offend Grant. The first Sunday after she'd been restored to her home, she decided to drive his car to morning worship. The night before he'd asked her to have breakfast with him in the garden room.

"Sunday morning is the only time I eat a leisurely breakfast, and I'd like for you to join me."

"It depends on how leisurely you'll be," she responded with a smile. "I'm going to church, and I have to be there by ten o'clock."

"Then we'll eat at eight."

"Since I'm joining you for breakfast," she said brightly, "will you go with me to church?"

"No," he hesitated, "I don't think so. I haven't been to church for several years." And defensively, he added, "But I do read my Bible and pray."

"Plan to go with me next week. The pastor is a young seminary student, and his messages are challenging."

He didn't promise, but when she was ready to leave, he walked to the garage with her in case she needed help with the car. Since she'd asked him to church, that sounded as if she wasn't ashamed to be seen in his company. Did he dare to ask her for a date? Days spent in Beauty's company were healing Grant in places he didn't even know he'd been injured.

Each Sunday after breakfast, Grant gave his household staff the rest of the day off. He'd noticed that Beauty had spent her other Sundays with Mrs. Fillmore, but when the housekeeper left the estate soon after Beauty started to church, he hoped that he and Beauty could have the rest of the day to themselves.

When Beauty returned, he heard her enter the kitchen. The cook had left sandwiches and salads in the refrigerator, and he knew she would start to prepare a light lunch. Grant wandered in before she chose anything.

"Hi," she said. "You caught me raiding the refrigerator."

"We could go someplace for lunch, if you prefer."

"Thanks, but I need to catch up on some computer work this afternoon. Father keeps asking when I'm coming home."

"Don't you have two sisters to care for him?"

"You don't know my sisters! They've been spoiled, and they're always complaining to Father, blaming him for their troubles. To hear them talk, you'd think farm life is worse than living in Siberia."

He watched her closely. Why had she refused to go out to lunch with him? She'd invited him to church. Was that different than going elsewhere with him? He'd gotten used to people staring at his scars, but it might bother the kindhearted Beauty.

"I'm going to eat a snack in the pergola. Do you want to join me?"

"Yes. I'd like that."

She filled a tray with two wrapped sandwiches, oranges, and bottles of juice. Grant picked up the tray and carried it to the pergola, where they sat at a small glass-topped table.

"When we were children," she reminisced, "we had company every Sunday. Father's parents were living then, and we had several cousins in the area. Do you have any family, Grant?"

"My older brother lives in the family home in Norfolk. His children are active in sports and other school activities, and we don't visit a great deal. He's on the board of directors at the bank, so we see each other quite often. My sister lives in Florida with her family. She visits us once or twice each year."

After lunch, he went to the warehouse with her, and

although he praised her efficiency, he was disturbed when he saw all of the work she'd completed. In a few weeks she'd be going out of his life. Was he ready for that?

At five o'clock, Beauty said, "Time to stop for today. The church is having a spaghetti supper this evening to raise money for youth activities. I'm going. Do you want to come along with me?"

"Yes," he answered, not willing to turn down an opportunity to be in her company. He indicated his shorts and knit shirt. "Like this?"

She nodded her head, smiling, apparently pleased that he would go with her. "We'll be eating in the picnic grove. You look fine, but I've gotten my blouse dirty, so I'll change into clean jeans and a shirt. Want to meet me at the garage in a half hour?"

Grant's pulse hammered as they walked up the circular staircase together, and his heart rejoiced. She must not be ashamed to be seen with him.

"I'll drive the van," he said, leaving her at the door to her room.

About fifty people had congregated in the churchyard when they arrived. Beauty introduced Grant to the pastor and the people she knew, many of whom had worked at Barwood when the Bartletts owned the estate. With Beauty at his side, Grant didn't mind the curious glances in his direction. After all, he'd lived in the area for almost a year, and the only glimpse his neighbors had of him was when he drove back and forth to work. Grant had never been class conscious, and his business interests brought him into contact with the public, so it was easy for him to be pleasant to his neighbors.

A sense of well-being settled over him, and after they left the churchyard, he traveled along country roads, taking the long way back to Barwood. They drove with the windows down, enjoying the peace of the twilight. Grant said good night to Beauty at the foot of the steps and turned toward his office. He stopped by the drawing room and studied Beauty's portrait for a long time.

"Thank You, God, for bringing her out of that picture. Her Christian spirit is changing me. The bitterness of the past is slowly disappearing and being replaced by hope and trust—the attitude You expect in Your followers. Thanks again, God."

The next night, while they were eating dinner, Grant mentioned, "The Virginia Wind Symphony will be at Ocean View Beach Park tomorrow night. You've probably heard their performance."

"Yes, many times."

"I have tickets. I'd like for you to go with me."

She hesitated, and without meeting his eyes, she shook her head. "No, I can't go."

When he clammed up and hardly spoke during the rest of the meal, she knew she'd hurt him. When he went to his office instead of following her to the garden room, she suspected he'd taken her refusal to mean she was ashamed to be seen with him. How could she convince him that it wasn't the reason without mentioning his disfigurement, which had never been named between them? She'd asked God to help her ignore his scars, and she didn't even notice them when they were together.

He still hadn't sought her presence by the time she usually went to her room, and Beauty walked down the hallway to his office. The door was open, and he sat idly at his desk, staring into space. She paused by the door, and he looked up at her with the guarded expression she hadn't seen in his eyes for several days.

"Please believe that my refusal wasn't personal—it had nothing to do with you." She paused, wondering how far to go. "I enjoy your company." When his eyes softened, she walked into the room, standing with her hand on his desk. "It was customary for my family to attend every performance of the symphony. As did our friends. If I go with you tomorrow night, I'll see a lot of my former friends, and I'm not ready to face them."

"Did your friends abandon you when your father's fortune declined?" he asked, his blue eyes piercing in their intensity.

"No, or at least most of them didn't. They telephoned until I stopped returning their calls, but we no longer had the familiar ties to bind us together. It's pride, I suppose, but I can't meet them now and have them ask questions and peer at me to see how I've changed."

If anyone could understand how she felt, certainly he could.

Grant said softly, "It's all right, Beauty. I shouldn't have been grouchy about it."

"The Bible warns Christians against pride, so I suppose I'm failing there, but I hope I can finish my work and return to Kansas without meeting anyone I used to know."

"You intend to go back?" he asked.

Startled, she said, "Of course! Every time I talk to Father, he asks when I'll be home. I should be finished in less than a month, and you can start advertising the collection for sale. When those artifacts are gone, that will be the last tie to our former lifestyle, and I'll be relieved. With the past behind me, I can start a new life."

"I didn't mean to make you feel bad, Beauty. I thought you needed a break and that you'd enjoy the music."

"I would have, but right now, I'm content to stay here." *Stay here with you,* she almost said, surprised at the turn her thoughts were taking.

Grant was heartened by her words that evening. He didn't want her to leave, but her quick response had assured him that her even temperament and kindness weren't feigned to worm her way into his favor. Not a day passed that he didn't understand more and more why she'd received her nickname.

The rest of the week, Grant tried to think of someplace he could take Beauty that wouldn't rake up memories of the past. At the spaghetti dinner, he'd been received well enough, so on Sunday morning, he went to church with Beauty. When they returned to Barwood, she prepared a light lunch, which they shared in the pergola. Grant looked forward to these relaxing hours with Beauty like a kid waited for Christmas. He was continually thinking of ways to keep her with him. Today, she wore a dress of some kind of soft material with a muted floral pattern, and he marveled at the difference she'd made in his enjoyment of Barwood. Before she came, it had just been a house; now it was a home that he eagerly returned to when he completed his day's work.

They'd finished their lunch and were sipping cups of hot tea when Dallas Winthrop sauntered into the pergola. His entrance annoyed Grant. Dallas was in the habit of dropping in unannounced, but Grant knew that this visit was designed so his friend could see Beauty. But Sunday afternoons when he and Beauty were alone in the house had become special for Grant, and he didn't want anyone to intrude.

Grant made the introductions, resenting the way Dallas appraised Beauty, as if assessing her worth.

"Would you like a cup of tea, Mr. Winthrop? And could I make you a sandwich?"

"I had a late breakfast, so I'm not hungry," Dallas said, "but I'd like some tea."

"I'll bring another cup," she said and went into the house.

"No wonder you've been keeping her to yourself," Dallas said softly.

Angrily, Grant responded, "I hope your curiosity is satisfied now."

"Oh, I've seen her before. I watched Miss Bartlett christen one of her father's ships when she was just a girl. She was a beauty then, but nothing compared to what she is today. Maturity and adversity have done wonders for her."

The conversation halted when Beauty returned with the cup and served Dallas. "Do you want more tea?" she asked Grant, and he shook his head.

"Then if you'll excuse me, I'll go upstairs. I want to write to my father. It's nice to meet you, Mr. Winthrop."

Dallas stood and shook hands with her.

"Grant tells me you've been working very hard, so perhaps it's time you took a break. I'd like for you and Grant to join me for a meal at Fisherman's Wharf sometime this week."

Beauty darted a quick look at Grant. "Well, I don't

know," she hesitated. She'd likely meet as many of her friends there as she would have at the symphony. "I'll think about it, and Mr. Palmer can let you know."

Silence marked Beauty's exit, and when he was sure she was out of hearing, Grant said angrily, "Why did you do that? I'm not sure she wants to be seen out with me."

"Are you sure *you* want to be seen out with *her*? You haven't dated anyone since Callie Stevens dumped you five years ago. Are you sure you've gotten over her? If you haven't, I'll tell you that Callie would like to come back to you. She's recently divorced, and when I saw her last week, she asked if you were dating anyone."

"I have no interest in Callie."

"No," Dallas drawled, "because you've fallen for Beauty. But I just wanted you to know that Callie may have had a change of heart."

"Let's go watch the golf match on TV. If we stay here, we'll argue all afternoon."

They walked into Grant's office, he turned on the big-screen television, and Dallas said, "Think about this trip to Fisherman's Wharf. I'll get a date, and you might have an enjoyable evening."

When they had finished dinner the next day and had moved to the garden room, Grant wandered around the room restlessly until he stopped at one of the sliding doors and looked out over the neat lawn.

"Do you want to accept Dallas's invitation to Fisherman's Wharf?" he asked without looking at her.

Beauty had lost sleep last night trying to make a decision. For herself, she was content to remain at Barwood, because in a few more weeks, she'd have to leave it and this time there would be no reason to return. But she considered Grant. Did he take refuge in the house to hide his scarred visage from the public? Or was there another reason?

"I'm willing to go if you are," she said, and he whirled toward her, a glad light in his eyes. "I've decided it's cowardly to pull this house around me like a shield to avoid unpleasant encounters with people I used to know," she said pointedly, in case this was the reason he'd become a recluse.

"Shall I tell Dallas to make reservations for Thursday night?"

"That will be fine. I've also hesitated to go anyplace, because I don't have any new clothes. If I see anyone who used to know me, they'll probably notice that I'm wearing clothes that are no longer stylish. But I've decided that's foolish, too. I'll never again be the pampered daughter of Simon Bartlett with a credit account in Norfolk's finest stores, free to buy a new dress for every occasion."

"I guess I've not really understood how your father's downfall changed your life, too. And yet you've handled it without bitterness."

"Oh, I've had my bitter moments," she said, with a weary smile. "But faith in God has brought me through it. I've accepted the fact that my life has changed. When my father's health improves, I'm going to launch out on my own. I will not spend the rest of my life dwelling on the past."

"That's a lesson you'll have to teach me. I'm very resentful of the blows life dealt to me."

That was the closest he'd come to referring to his facial scars, but he'd have to be more specific than that if he wanted her to comment. The accident that had disfigured him was obviously a touchy subject, and she feared she'd say the wrong thing.

Chapter 5

When Beauty entered her room the next day, after coming from the warehouse, a red dress was spread out on her bed. A beautiful one-piece, scallop-edged lace top with a gored chiffon skirt from one of Norfolk's exclusive shops. At first, Beauty was humiliated that Grant thought she'd been hinting for him to buy her some clothes. Then she became angry. She snatched up the dress, ran down the staircase, and confronted Grant in his office. She pitched the dress onto his desk, turned on her heel, and left swiftly without saying a word.

Grant vaulted out of his chair and caught her in the front hall before she reached the stairs. He grabbed her arm, and she turned furious eyes on him.

"What brought that on?" he asked.

"How dare you!" she said, her voice shaking. "Do you have such a low opinion of me that you think I was hinting for you to buy me a dress?"

"No, I didn't think that," he said slowly. "I wanted to buy you a gift. I keep thinking that if it wasn't for me, you'd still have lots of clothes."

She stamped her foot. "Will you stop belittling yourself? I've told you before that if you hadn't bought

Barwood, Father might have ended up in prison for defrauding his creditors. I've never blamed you personally for what happened to us."

She jerked her arm out of his grasp and had run up several steps before he said, "I'd like for you to keep the dress."

She stopped and faced him. "I will never wear that dress, so you might as well return it."

"Are you still going out with me Thursday night?"

"That's up to you. If I go, I'll choose my own clothes."

"Which I'm sure will be appropriate."

The incident wasn't mentioned when she came down for dinner, but their evening was strained for she was still angry and Grant was contrite.

Beauty spent a lot of time thinking about what she would wear on Thursday night, for she wanted to be as presentable in her old clothes as she would have been in the red dress. She didn't have much choice, but she decided on a sea green outfit of pants, a sleeveless tank top, and a sheer matching vine-print tunic. As a peace offering, she attached the rose pin he'd given her to the tunic.

Dressed in a beige suit and a blue polo shirt, Grant waited for her at the foot of the staircase. He took her hand and pulled her close, stopping just short of an embrace.

"You look beautiful, and I like you this way much more than if you'd worn the red dress. Forgive me?"

Flushing slightly, Beauty said, "Forgive *me* for getting angry. I thought I'd stifled my pride, but that incident proved it's still simmering below the surface. I can't be in the position of begging for favors."

"I won't make that mistake again," he said, and as they walked to the car, she thought he wouldn't have much more opportunity. Her work would be finished within two weeks.

Fisherman's Wharf, overlooking historic Hampton Roads Harbor, was one of Norfolk's largest and finest restaurants, famous for the buffet featuring a wide selection of seafood. Grant asked for the reservation in Dallas's name and rested his hand beneath Beauty's elbow as they were escorted to the table where Dallas sat with a redheaded, petite woman. When Dallas stood, Grant muttered under his breath, and his face flushed, causing his scars to be more prominent than usual. His hand tightened on Beauty's arm.

"Good evening," Dallas said. "Beauty, this is Callie Stevens. Callie, Annabelle Bartlett, better known as Beauty. Grant, I believe you and Callie are acquainted."

"I'm pleased to meet you, Beauty," Callie said. "I've heard of you."

As Grant seated her, Beauty said, "Hello, Callie. It's nice that you could join us for dinner. I haven't had a good seafood meal since we left this area and moved to Kansas, which is a long way from the ocean."

She'd determined, when she agreed to accept this invitation, that she wouldn't hide from the past anymore. The decline of the Bartletts wasn't her fault, and she would no longer turn away from her family's misfortune.

"In what part of Kansas do you live?" Callie asked, as if she were interested.

The waiter came for their order, and before they moved to the buffet table, Beauty said, "My mother inherited a farm not far from Topeka, Kansas, and she willed it to her children with Father as the trustee. Since it was in our names, it wasn't included in Father's assets when he lost his shipyards. My father and I like the farm, but the rest of the family don't share our opinion. My sisters want to go to college, but they aren't willing to work to pay their way, and of course, Father isn't financially able to send them."

After making that admission at the outset, Beauty enjoyed the rest of the meal, since she wasn't dreading that someone would ask her questions. She and Callie chatted amicably, but it was obvious that Grant was angry, and he answered in monosyllables when Dallas tried to draw him into the conversation.

A few acquaintances stopped by the table and seemed genuinely glad to see Beauty. The evening would have been a satisfying occasion if she hadn't sensed Grant's discomfiture. The food was excellent, and both Dallas and Callie were good conversationalists. But Grant hardly spoke, and when he did, his voice was harsh, unlike his usual pleasing voice.

When Callie and Beauty went to the rest room before dessert was served, Grant turned angrily on Dallas.

"What do you mean by inviting Callie? If I hadn't had Beauty with me, I would have left immediately."

"Simmer down," Dallas said soothingly. "You haven't seen Callie since she broke your engagement, and I thought you should meet her again. It's a good idea for you to see her and Beauty together, so you'll know which one you should choose. I did this for your own good."

Grant groaned. "Deliver me from friends who meddle in my affairs for my own good! Beauty has handled it well, but I'm sure she knows I'm angry and she's bound to suspect something. It's hard to tell what Callie might say to her."

"Here they come now, so relax and act like you've got some intelligence. Someday you'll thank me for getting you out of that shell you've built around yourself."

Driving back to Barwood, Grant still wasn't talkative, but Beauty chatted about the evening.

"I enjoyed being out again," she said, "so I'm glad Dallas invited us. It wasn't a bit difficult to meet my old friends. I had a good time."

"I'm glad you did. Obviously, I didn't."

She laughed softly. "I noticed that."

"Do you know anything about Callie?"

"I think I've seen her name in the papers, but I'm not sure. I liked her."

"Callie is from Portsmouth, and we were engaged once. She broke the engagement when. . . ," he paused, and she sat close enough to him that she felt his muscles tightening, "when I had my accident."

So Callie had left him when he'd become disfigured! If his scarred face had bothered her in the past, that hadn't seemed to be a problem tonight. Beauty had been aware of Callie's attempts to charm Grant out of his bad humor.

"She married someone else and moved away. Dallas told me a few days ago that she's divorced and is living in Portsmouth again. I've never forgiven Callie for the way she treated me, and I'm angry because Dallas invited her tonight."

Beauty laid her hand on his arm. "Perhaps it's just as well you did meet her. How else could you know if you still have feelings for her?"

"That's what Dallas said, and his experiment worked in that regard. The feelings are gone. I was as dispassionate in her presence as if she'd been a perfect stranger."

Beauty wished his words hadn't brought so much pleasure to her.

"Then tonight has been a new beginning for both of us. Once I admitted that my former way of life was gone, it was easy to talk about the change in our economic and social status. It's taken me a year to recognize that material wealth isn't the road to happiness."

Grant put his arm around her waist as they walked into the house from the garage, and she didn't resist. He'd come close to telling Beauty how hurt he'd been when Callie turned against him, but when Grant left her at her bedroom door and went to his room, he told God instead.

"God, I've known all along that my bitterness toward Callie kept me out of fellowship with You. I don't even know if I ever loved her, but whatever I felt for her is gone. I've tried to compare my association with Callie to how I feel about Beauty now. Am I in love with Beauty? If so, am I attracted to her because of her physical perfection or because of the loveliness of her spirit? God, if I ask her to marry me and she turns me down, I'm not sure I could ever recover from that."

The phone rang, and Beauty wiped her dusty hands before she answered. It must be Grant, for no one else ever telephoned the warehouse, and he must be calling from the van for he wouldn't have had time to reach the office.

With a smile in her voice, she said, "Hello."

"Beauty, this is Dallas Winthrop. Don't be concerned, but Grant has been in an accident."

Her heart plummeted. "How badly is he hurt?"

"I don't know yet. We met for breakfast, and as he was pulling away from the restaurant, a truck veered out of control and struck the driver's side of the van. They're loading him in the ambulance now. I'll telephone as soon as I know something."

"Where are they taking him?"

He named the hospital where the Bartletts had doctored, and Beauty said, "I'll leave right away and meet you at the hospital."

"That isn't necessary. . . ," Dallas started, but she replaced the phone receiver. If Grant was injured, she wanted to be with him, and she didn't have time to argue with Dallas.

An hour later, she walked into the crowded waiting area adjacent to the emergency room. Dallas leaned against the wall.

"How is he?" she demanded breathlessly.

"No word yet. I tried to call his brother, but he's not at home. It was good of you to come."

She didn't answer, and he pointed to two empty seats. "We can sit there."

"Thanks for telephoning me," she said. "I told Mrs. Fillmore about the accident, for I didn't want the household staff to hear about it otherwise."

The times she'd seen Dallas, Beauty had taken him for a happy-go-lucky fellow who didn't have a care in the world, but his face was wrinkled in concern this morning.

"I keep thinking about his other accident and what that did to him. He'd been a handsome man, and I was with him the first time he looked in a mirror after his bandages were removed. I'd never cried since I became a man, and I haven't cried since, but I bawled like a baby when I saw what had happened to his face. He didn't shed a tear."

"I'd like to know what happened," Beauty said. "He's never mentioned his disfigurement to me."

"Grant had taken up car racing, and he was pretty good at it, but one day his race car went out of control. The vehicle exploded into flames just as his crew pulled him to safety, but not quite soon enough. One flash seared the left side of his face, and that was his only serious injury."

Beauty covered her face with her hands. Dallas took a photo from his billfold. "This is a picture of Grant and me when we were in college. He got rid of all of his pictures, and he'd be furious if he knew I still carried this one."

She'd often wondered how Grant would have looked before the accident, and her hands trembled as she took the photo. He had been handsome when the left side of his face was smooth and blemish-free, but the greatest change was in his expression. The camera had caught a look of pride, serenity, and optimism—traits she hadn't seen in Grant. She shuddered and handed the photo back to Dallas.

"Such a tragedy!" she said.

"Grant refused to have plastic surgery. He said people would have to take him as he was, but he's become a recluse. He used to play golf, and we'd go sailing often, but after he bought Barwood, he stopped all social activities. Last week was the first time I've persuaded him to go anywhere in the evening, but he's changed a lot lately," Dallas added pointedly.

Beauty was spared a reply when a green-suited doctor, with a protective cap still on his head, stepped into the waiting room.

"Grant Palmer's relatives?" he asked, scanning the room, and Dallas stood up.

"Here."

The doctor came toward them, and Beauty remained seated, but her hands tightened on the arms of the chair.

"Mr. Palmer's injuries are not extensive," the doctor said, and Beauty expelled a deep breath. "He had a hard blow to his head, but it's not a concussion. No doubt, he'll have a sore head as well as painful muscles. He can go home shortly, but he should have someone monitoring him for the next twelve hours. If he sleeps, he should be awakened every two hours. You can see him now, if you like."

"Maybe I'd better not go in," Beauty said to Dallas, fearing she might have overreacted by rushing to the hospital. What would Grant think?

"You might be the medicine he needs," Dallas objected. "You can drive him home when he's ready. I'll need to check out his van and call his insurance company."

With that reason for being there, Beauty didn't hesitate, and she followed Dallas into a large room separated into small cubicles by curtains. Inside one cubicle, Grant lay on a hospital bed, his eyes closed, the right side of his face as white as the sheet, contrasting vividly to the scarred left cheek.

Dallas laid his hand on Grant's shoulder. "Hey, buddy, you can't sleep in the middle of the day."

"I'm not asleep," Grant growled lowly. "My head hurts, and it's less painful if I keep my eyes closed."

"I'd open them if I were you," Dallas advised.

Grant slitted his eyes, then opened them wide when he saw Beauty. He held out his hand, and Beauty gently squeezed his fingers.

"The doctor says you can leave the hospital soon. I came to take you home."

He returned the pressure on his hand, saying to Dallas, "Why'd you bother her?"

Dallas laughed. "You're a hard man to please. I'd think you'd be glad to have a beautiful woman hold your hand and wipe your fevered brow."

He pushed a chair close to the cot for Beauty. "Since Beauty is here to look after you, I'm going to check out the accident site and tend to the van."

"Was there much damage?"

"Quite a lot to your vehicle—not much to the other man's truck."

"I don't know what happened."

"The truck blew a tire and careened across the yellow line into your lane. I doubt there'll be any citations, but I'll check it out."

Grant smiled. "Thanks, Dallas. You're a good friend, even if you do annoy me sometimes."

With an airy wave of his hand, Dallas left them alone. Still holding Grant's hand, Beauty said, "Thank God you weren't hurt badly."

"Yes. I've thanked Him, too." He closed his eyes. "They gave me some medicine that's made me woozy."

"Apparently it's all right for you to go to sleep. I'll be here if you need anything." But he didn't make a sound.

Was it worth an accident to find out how much he cared about Beauty and how concerned she was about him? He couldn't remember when he'd been so relaxed and easy in his mind. Was it the medication or Beauty's hand holding his that made the difference?

Chapter 6

The doctor didn't discharge Grant until after lunch, and it was midafternoon when they reached Barwood. Since the doctor recommended bed rest for twenty-four hours, Grant went to his room as soon as they got home.

"I won't go to the warehouse, so I can check on you periodically," Beauty told him. She brought a silver bell from her room. "This is the bell I used to ring when I needed my mother, so you can use it if you need anything. Either Mrs. Fillmore or I will hear it."

"I have a headache, but there's nothing else wrong with me. I'm not going to spend the rest of the day in bed."

"Yes, you are," she said saucily.

"Are you going to sit beside me?"

"That isn't necessary."

"Will you eat dinner with me up here?" he asked.

"Certainly. But I'm going to leave now so you can rest."

"I'm feeling fine."

"Regardless, the doctor said you were to take it easy, and I'm to see that you do." She grinned. "I'm the boss for the time being."

"I can't think of anyone else I'd rather have for a boss," Grant dared to say, and he laughed when she blushed.

When she returned at the dinner hour, carrying a folding table, he had changed into blue sweats and was lounging on the bed, watching television. She unfolded the table and had placed it near the bed by the time Mrs. Fillmore walked in with a loaded tray.

"Just a light meal tonight," the housekeeper explained. "Broccoli soup, garden salad, toasted bread, and strawberry yogurt."

"Sounds great to me," Grant said.

Beauty spent the rest of the evening in his room, sitting in a chair beside the bed where he lounged, propped up by pillows. While surfing for a program, Grant came across the animated version of the fairy tale, *Beauty and the Beast*, and he said, "This movie received a lot of awards. Shall we watch it?"

Although she was uncomfortable with the subject, Beauty agreed. Did Grant see any connection between the fable and their relationship? Had he chosen the movie deliberately to see her reaction?

The movie depicted the story of the fabled Beauty, who sacrificed her freedom to save her father. Of the prince who'd been turned into a monster, waiting for the kiss of a beautiful woman to restore him to his normal character. Of Gaston, the village youth who was determined to have Beauty for his bride.

Once, Grant turned to Beauty and asked, "Is there a Gaston in your life?"

She shook her head. "No."

"Has there ever been?"

"No."

The movie ended when the mythical Beauty's kiss brought the Beast to his former self. Grant turned off the television.

"Too bad it's a fairy tale," he said grimly.

Beauty stood up and rolled the chair away from the bed.

"It's been more than twelve hours since the accident, so you can go to sleep," Beauty said. "I'm going to my room, but you should leave your door open tonight, as will Mrs. Fillmore and I. Ring the bell if you need anything, and one of us will hear."

Grant reached for her hand, lifted it to his lips, and kissed it gently.

※

"Help! Help!" Grant's frantic calls echoed through the house and catapulted Beauty out of bed. Grabbing a robe, she ran down the hallway. Mrs. Fillmore was already in Grant's room, standing at the foot of his bed.

"He's not awake," she said.

Grant rolled back and forth under the light blanket, hand held to his blemished cheek. "The burn is terrible. Do something," he pleaded.

Beauty turned troubled eyes toward Mrs. Fillmore. "Should we telephone the doctor?"

"Not just yet," she advised. "Some people can't take pain pills without having nightmares. I think that's his problem. What happened today probably made him remember the other accident when he was burned. I'm going to rouse him."

Mrs. Fillmore put a firm hand on Grant's shoulder, and he quieted immediately. She shook him gently, and he opened his eyes.

"Do you need anything, Mr. Palmer?" she asked.

He shook his head and winced. "No. I'm all right," he said and went back to sleep.

Beauty rolled the lounge chair close to his bed. "I'll stay with him awhile. I won't be able to go back to sleep now, and I might as well sit here."

Mrs. Fillmore nodded. "Let me know if you need me."

Grant relaxed on his back, and Beauty picked up his hand and kissed it. He stirred and said sleepily, "Go to bed, Beauty. You need to rest. I'm all right."

She didn't answer, and a delicate snore soon assured her that he was resting. In the quietness, she assessed her reaction to Grant's accident. She hadn't hesitated about going to him. At first, she'd tried so hard to be impersonal toward Grant, not to expect anything from him except the same consideration he'd given her father. But since he'd insisted that she resume her former position in his house, she was content with the status quo, wondering how much Grant's presence added to that contentment. After her mother had died, there had been a lot of grief in the house. Relations between the Bartletts were often tense. And the days when the shipyards had been destroyed and Simon had realized that he'd lost everything had been tragic! With some shame, she admitted she was happier at Barwood with only Grant for company than she'd been since her mother's death. Why?

She loved her father and had every intention of going back to Kansas, but as the time neared for her departure, she knew this second leave-taking would be more difficult than the first one. Did she dread leaving the familiar surroundings of home? Or was Grant the lodestone that tied her to Barwood this time? The incident today had left Beauty with a lot of questions but no answers.

Before she left the room, Beauty looked intently at Grant. She leaned over, cupped his face in her hands, and kissed him gently, but his arms lifted swiftly and pulled her down on his chest, intensifying the caress. Quickly freeing herself, Beauty ran out of the room, alarmed at her reaction to their kiss.

Beauty dressed and showered before she went to Grant's room. It was vacant, and Anna was making the bed.

"Where is he?"

"Went downstairs to breakfast about fifteen minutes ago," the maid said.

Beauty ran down the steps to accost Grant in the dining room sipping on a cup of coffee.

"You shouldn't be up yet."

He looked at his watch. "The doc said twenty-four hours, and it's been almost that long. I'm tired of lying around."

"You surely aren't going to work today?"

"Not unless there's an emergency. Sit down and have breakfast. Mrs. Fillmore's bringing me toast and jelly. She'll fix what you want."

"I prepare my own breakfast."

"Not this morning," he said, and his right eyebrow slanted upward. "I'm an invalid, and you're supposed to look after me."

"How did you rest?" she asked, taking a seat beside him. A flush stained her cheeks. How much did he remember about last night?

"My neck is stiff, my shoulder is sore, and I've got a knot on my head," he said, "but I may have rested. I dreamed a lot. Dreamed I had died and a fairy princess kissed me and I came back to life again."

Had he really dreamed that or did he know what she'd done?

"You don't believe in fairy tales, do you?"

"No," he said reluctantly, "but that's one tale I'd like to be true."

Mrs. Fillmore brought a breakfast tray and forestalled any further talk about kissing, much to Beauty's relief. The housekeeper had enough toast for two, and she brought a glass of orange juice for Beauty.

Wishing she could do something special for Grant before she returned to Kansas, Beauty had been toying with an idea for several days. With Grant in this relaxed attitude and in no rush to go to work, perhaps now was the time to broach the subject.

They left the dining room, and before he went to his office, she said, "Since Dallas took us to Fisherman's Wharf and he was so helpful when you had the accident, would you like to ask him and Callie for dinner some evening? I'd be glad to plan the meal—I used to do it for Father's guests."

Grant considered a few minutes. "To be honest, I see people all day long, and when I come home I'd rather be alone with you."

Beauty's face flushed, but her heart warmed. She felt the same way, but she was bothered about Grant's relationship to Callie. Had he really gotten over his love for his former fiancée? Was his avoidance of her an indication that he hadn't forgiven Callie for rejecting him?

"But Dallas is a great guy," Grant continued, "and he'd jump at the chance to dine at Barwood. I'm not particular about having Callie, but it's okay to ask her."

"Will you contact them and let me know what evening? Do you want to approve the menu?"

He turned startled eyes toward her. "No. I've never been much for social events, so you'll have to take care of all the details. I trust your judgment. How formal is this dinner going to be?"

"Oh, you won't have to wear a tux, but it won't hurt you to wear a suit and tie."

"I wear a suit and tie all day at work. When I come home, I want to get into casual clothes," he grumbled.

Her gray eyes sparkled merrily. "Won't you do it to please me?"

"All right," he capitulated easily, "if you'll do something to please me."

She looked at him warily.

"I don't want you to throw a fit like you did when I bought that red dress for you, but please go to a shop in Norfolk and buy a new dress for the occasion."

Beauty wouldn't meet his eyes. Did he suspect how much she wanted a new dress? She would like to look elegant, to grace Grant's table in the way he deserved. And she dreaded having Callie see her in another garment that was several years old. *Pride goeth before destruction,* Beauty admonished herself.

She shook her head. "It isn't appropriate."

He lifted her chin and made her meet his gaze. "There are no strings attached to my offer, but it would make me very happy."

He still held her chin, but she closed her eyes.

God, she prayed inwardly, *we're supposed to shun all appearances of evil. Am I opening the door to other advances?* Still, Grant had been an example of propriety since she'd been at Barwood, and she found herself nodding slowly. She opened her eyes and met his gaze unflinchingly.

"I'm not sure I should, but I'll accept your offer."

His scarred face wrinkled into a wide grin as he pulled her into a brief embrace. He reached in his pocket, pulled out several folded bills held together by a money clip, and handed them to her. A hundred-dollar bill lay on top.

"Pay cash, and no one will ever know about this except the two of us. Don't look at the price tag until you find what you want."

"You might be sorry," she said.

"No, I won't."

Grant returned to work the next morning, and Beauty made plans for the dinner. She asked Mrs. Fillmore to have the silver polished, the china and crystal washed. She wanted this to be an event that Grant would remember after she was gone. It would be almost like a swan song for her, too, giving her something to remember when she was no longer at Barwood.

She tried to stifle any pride in being the hostess, but she would be glad to have Dallas and Callie see Beauty Bartlett at her best. Having second thoughts, she wasn't sure she wanted Callie to see what she'd missed in turning Grant down, but it was too late to fret about it, because Grant telephoned midafternoon and said that both Callie and Dallas had accepted the invitation.

Beauty suspended work at the warehouse until after the dinner. She presented the kitchen staff with a traditional Bartlett menu often served when her father had entertained at a formal dinner.

For starters, they'd have oysters on the half shell and clear chicken soup, to be followed by broiled fish with anchovy, crown roast of lamb, duchesse potatoes, brussels sprouts with lemon butter, celery hearts, stuffed endive salad, and baked Alaska for dessert.

Beauty didn't shop for the new dress until the day of the dinner. She finally chose a white, sleeveless, knee-length shift with a scoop neckline in a soft cotton blend. She didn't look at the price tag until she had chosen the dress, but even then, she hesitated before she gave the clerk three hundred dollars.

She brushed her hair back from her forehead and twisted it into a snug chignon at her nape, held in place with a diamond-studded comb that had once belonged to her grandmother Bartlett. She fastened her grandmother's diamond choker around her neck—this jewelry was one of the few things left to remind Beauty of the glory days of her family.

She was in her room when Grant came home, and she didn't see him until she went to his office ten minutes before the guests were to arrive. He was dressed in a navy suit, a light blue shirt, and white tie. Viewed from his right profile, Grant was extremely handsome, but when he turned his head, his ruined visage became visible, and Beauty felt like weeping. But judging from his kindness toward her family, she knew the inward scars had not gone very deep, and she was thankful for that.

He came around the desk like one in a trance, and he circled Beauty, noting each facet of her appearance.

"You could have stepped off the page of a model's magazine. You're stunning."

"Thanks to you," she said, handing him back the

money clip. He dropped it in his pocket without even checking to see how much she'd spent.

The doorbell rang, and he said, "Why did we invite the others? You're all the company I need."

Trying to remember her lowly position in the house, Beauty stayed behind until Grant had greeted his guests.

"Dinner won't be served for a half hour," Beauty said. "Won't you come into the drawing room?"

A tray of cheese snacks had been placed on the table, and Beauty served glasses of spiced rhubarb cooler, made from her mother's recipe. When Callie looked pointedly at the large portrait of Beauty hanging over the mantel, Beauty wondered if they shouldn't have received the guests in the less formal living room.

"A good likeness of you," Callie said. "Who was the artist?"

"A student from France who came to study in the United States one summer. Father commissioned him to do portraits of my sisters and me. Grant bought the property as it stood. These portraits wouldn't have fit into our farmhouse in Kansas, anyway."

The conversation shifted to less sensitive subjects, and Mrs. Fillmore soon announced dinner. Seating hadn't been discussed, but Grant placed Callie to his left side where she'd have to look at his scars, and Dallas held the chair for Beauty to sit opposite Grant.

The delicious food was served skillfully, and the guests were complimentary. After dinner, Dallas asked for a tour of the warehouse, and the four of them walked through the garden to look at the rows of artifacts that Beauty had arranged. She acknowledged Grant's praise for her skill and hard work with a sinking heart. It must be plain to everyone that she didn't have much work left to do.

Returning to the house, Beauty and Dallas strolled ahead, leaving Callie and Grant together. She chatted about the magnificence of the Barwood gardens, but Grant hardly heard what she said. He admired Beauty's even stride, her rounded slenderness, and the smoothness of her neck, marveling that even her back was beautiful.

He became conscious that Callie had stopped talking. Embarrassed, he shifted his attention back to her. After all, the woman was an invited guest.

"Will Beauty be leaving Barwood when her work on the collection is finished?"

"Not if I have anything to say about it," Grant said, and his attention shifted to Beauty again.

"I should think you'd have a lot to say about it."

When he didn't respond, she said, "It isn't easy to admit my mistakes, but I made a big one when I broke our engagement. It's obvious that I waited too long to learn that."

Dallas paused on the path and turned toward them, sparing Grant the necessity of answering. He had no desire to discuss his feelings about Beauty with anyone.

Grant and Beauty stood together and watched their guests leave. He put his arm around her shoulders as they entered the house.

"This has been a wonderful evening," he said. "Thanks for suggesting and arranging it."

"It was a privilege for me. Father used to entertain a lot, and after Mother died, I was his hostess. I'm glad I have this to remember when I go back to my family."

"You don't have to leave," he said softly.

"Good night, Grant."

He wanted to kiss her, but he wasn't sure Beauty would accept his caress. He lifted her right hand and kissed each finger softly before he released her.

Chapter 7

Three days later, she'd done everything she could possibly do. All of the items were inventoried, cataloged on the computer, and sorted into groups. Grant had helped her move many of the larger items, but she had to decide what to do with the masthead of the *Mary Smith,* an eighteenth-century schooner that had served as a privateer in the American Revolution. The masthead was fastened on the wall of the warehouse, and it would be easy enough for a prospective buyer to examine it in that position, so she spent the day cleaning and polishing the wood. Everything she'd come to do was finished, but she hesitated to go.

She dallied one more day, and it was almost a relief when the decision to leave was taken out of her hands. She and Grant had finished dinner and were starting for a walk when the phone rang.

"I'm tempted to ignore it," Grant said. "I've spent most of the day talking on the phone, but perhaps I shouldn't. Wait a second."

He went into his office and soon returned, handing the cordless phone to Beauty.

"Hello," she said, and her sister, Etta, answered.

"Father had another stroke today. He's in the hospital at Topeka."

Beauty sat down suddenly on a hallway bench. It did seem as if Etta could have broken the news more gently. "How bad is he?"

"I don't know. Frances went with him to the hospital, and she said you could call her there if you wanted to." Etta reeled off the name of the hospital, and Beauty interrupted her.

"Wait a minute. I have to find a pen and paper."

Grant had been standing close, and he handed Beauty a pen from his pocket and held a notebook for her. Trembling hands jotted down the information, with Grant reading as she wrote.

"I'll come home as soon as possible," Beauty said.

Grant knelt beside her. "What's happened?"

"Father's had another stroke. I must go to him. I'll telephone the bus station and find out what time I can leave tomorrow."

He pulled her into his arms, patting her on the back and comforting her.

"I'll make arrangements for you to travel by air, and it won't take any time for you to get there. But I'm going to buy a round-trip ticket."

"No," Beauty said. "I've finished my work at Barwood. I intended to tell you tonight. Even if Father wasn't in the hospital, it's time for me to leave. But I would appreciate having you arrange a plane trip for me—someday I'll pay you back for all you've done for me."

"I've been in *your* debt since the first day you walked into my office." He patted her shoulder. "But we'll discuss that later. You go pack, and I'll see what kind of schedule

I can arrange for you."

Beauty told Mrs. Fillmore she was leaving, but when she went upstairs, she sat on the side of her bed. It had happened too fast. She'd hoped for a few more days to get used to the idea of leaving Grant. She was conscience stricken that she should hesitate at all when her father was ill. How much did she really care for Grant?

She still sat on the bed a half hour later when he tapped on her open door.

"Packed yet?"

She shook her head.

"You'll leave at ten thirty in the morning and be in Topeka by six o'clock tomorrow evening. That's not a bad schedule, considering you'll have two changes to make. I also took the liberty of reserving a hotel room for you not far from the hospital."

"I'm not thinking very well," she said. "I should have telephoned my sister at the hospital to see what his condition is before you made those arrangements."

"Telephone her now—it will ease your mind."

She did feel better after she talked to Frances, learned that Simon's stroke had been a minor one, and that he would be going home as soon as the doctors regulated his medication to prevent future strokes.

"Why don't you stay a few more days until he goes back home?" Grant insisted, but she shook her head.

"I promised Father I'd come back to him as soon as my work was finished. I'm sure he's anxious about me."

"Will you come downstairs after you've packed? It's still not too late for us to take a walk."

She agreed and set about the distasteful chore of packing. When Mrs. Fillmore came in and offered to help,

Beauty said, "I had intended to take everything with me, but if you don't mind, I'll just pack enough for a few weeks, and you can ship the rest to me later."

"Surely you're coming back."

Beauty shook her head. "I've finished my work at the warehouse. I have no reason to stay."

"I don't believe that. I have eyes in my head."

Beauty ignored her remark, and Mrs. Fillmore said, "I'll send anything you want, but I beg you not to make any hasty decisions."

"The decision was made before I came here. I told Father I'd stay only long enough to complete his work. I've done that."

Knowing that she'd want to go to her mother's grave, Grant headed in that direction when they left the house. Beauty took in every aspect of Barwood, as if she'd never seen it before. She picked a rose when they entered the garden surrounding the grave, knelt beside her mother's headstone, and laid the sweet-scented pink bloom on the grass. Grant hunkered down beside her, his hand on her shoulder, and when she started to rise, he took her hand and assisted her. He didn't let go of her hand as they strolled on toward the creek.

"I'm going to miss you," he said.

Beauty sniffed.

At the creek, they sat on the grass, watching a family of white ducks drifting lazily in the quiet current. Grant turned Beauty's face toward him, and he saw sorrow in her eyes. Was she sad because of her father's health or because she would miss him? He couldn't let her leave until he knew.

"I understand that you have to go to your father, but promise me you'll come back."

She lowered her eyes. "I can't promise that. If Father doesn't get well, I'll have to look after my sisters."

"You have several brothers who can take some responsibility for their sisters. It's time you thought of your own happiness. And mine. Beauty, I want you to marry me and live at Barwood as my wife. I love you. The past two months have been the happiest I've ever known. It's because you're here."

Her eyes filled with tears. She shook her head, still not meeting his eyes.

He lifted her chin. "Look at me. I have to know. Are you refusing me because of my scars?"

Her eyes widened in surprise. Then she smiled and moved her hand across the roughness of his blemished cheek. "What scars?" she said, and she kissed several of his unsightly flaws.

Grant pulled her into such a tight embrace that she feared he might crack her ribs.

"My sweetheart!" he whispered over and over as he laid his rough cheek against her face. "It's no wonder I love you." Then he kissed her long and tenderly, his dry skin against her face.

"If it isn't my scars, then why won't you marry me?"

"I want to marry you," she said, "but I must be sure *why* I want you. Would I marry you because I want to come back to Barwood or because I'd want you even if we had to live in a hovel?" She laughed a bit. "Or on a farm in Kansas? Until I know that for sure, I won't promise to marry you."

"I want you so much, I'll take you no matter why you

marry me, but I can understand why you have to be sure. You will keep in touch? Call me every night?"

"Please don't tie me to promises. I'll go to Kansas and see what's going on. I'll keep in touch, but I don't know how often."

Twilight was falling around them, and Beauty stirred in Grant's embrace.

"I still have some packing to do before morning, so let's go to the house."

"I love you," he whispered again. "If things get tough for you in the next few weeks, always remember that I love you."

Telling Mrs. Fillmore good-bye and leaving Barwood was almost as bad as it had been a year ago. Crying openly, the housekeeper hugged Beauty and then bolted toward her office. No doubt realizing how difficult it was for Beauty, Grant didn't speak as he opened the door for her and stored her luggage in the sedan. Their drive to the airport was made almost in silence. Beauty knew if she tried to talk, she'd start crying, and she didn't want Grant to remember her with red eyes and a runny nose.

Grant had said all there was to say last night. The next move was up to Beauty, and he knew she wouldn't make any decisions until she'd seen her family. As he drove, he silently prayed for her speedy return to Barwood.

He stayed with her until she was checked in at the airport, went through security with her, and got her settled in the waiting area. Since he'd learned that Beauty was receptive to his caresses, Grant didn't care what others thought. He smiled and held out his arms. She put her hands on his shoulders and snuggled close to him, looking intently into his eyes, taking in every detail of his features.

"I can't bear to stay and watch the plane carry you away from me," he whispered, "so I'll go to work. I don't think I'd get over it if you don't return, but I know you will. I believe God wants us to be together."

Her hand tenderly caressed his blemished face, and she spoke softly. "May the Lord keep watch between you and me when we are away from each other. Kiss me now and go. This good-bye is tearing me apart."

He kissed her and gave her one last squeeze. "It isn't good-bye, sweetheart. I love you, and I won't let you forget me."

Chapter 8

Beauty wakened terrified. Something was wrong with Grant, she knew there was. The dream had been so vivid. He was lying in bed, swathed in bandages. Had he been in another accident? She switched on the light beside her bed. Five o'clock in the morning—too early to call. Then she realized it would be six o'clock in Virginia. These dreams had occurred frequently during the three months she'd been in Kansas. Every dream was different, but in each one Grant was in a doctor's office or in a hospital bed. After each dream, the desire to be with him was so overpowering that Beauty no longer doubted that it was Grant she loved rather than the opportunity to return to her former home.

Even if she'd wanted to, she couldn't have forgotten Grant, for he'd contacted her every day. If he didn't telephone, he sent her a gift. Every Monday, a florist delivered seven roses to her door—a rose for each day of the week. Evidence of his love was all around the room. The pink robe lying on the foot of the bed was from Grant. He'd sent her jewelry, books, perfumes, and music boxes, making her sisters wild with jealousy.

But her father's health had improved, and Beauty was

free to go to Grant. Although she'd longed to confide in him, she'd never let him know how unhappy she'd been with her family.

She could imagine his reaction if he knew how Etta and Frances had made life miserable for her. Although they easily could have cared for Simon, they kept inventing reasons to keep Beauty in Kansas, and she didn't want to leave anyway until her father was able to look after himself. Grant had sold Simon's nautical collection for enough to pay off his final debts, leaving enough for another beginning for Simon, but Etta and Frances had tried to get their hands on the money. They were furious when Simon had put the money in a trust fund, which wouldn't pass to his children until his death. Beauty had stayed on to keep the two girls from badgering their father until he was well again.

Simon had met a woman whose son was his roommate at the hospital. The woman lived in Florida, but she'd come to Topeka to care for her son. After he'd returned to the farm, she and Simon had kept in touch, and Beauty was pleased to see a romance blossoming between the two. Her mother had been gone for several years, and Simon was lonely. This, too, displeased Etta and Frances.

At first the sisters were determined that Beauty should stay on the farm, but when they realized that Grant was in love with Beauty, they encouraged her to marry him, thinking this was a good way for all of them to return to Barwood. Beauty finally appealed to her oldest brother, who suggested selling the farm in Kansas and dividing the proceeds between the heirs, which could be done as soon as Etta, the youngest sister, turned twenty-one in November.

Knowing she wouldn't go back to sleep until she

learned that Grant was all right, Beauty put on her robe and tiptoed downstairs to the kitchen. She dialed Grant's number on the rotary phone, holding her breath, fearing he might not answer.

Thank God, she thought, when the receiver was lifted and he answered sleepily.

"Good morning!" she said brightly. "Time to get up."

She envisioned him sitting up in bed and pushing his thick blond hair back from his forehead.

"Beauty! Why are you calling so early? Is everything all right?"

"Yes, now that I'm talking to you. I keep having bad dreams about you, Grant, as if you're sick. Have you been in the hospital? Are you all right?"

Did he hesitate? "Yes. I'm fine."

"I love you," she said softly.

She envisioned the surprise on his face. "What did you say?"

"I love you."

"That's what I thought you said. Well, praise the Lord and hallelujah! What a beautiful morning! My prayers have been answered."

"I'm miserable being away from you. I think that's why I keep dreaming you're sick, and when I awaken, I'm so worried that you need me and I'm not there."

"I need you, and you're not here," he said promptly, and she knew he was smiling.

"I know now it's *you* I want, not Barwood. Is that offer of marriage still open?"

"I'll marry you today. Do I hop on a plane and come to Kansas, or are you coming home?"

"Not so fast," she said. "I didn't mean today. It might

be a couple of months before I feel free to leave here."

She explained to him about the possible sale of the farm and that Simon might remarry. "He's old enough to retire, and he'll have some income from the trust fund. The woman he's interested in owns a house near the waterfront in Pensacola, Florida. Father will feel right at home."

"I'll help any way I can. I'll let your family move back to Barwood if necessary. That would be a small price to pay for having you."

"No, thank you," she answered. "My sisters aren't easy to live with. Our farm is near Topeka, and a developer wants it badly enough to pay a high price. My sisters will receive a good sum of money for their share, and it's time they start fending for themselves. Besides, I'm selfish enough to want you to myself."

"I prefer that, too. Beauty, I miss you so much. I can hardly bear to come home at night when you're not here, and it really isn't a home without you. More than once, I've picked up the phone to make reservations to come and get you, but I've tried to be patient. I don't want to wait much longer."

"I'm planning to spend Christmas at Barwood," she assured him.

After seeing her father married and on his way to Florida and carrying a cashier's check for her portion of her mother's estate, Beauty boarded a plane to return to Virginia on the sixth of December. The months of waiting had seemed interminable to both her and Grant. He'd made arrangements for a quiet ceremony in the small church near Barwood, and their wedding would take place as soon as she arrived.

Beauty could hardly restrain herself when the plane landed, and she was out of her seat, standing in the aisle, even before the seat belt sign was turned off. She fidgeted while the attendants opened the door and attached the walkway to the plane. Pulling her carry-on bag behind her, she hurried toward the terminal, where she scanned the faces of people in the waiting room. Her heart plummeted! Grant wasn't there, even though he'd telephoned early that morning, saying he'd be waiting.

"Beauty," she heard him call. The voice was Grant's, but the face of the man looming over her was that of a stranger. She dropped the handle of her suitcase, and Grant pulled it out of the way of the deplaning passengers. She ran her hand over the left side of his face where the skin was as smooth as a baby's.

"I don't understand," she said.

"The miracle of modern medicine, sweetheart. I've been spending a lot of time with a plastic surgeon. I didn't want you to live with my scars the rest of your life."

"But, Grant, I'll miss the way you used to be. Your scars didn't bother me."

"But they bothered me, and I did it for you. I hope you aren't disappointed," he added worriedly.

"Oh, no," she said. "You're handsome, but it's going to take awhile to realize who you are. I love *you*. My love has nothing to do with your outward appearance."

Grant noticed that people had grouped around them, staring, and he laughed. "We're making a spectacle of ourselves. Let's go home."

By Christmas Eve, they'd been married two weeks. Mrs. Fillmore and Beauty had spent every day decorating

Barwood in the Bartlett tradition. A huge tree stood in the drawing room. Candles gleamed from every window. Several trees on the lawn glowed with strings of red bulbs. The service employees had been given generous bonuses and granted two days' leave. The cook had prepared food in advance, and all Beauty had to do was heat and serve what they wanted.

One of Grant's gifts to Beauty was a floral arrangement of fifty red roses, which she'd placed on the marble-topped table in the entrance hall. They opened their other gifts and sat on pillows in front of the fire in the family living room. The house was quiet.

"Just the two of us," Grant said. "I've been dreaming of this for months. I have one more gift for you." He handed Beauty a box that had been hidden behind a chair.

Removing the Christmas wrapping, Beauty took out a beautifully illustrated children's book—*Beauty and the Beast*. She didn't know what to say.

"When we watched the video version of this story, I commented, 'Too bad it's only a fairy tale.'"

Grant took the book from her hand and turned to the first page. "In the original fable, an evil sorceress cast a spell on a young prince and turned him into a monster. The prince could never regain his features until a beautiful, truehearted maiden promised to marry him."

A log snapped in the fireplace, shooting sparks toward the chimney, and a brisk wind blew sheets of rain against the windows. Grant stared toward the flames, thinking of the changes Beauty had brought to his life.

"The story reminds me of our relationship. It was almost like a fairy tale come true when you promised to marry me."

Grant closed the book and gazed tenderly into Beauty's eyes.

"But it was God, not a sorceress, who brought us together," he continued. "When you came to me, not only was I scarred on the outside, but my bitterness had left scars within. Your sweet Christian spirit healed me inside, and my faith in God was born anew simply because of your example. When you said you'd marry me, I felt like the beast in the story who had shed his old self. I was good enough for you on the inside, so I wanted to be physically whole, too."

Beauty touched his unblemished left cheek. "I love you the way you are now, but I loved you the way you were."

"I know that, but I wanted you to have the best of me. I'm convinced that God will give us a future as wonderful as the fabled Beauty found with her prince."

"And they lived happily ever after," Beauty said as she lifted her lips for his kiss.

IRENE B. BRAND

Irene is a lifelong resident of West Virginia, where she lives with her husband, Rod. Her first inspirational romance was published in 1984, and since that time she has had over twenty titles published. She is the author of four nonfiction books and various devotional materials; and her writings have appeared in numerous historical, religious, and general magazines. Irene became a Christian at the age of eleven and continues to be actively involved in her local church. Before retiring in 1989 to devote full time to freelance writing, Irene taught for twenty-three years in secondary public schools. Many of her books have been inspired while traveling to forty-nine of the United States and thirty-four foreign countries.

The Shoemaker's Daughter

Lynn A. Coleman

Dedication

I'd like to dedicate this story to my daughter, Sarah. You've been a wonder since the day you were born, and you've been our Princess. May God bless you as you mother those three darling daughters of yours.

All my love,
Mom

Chapter 1

M arissa!"
     Marissa cinched the straps holding her surfboard in place on the roll bars of the jeep. *"Buenos dias, Tia Rosa."*

"I was hoping to see you this morning, child. I've been hearing some very disturbing things and thought you ought to know."

"Disturbing" to Aunt Rosa could mean anything from a mosquito bite to the world coming to an end. Marissa held back a smirk and proceeded to tie her long black hair back into a ponytail. "What's the matter?"

Rosa wiped her hands on a cloth and forked some stray, gray strands behind her ear, placing the cloth on the white coral border surrounding a mound of impatiens. Rosa's yard was a testament to tropical flowers all year long. "It's your father's business, dear."

"Daddy sold the business a year ago. You know that."

"My gracious, child, of course I know that. I'm not senile. But the young man who purchased it. . .well, he's running it into the ground." Rosa placed her hands on her ample hips and wagged her head back and forth. "Such a shame. It's not like it's all his fault, mind you. . . ."

Marissa half listened, but mostly she thought of her father's shoe repair business, how hard he'd worked, how hard the entire family had worked. Thirty years in one location. He always had time for his customers, although that meant he often didn't come home until well after dark. But he reminded the family that keeping the customers happy, showing them concern, was part of what kept them clothed and fed. Of course, the fact that her father was one of the best cobblers this side of the Atlantic didn't hurt either.

"He does love her so," Rosa rambled.

Love? What does that have to do with the business? "Who?"

"Mr. Flynn's mother, dear."

His mother? Maybe she should have paid more attention to Aunt Rosa.

"You weren't listening, were you?"

"Afraid I got sidetracked."

Rosa's eyes twinkled. "You always did have that problem. Okay, let me try again. Mr. Flynn, the owner of your father's business, hasn't been keeping up with orders. His mother's car accident—which left her in a wheelchair—is the reason, and people were patient at first. But you know how folks are today—rush, rush, rush, everything has to be done yesterday. Anyway, he's losing customers left and right, and I just thought you ought to know."

"I'm sorry to hear that." And Marissa truly was sorry for the man's troubles. But what did they have to do with her? It was his business now, not her family's. Her parents, RVing around the country, certainly wouldn't care. Perhaps that wasn't quite true. The business meant more than money to her father. "Thank you for telling me, *Tia* Rosa.

The next time I talk with my folks, I'll let them know."

"Such a shame. He's a fine young man. Just had a peck of trouble since he bought the business."

Trouble? What else had happened? Granted, a car accident that left a family member in a wheelchair would be hard, but what other trouble had this man experienced?

Marissa had avoided going back to the store since she had come home from college. It wasn't theirs anymore. It didn't feel right. A gentle breeze fluffed her sleeves, reminding her of what she was doing up so early this morning and bringing her back to the immediate. "I need to get going, Tia Rosa. We'll talk some more when I get back."

"Going surfing?"

"Yup. Small-craft warnings are up for the Gulf Stream, so you know that means some waves are hitting the beach."

"Be wise, child. I know you've been surfing since you were a *niña*, but you're far smaller than a small craft." Rosa winked.

"Thank you, I think." Marissa kissed Aunt Rosa on the cheek and jumped into her jeep. Waves in Miami were few and far between, and anyone with a mind to surf had to get them when the getting was good. And all indications were, they were definitely good.

Her seat belt clicked as she settled into place. She turned the key, and the engine purred to life. She patted her board and drove toward the beach. The house was only a few miles from the beach, just far enough from the business so Daddy felt like he was away from work on his days off.

When her folks first arrived in Miami, shortly after they were married, they lived in the small apartment behind the store. But that was years before she was born. Eight, to be precise. Her grandfather had taught her father the trade, and he would teach his son. But a son was never born. Five daughters, all of whom made him very proud, but none of whom wanted, or married, a man who would take on the family business. As the baby of the family, Marissa had been in college when her parents retired. Last year, after her father suffered from chest pains, the folks decided to retire early, enjoy life, and do some of the traveling they had always hoped, but never had the time, to do before.

Marissa wormed her way through the traffic, mentally shifting gears, and focused on the awaiting waves.

Cameron tossed the hammer and the awl down on his workbench. Too many uncompleted orders, and everyone demanded immediate service. His mother tried to be patient, but she had needs, too. Doctor appointments, therapy sessions—all of those took time, valuable time. Time he didn't have. If he hadn't paid out so much up-front capital, maybe he'd have enough to hire an assistant.

But he had needed to put down most of his savings to get an affordable monthly payment. Thankfully, Sam Jones charged him a low rent for the prime real estate. Sam had bought up large sections of Miami Beach and North Miami Beach in the early seventies, when everything was falling apart. But the new life that Miami was experiencing had made Sam a wealthy man. Fortunately for Cameron, Sam also loved his chosen profession, a cobbler, a shoemaker, his family heritage. But Sam would not be pleased to see thirty years of his hard-earned business whittled away in one year.

Cameron stretched his back and groaned. He'd come

in at six to get a jump on the orders that should have been done last week. Working with leather had been a hobby he'd started in high school. During college he had worked for an old cobbler in Connecticut. After college he found a job working nine to five in business management. The pay was great, but the job itself didn't give him pleasure— not the way working with leather had.

Finally he gave up the white collar job and pursued an apprenticeship with Mike. Cameron snickered as he looked at a weather-curled photograph of himself with the burly and bushy, white-haired, balding Michael Perrione. In Cameron's hands were the first pair of shoes he ever made from the soles up, a gift to his father for graciously under-standing he wasn't cut out to be a high financier on Wall Street.

For three years he had scrimped and saved so he could buy his own shop. His parents had allowed him to live at home and put just about all of his earnings away for a down payment. Unfortunately, his father never saw the day when he purchased his own shop. But his mother had, and she had even moved to Miami to be closer to him, her only remaining family.

Cameron let out a sigh. "Reminiscing isn't getting your work done, old boy. Get moving." He grabbed the woman's shoe he had been repairing, replacing the leather on the heel. Once the glue was set, he brought it to the nibbler and removed the excess before bringing it to the sander.

He flipped the off switch of the sander and heard a car pull into the back alley parking space. Most customers came through the front, but some of the regulars knew they could generally find a spot or two behind his shop. Cameron wiped his hands on a rag and straightened his apron. Inwardly, he prayed he had this customer's order ready. Outwardly, he put on the biggest smile he could muster and waited.

And waited.

His plastic smile slipped and curiosity got the best of him.

Marissa pulled into her familiar parking spot and noticed a bright red classic convertible with white leather interior. Having worked with her father during her summer vacations and any other school vacation, she'd come to appreciate high quality and finely crafted leather. If this leather wasn't original, then whoever had replaced these covers sure knew what he was doing.

Instinctively she reached out and caressed the fine, smooth surface. And if she knew her materials, it was some of the nicest Italian leather she'd ever seen, smooth as a baby's bottom and inviting as a fluffy comforter on a chilly morning.

Marissa scanned the skies. There was no threat of rain, but whoever owned this car ought to put a cover over these seats. The sun would kill the leather. Unless, of course, the owner knew that and kept the leather well oiled and polished.

Marissa looked at the back door to her father's old shoe repair business. It seemed much the same, and yet also looked so different. Had it really been a whole year since he'd sold it? What surprised her most about her life was the fact that she hadn't accepted her father's offer to give her the business. In the end, he'd sold it to a New Englander who had apprenticed with an old cobbler up there for several years. And, apparently, according to Aunt

Rosa, Mr. Flynn was having some troubles.

The surf crashed behind her. "Enough musing for one day, girl," she reprimanded herself. "The surf awaits."

Marissa stepped on the running board of her jeep and unfastened her surfboard. Before removing the board, she looked around, then hid her keys in a secret leather pouch hidden by the natural curve of the driver's seat.

Now—she was set to go surfing. How long had it been? A year? No, it hadn't been that long; it only felt like it. In fact, this past year's hurricane season had been wonderful. Plenty of storms, too far out to do Miami any damage, but close enough to bring in some great waves. Miami was not known for its surfing. The temperature of the water was fine, but the Bahamas created a natural breaker and protected the shore from the full force of the Atlantic. So the few days when it was remotely possible to get a good ride, surfers were always out there.

Her finely polished board glistened in the morning sun. Marissa stepped back up on the runner, lifted the board slightly and pulled it down, then stepped back to the pavement in one fluid movement. Joy swept through her. She loved to ride the waves.

"Hey!" a voice bellowed from behind.

Marissa jumped, flinging her board around with her. "You can't—"

The sound and feel of her board making contact with some—one—sickened her. Whom had she hit? She lowered the board slightly.

A man sat on the pavement moaning and holding his nose with both hands. Marissa's stomach flip-flopped. Blood was everywhere—down the man's white shirt, streaming out through his fingers, down his hands, and trickling down his forearms.

"I'm so sorry," she gushed. Dropping her board, she came to the man's aid.

Tears pooled in the deepest blue eyes she'd ever seen. His face reddened with anger, but to the man's credit, he didn't yell.

"I'll call 9-1-1."

"You broke my nose," he moaned.

"I'm sorry. I didn't mean to."

A sound of restrained pain escaped his lips.

Marissa grabbed her towel and handed it to him. He didn't accept it, but then again, he was holding his nose with both hands. How could he take it? She laid it gently in his lap, then hustled back to her car, retrieved her keys, and unlocked her cell phone from the glove compartment, calling 9-1-1.

"Marissa Jones," she responded to the operator.

Jones? Cameron looked at the wild woman and wanted to scream. She had to be one of the former owner's daughters. Who else would be so bold as to park in his limited customer parking? The fact that it was hours before anyone would come to the shop didn't matter. All he'd seen was a surfer trying to take advantage of free parking in his limited back lot.

The pain pulsated through his entire body as Cameron listened to Marissa give the operator directions, then click her phone shut.

"They'll be here in a moment. I'm so sorry."

She knelt down beside him, holding an ice pack in her hand. Where she'd come up with an ice pack, he didn't have a clue, but who needed to figure that out now? Now he needed pain killers. Ice would have to do until the paramedics arrived.

"Here. I know it will hurt, but it will keep the swelling down," she offered.

Cameron grasped the ice and noticed the blood on his hand. It was everywhere. He slowly closed his eyes. He wasn't one given to a queasy stomach but. . .

"Let me." Her steady hand cupped the back of his head. Tenderly she placed the ice on his crushed nose. He gasped for breath. The pain was excruciating. His eyes focused on a pair of beautiful dark brown eyes, looking like a deer's trapped by a driver's headlights. Nausea fluttered in his stomach. He held it back and closed his lids. Now was not the time to pass out. Cold sweat beaded on his body, and Cameron felt himself spiraling downward.

Chapter 2

An eternity passed while Marissa paced the hospital's waiting room floor. Why was she still there? *Because you're the one who sent the man to the hospital,* she reasoned with herself. Guilt, mixed with the horror of what she had done, demanded that she see Cameron Flynn through this. He had passed out in her arms. She had continued to hold him until the ambulance arrived and while the EMTs pulled out his wallet to determine his identity. The poor man's troubles, as Aunt Rosa put it, had just increased. She'd have to call her parents tonight. Maybe her father could give her some insight into helping him.

In spite of his injury, she noticed he was a very handsome man. His ash-blond wavy hair, strong cheekbones, and squared jaw, all added to his attractiveness. The mass of red blood streaming down his face had distorted the rest of his features.

Marissa looked at her watch and flipped open her cellular phone. "Hi, Bill. This is Marissa. Sorry I'm late, but I. . ." How could she explain this? "I had to bring a friend to the hospital this morning. His nose was broken."

"When do you think you'll be able to come in?" Bill asked.

"I'm hoping noon, but you know how hospitals are. I've been here for a couple hours already."

Bill whistled. "All right. Did you have any meetings set up this morning? Do they need to be canceled, or can I assign someone else?"

"Nothing in the morning." But she did have a one o'clock, and if she wasn't there, she'd lose the account. On the other hand, if Bill or someone else went in her place, they would save the deal. Realizing it was better for the company for this appointment to be kept, she sighed. "Bill, I do have a one o'clock, and even if I get there by noon, I'm not certain I'd be ready for the presentation."

"The Watson account?"

"Yes. Muriel should be able to print out the proposal, but I should have you or Jim run with this one. Jim's quick and he'll see where I was going with my pitch."

"Jim's a good choice, Marissa. I hope your friend is feeling better soon. How'd he break his nose, anyway?"

"Uh, I kind of slammed my surfboard into it." She winced at the memory of the horrible, cracking thud.

"You sure he's still a friend?" Bill laughed.

"Actually, I've never met the man before. He's the gentleman who bought my father's business."

"Stop, you're killing me," he chortled. "You've hit a perfect stranger in the head with your surfboard and you're waiting for what? Your reprimand?"

"I'm sure the man's upset. But no, I needed to find out if he's going to be okay. It's my fault. The least I could do is drive him back to the shop."

"Marissa, if it was me and I didn't know you—trust me, Honey, I wouldn't want to see your pretty face right away."

"Oh. Well, he hasn't a choice. I'm here. I'll be in as

soon as I can. Bye, Bill."

She could still hear Bill chuckling when she hung up the phone. Bill was a man of the world, and possibly he was right about Cameron Flynn not wanting to see her. . .but she needed to see him. She needed to know he'd be all right. Somehow she'd have to pay for this emergency visit, too. She wondered if her car insurance would cover this? Would any of her insurance policies cover this? Probably not. She hadn't taken out a policy on her surfboard and any bodily injuries that it might cause. "Guess I'll be staying in the folks' house for a few more months," she moaned.

She walked up to the nurse's desk for the fourth time. A middle-aged nurse in white slacks and a blue top smiled as Marissa approached. "He's coming out of X-ray. The doctor should be fixing him up real soon."

"Thanks."

Marissa walked back to the waiting area and sat down, thumbing through ancient magazines. "Why is it they never have anything current?" she asked no one in particular.

"Probably because current magazines would grow feet," smiled a blue-gray-haired lady sitting in the corner.

Marissa chuckled. "You're probably right."

A doctor clad in rumpled surgical blues with a shock of mousy brown hair escaping from under his surgical cap scrubbed his hands.

"Mr. Flynn, you're a fortunate man. The break is clean and it should reset just fine."

"Thanks," Cameron muttered.

"From what you said about the accident, your nose could have been crushed. Be glad that the most you'll be dealing with is a slight crook of the bridge." The doctor washed his hands, then sat on the stool and rolled it over to Cameron.

"There was so much blood." Cameron looked at the now browning stains on his shirt and pants.

"Head wounds are like that. I stitched up the wound with tiny sutures. You have twenty, as opposed to the five you would have normally been given. The scar will be visible for a while. Remember, once it's healed, to keep sunscreen on it so the scar tissue doesn't turn gray."

Cameron nodded. His head throbbed. He raised a hand to stabilize his head.

"No driving for twenty-four hours. You were unconscious when the paramedics arrived and you have a slight concussion. Like I said, you were a fortunate man. Besides, you have a beautiful woman out there pacing and bothering my nurses every twenty minutes or so. A man can't be all that unfortunate with a woman like that," the doctor winked.

Cameron groaned. "She's the one with the killer surfboard."

The doctor slapped his knee and laughed. "You'll be fine, Mr. Flynn. Make an appointment with your orthopedic surgeon and have him follow up. I've written out your orders. Read them to remind yourself how to take care of the wound. After a day you'll be up and around just fine."

His orthopedic surgeon was also his mother's. Maybe he could schedule appointments on the same day. Today was shot. He wouldn't be able to work. He could wait on customers, hand out completed orders, but he couldn't get any new orders out. His mother! "Oh, man," he mumbled as he looked at his watch. It was long past ten o'clock and her appointment.

"I need a phone."

"There's a pay phone in the waiting area."

"I don't have any change. Can I use the one at the nurses' station? I was supposed to bring my mother to her doctor appointment an hour ago. She'll be worried sick."

"No problem, just tell the nurse I said it's okay."

"Thanks." Cameron hopped off the bed. He felt dizzy. He fumbled, grasping the bed.

"Slowly, Mr. Flynn. You've got a concussion, remember?" the fiftyish doctor admonished.

The staff had plopped Cameron into a wheelchair in mere seconds. Then they rolled him to the desk, where he placed the call to his mother.

"No, Mom, I'm fine. I'll be home shortly. Reschedule your appointment."

"Okay, son. But how on earth did you break your nose?" He was relieved to hear that the apprehension in her voice had calmed tremendously.

"Long story; I'll tell you when I get home."

"Okay. Be careful."

"I will. Bye, Mom."

"Bye."

He listened for the gentle click of his mother putting down the receiver and handed the phone back to the nurse.

"Thanks."

As a male orderly wheeled him to the waiting area, Marissa Jones jumped up. "Beautiful" may have been an understatement on the doctor's part. The brilliant, dark black hair and lightly tanned olive skin revealed her Italian heritage. *She may be beautiful, but she's also a klutz,* he reminded himself.

"Mr. Flynn, I'm so sorry. What did the doctor say?"

"He said I was fortunate." He'd let her stew for a moment with the gravity of her careless behavior.

Her eyes sparkled with tears. "I'll pay the hospital bills."

"I have insurance, but you can pay the deductible." He kept his voice tight. She might be beautiful, but he wasn't going to be a man who was fooled by a woman's attractiveness. No, she was self-centered and reckless. He didn't need that in his life.

"No problem. Can I drive you back to the shop to pick up your car?"

Did he want to drive with this woman? Was she safe? "No, thanks. I'll order a cab. Doc says I can't drive for twenty-four hours."

"Oh, all right. Well, I'm staying at my parents' house. If you need anything, call me."

Calling her would be the last thing on this earth he would do. He had enough problems. Inviting more trouble into his life would be suicide. And this woman with the brilliant black hair, well-shaped body, and killer surfboard was trouble with a capital T, no question about it. "Good-bye, Miss Jones."

"Good-bye. And again, I truly am sorry."

The man is a jerk, Marissa assessed. Handsome, even with his nose bandaged, but a jerk nonetheless. Was he afraid that she couldn't drive a car?

She didn't have to stay at the hospital and wait for him. But then again, she really did it for her own sanity. It wasn't like she expected the man to just forgive her at the drop of a hat. But she'd apologized half a dozen times. Not once did he say "it's okay" or "you're forgiven."

Wasn't a person supposed to do that? The most she got from him was groans and daggers. He certainly had a temper, controlled, but a temper. So why did this bother her so much? Hadn't Bill warned her the man wouldn't be all that pleased to see her?

Marissa drove home and placed her unused surfboard in the garage. Upstairs, she showered and dressed for work. If she hurried, she could go with Jim to present her proposal to the Watsons.

Her body was tense. She was angry, she was hurt, and she grieved for the pain she had caused Cameron Flynn. If she was going to be of any worth to anyone today, she needed to take a few minutes and have some one-on-one time with her Lord. Marissa sat at the foot of her bed and silently began to pray.

Okay, Lord, I blew it. I'm sorry. I didn't mean to hurt the man. Please forgive me, and please let Cameron Flynn know I meant him no harm.

She rose from the bed, then sat right back down again.

Oh, and work something out for him and his business. Rosa says it's a mess, but You know what's really happening and what he really needs, Lord. Thanks.

Marissa nodded at her reflection in the mirror—her hair in place, her makeup light but perfectly blended. She looked fine, but inside she still needed God's peace and forgiveness. She knew it would come. She just needed to wait.

A familiar verse of scripture came to mind. "Through Jesus, therefore, let us continually offer to God a sacrifice of praise—the fruit of lips that confess his name. And do not forget to do good and to share with others, for with such sacrifices God is pleased." Quickly she opened the Bible on her nightstand and found the remembered verse from Hebrews 13:15–16.

It really would be a sacrifice to praise God now, but she knew it often worked. She clasped her keys from her dresser and began singing, in full voice, "We bring a sacrifice of praise. . . ," as she bounced down the stairs to the garage and into her jeep.

The one o'clock appointment and hurrying to team with Jim kept her so busy she hardly thought of Cameron Flynn and the damage she'd done to his handsome face. As the afternoon wore on and jokes about her being "the crusher" surfaced, she couldn't help thinking about Cameron. At one point she looked up his work number, only to discover it was the same number her father had used for the past thirty years. Marissa tapped her finely polished nail on her desk. If she had gone surfing as planned, her nails would be chipped and possibly broken. Marissa smiled. At least she didn't need to schedule another manicure this week.

"Great job on the Watson presentation," Jim declared as he stood in the doorway to her office.

"Thanks."

His million-dollar smile aimed right for her. Marissa braced herself. She'd seen that smile before.

"I think the two of us work well as a team. What do you think about us doing some more proposals together?"

Marissa held back her laughter. "We did do well together today. However, a team would mean more than you coming on at the last minute to pinch-hit when I get tied up."

"I was more than happy to help out."

He wasn't a bad looking man with his dark hair and

large frame. He stood about six-foot, she guessed, and had a bit of a paunch.

Goodness, he wasn't getting it. "Thanks for your willingness but. . ." Marissa tapped her desk a little harder with her fingertips. "I think I'm doing okay with my presentations, scouting out potential new customers, and working up advertising proposals and pitching them."

"You're doing fantastic. You've been here less than a year and have landed some good contracts."

He still wasn't getting it. She'd been the one to do all the legwork, and now she'd have to share a percentage of her commission because of her reckless behavior. "I'll keep it in mind, Jim. But I don't mind telling you, I like working independently."

That did it. His million-dollar smile slipped a couple thousand, and the worry line shot up on the center of his forehead. "I understand, feel the same way myself."

"Thanks, Jim, and I do appreciate you filling in for me. I'll definitely be calling you if I run into a jam again." *Oh, but Lord, please keep me from running into more jams,* she silently prayed.

"No problem, glad to help." Jim lightly knocked on the door frame. "Well, guess I'll be going now. Again, congrat's on the Watson account."

She nodded.

It wasn't long before Bill walked in wearing an enthusiastic smile. "I just went over the figures on the Watson account. Great job!"

"Thanks."

"You've certainly proved to be a valuable asset to this company. I'm glad I hired you."

Marissa chuckled. "Me, too."

"I'm not sure, but I don't think I've ever had a first-year employee do as well as you. You're a go-getter, and I like that. And you're creative, which only helps the firm. I appreciate that."

Marissa didn't mind being complimented, but it always left her a bit uncertain as to how to respond. She looked down at her desk, pulled a couple of pieces of paper together, and stacked them.

"Thanks."

"By the way, how's the man with the broken nose?" Bill's bald head glistened under the office lights, and his grin was brighter still.

"Fine." Marissa sighed.

"Heard you picked up a nickname today." He chuckled.

"Thanks for letting everyone know," she quipped, flinging her sarcasm back at him perhaps a bit too sharply, she thought.

Bill raised his hand to his chest in feigned innocence. *"Moi?* I'd never."

"Yeah, right."

"Good night, crusher. See you in the morning." Bill laughed and waddled off to his office.

Marissa glanced at the clock. It was well past five. She could leave and not feel guilty. Moments later she was working her way through the commuting traffic—sunglasses on with hair held back—and enjoying the refreshingly cool day. *Low seventies, perfect weather for Miami in January,* she pondered.

As she pulled into her driveway, she saw Aunt Rosa making a beeline right toward her. What did she want now?

Chapter 3

"Cameron, what on earth happened?" his mother's voice gasped out.

Cameron turned around and noticed his reflection in the hall mirror. Two swollen, dark black shiners stared back at him, accented by the white bandage surrounding his nose. Or rather, what was left of his nose. The doctor had said he was fortunate, but he also indicated a possibility of further surgery down the road to aid his breathing.

"A wild woman hit me with her surfboard."

"What?" Jean Ann Flynn took most things in stride, but Cameron knew when it came to him, she became very concerned. He watched her embrace the armrests of her wheelchair, a contraption she might never be rid of. She was making progress but. . . No, he wouldn't allow his mind to go there again, to the tractor trailer that had lost control on the northern bend of the Palmetto Expressway, hitting his mother's car broadside and causing her to flip her vehicle. He was fortunate to still have her alive.

"Well, maybe she isn't a wild woman, but it sure felt like it. Sam Jones has a daughter. Actually he has five, but this one apparently loves to surf. She pulled into the rear parking space at the shop and was taking the board off her jeep when I called out to her."

"But why did she hit you with her surfboard?" she asked.

"I'm getting to that, Mother." He patted her hand lovingly and gave her a kiss on the cheek. "Apparently I startled her. When I called out—"

"You mean, when you yelled?"

"Well, yeah, sort of," Cameron admitted, as he sat on the sofa next to his mother.

"Cameron James."

Cameron stiffened. Why was it, at twenty-six, his mother still had a way of getting to him? "I guess I yelled. But I can't have surfers taking up my valuable parking space by leaving their cars there all day."

"I suppose not. But haven't I taught you, 'a little sugar goes a long way'?"

"Mother." He paused and rubbed the back of his neck.

"Sorry, son. Does it hurt much?" She leaned closer, examining his bandages.

"Only when I breathe."

"Oh my."

"Seriously, Mom, I'll be okay. I just need to rest for a day. She gave me a mild concussion, too." He started to get up.

"Lay down on the sofa and I'll fetch you something to drink."

"I'm fine, Mom. Do you need anything?" he asked.

"No, this new nursing assistant is wonderful."

Cameron was grateful his mother's medical insurance covered in-home care. It made life and living with this accident so much easier.

Weariness washed over him and he patted his mother's hand. "I think I'm going to go to bed and take a nap."

"You do that, son. I'm sorry."

"Adds character, right?"

"Possibly." Jean winked.

She looked like she was carrying some humorous secret. What, he didn't have a clue, but he'd eventually find out. Now he just wanted to rest and try to salvage some of this horrible day.

"Marissa, what on earth did you do to that poor man?" Aunt Rosa placed her hands on her hips and took her standard stance. She was a sweet woman who had a mind of her own, though Marissa always thought she listened to more gossip than a person should. But Rosa never seemed to outright gossip. Like this morning, when she informed Marissa about Cameron Flynn's troubles. She didn't draw it out like some piece of juicy news. But how on earth had she heard about her clunking Cameron Flynn in the face with her surfboard?

"It was an accident."

"I told you about Mr. Flynn's troubles so you could pray and thought perhaps your parents might be able to help him in some way. I didn't mean for you to give him more."

"*Tia Rosa!*" Marissa quelled her temper. "I didn't mean to hit the man in the head with my surfboard. He startled me, and I just swung around to see who was yelling. I had no idea he was right behind me."

"Humph. I heard some wild woman hit him with a surfboard. And I knew you were surfing."

"I certainly am a woman, but I wouldn't call myself

wild. Besides, who called me that?"

"You know how it is, some of his customers asked how he hurt his nose, and apparently he said something about a wild woman and her surfboard. Naturally, I assumed it was you."

"Well, it was, but I wasn't willfully trying to hurt the man."

"No, I imagine not. So, what are you going to do to make things right?" Rosa softened her stance.

"What can I do? I apologized to the guy half a dozen times, but he wouldn't accept it. Not to mention, I waited at the hospital all morning to see how he was and even offered him a ride back to the shop. But he didn't want anything to do with me."

"He must have a temper."

"Apparently, but he controlled his anger when I first hit him. Of course, the fact that he went unconscious could have helped." She winced.

"Unconscious? girl, you need to fill me in. I've got some *arroz con frijolés negros ey carne ripada* for dinner. Would you like some?"

Marissa smiled. Rosa's Cuban beef was some of the best in Miami. How could she pass that up? "Sure."

"Great, you go change, and I'll have our dinner ready by the time you come over."

"Sounds wonderful. I don't feel like cooking for myself today."

"And I hate eating alone. I'm never happy when Manuel is out of town." Rosa's smile transformed into a distant, mournful look. Manuel and Rosa, longtime friends, had been more like family than neighbors.

"How long before he returns?" Marissa asked.

"Another week. I never understand why it takes him so much time to set up those South American bank computer systems. But apparently it does. You know he has to stay long enough to train the workers and to make sure all the bugs are out of the system."

"Yes, I remember." And for as long as she could remember, Manuel worked half the year in the States and half the year in some country in Central or South America. But if memory served her right, this was his last year before he retired.

"I'll be over shortly."

Rosa headed to her single story house. The yard was immaculate, her gardens exquisite. Marissa looked at her own yard. Without her mother tending to the garden, it was badly in need of some TLC. Perhaps this weekend she could make a dent—if she didn't bring work home from the office again.

Inside the cool house, she dropped her keys, picked up the portable phone, and punched out her parents' cell phone number.

"Mom, it's Marissa."

"Hi, sweetheart, is everything okay?"

"Yes and no. Work's going great, but I kinda broke a man's nose with my surfboard today."

"What?"

Marissa sat down in the overstuffed chair and proceeded to tell her mother the details, then retold the whole story again to her father.

"Oh, one other thing, Daddy. Rosa says Mr. Flynn's not doing well with the business. Something about his mother's car accident and not being able to keep up with the orders."

"I see. Do you know what happened to his mother?"

"Not a clue, but Rosa gave the impression it was serious."

"Hmm, let me pray about this, dear. Thanks for bringing it to my attention. You might want to pray, too. . .see if there is something you might be able to do to help him."

"Apart from helping him out in the shop, I can't imagine. But I don't have the time, and personally I don't think he'd want me."

Her father laughed in his hearty way. She smiled at hearing it once again. "But, sweetheart, you knocked the man out with a surfboard? I imagine anyone would be a bit defensive after that."

Marissa chuckled and answered, "You're probably right." She finished her conversation, telling him about her job, the compliments, and the ribbing she'd gotten today. Her parents informed her about their trip and how cold it was. They were going to head south to Texas after spending another day or two in the Utah Rockies.

Marissa looked at her watch. Rosa would be waiting on her. She quickly changed and headed over to her long-time family friend.

"I was wondering if I needed to send out the troops?" Rosa smiled, stirring a simmering pot of Cuban beef.

Marissa's stomach gurgled from the heavenly aroma. "Smells wonderful." Marissa reached in and snatched a piece of meat.

Rosa slapped her hand. "You haven't changed."

"Nope." Marissa grinned. "I called my folks before I came over and filled them in."

"I see, well now it's my turn. Start from the top. How on earth did you break that man's nose?"

Cameron woke for dinner and slipped back under the covers. Either she'd hit him harder than he thought or his body was plain worn out from everything he'd been through over the past couple months. Cameron rolled to his side. His nose touched the pillow. Pain shot through him like a dagger. "Grrr," he rumbled, reaching for the pain medication the doctor prescribed and taking another pill. Maybe trying to wait on customers hadn't been the wisest move he'd made today. Then again, what did he do today that had been wise?

He punched his pillow and lowered his head carefully this time.

After dinner Marissa returned home, only to pace back and forth as her father's words echoed in her mind. "Help him. . . ."

How? Why?

She groaned.

She knew why. Not to mention the verse from Hebrews that had come to her earlier that morning. The second part even echoed her father's words; "And do not forget to do good and to share with others, for with such sacrifices God is pleased."

"So what should I do, Lord?" she pleaded.

A familiar childhood fairy tale, *The Elves and the Shoemaker,* came to mind. Naturally enough, it had always been a family favorite.

"Lord, are You saying what I think You're saying?" She waited in anticipation of that still small voice.

Nothing.

Should she? Could she even get into the place? Surely

he had changed the locks and security system, hadn't he?

Marissa paced the white tile floor. She stopped and nibbled her left thumbnail. It was worth a shot, wasn't it? What was the worst that could happen?

"You could be arrested for breaking and entering," she said aloud.

Of course she could run off before the police came to check on the alarm. *But that's criminal, isn't it?* She gnawed the red polish off her thumbnail and started to work on her forefinger. She removed some chipped polish from her mouth and sighed. *Another manicure bites the dust.* At least she had this shade of polish and could redo it herself.

This is crazy, her inner voice chided. *This is larceny! Well, maybe not larceny, but breaking and entering, definitely.* "I can't believe I'm thinking these things," she muttered.

Marissa spied her keys on the glass coffee table. She could at least try. After all, what harm would it do? *The alarm shouldn't go off if I just press in the wrong code and don't open the door, should it?*

Marissa marched into her bedroom where her swimsuit and earlier clothing lay sprawled out on the Queen Anne-style double bed. Her room was the only one decorated with old things. The rest of the house was completely modern. There was something about wooden furniture she enjoyed. The smell and the feel were so natural. Of course, the white leather sofa and chairs in the living room were rather comfortable, too. And their coverings were genuine leather, the good stuff, not the pressurized strips fused together as bonded leather. Single hides carefully stitched, wonderfully tanned. Yup, she did enjoy working with leather—always had, ever since she was a child.

Marissa grinned at the prospect of working in her

father's old store again. But would she find the tools? Had the new owner laid out the shop differently? "You won't know until you get there," she admonished herself. Putting on some old clothes, she marched to the living room, grabbed her keys, and set out for Cameron Flynn's shoe repair store.

By the time she drove up to the back of the shop, all of her fingernails needed repolishing. But what did it matter? Shoe repair didn't treat things like nail polish kindly. She left her headlights fixed on the outer door and number pad.

Marissa scanned the parking lot, thankful no one was there. Slowly she eased herself out the jeep and walked over to the back door. She flipped through her keys and found the well-worn brass key that once belonged to her father's store. Should she?

"Try the key first," she whispered to herself. "But don't turn it," she cautioned.

Her heart raced.

Her hand trembled.

The key slipped right in. She smiled. *Could it be he hasn't changed the locks?*

Marissa looked up at the alarm keypad. The front covering was different, newer looking. She stopped her fingers before touching the surface and pulled her hand back.

This was definitely insane. What would she tell the judge tomorrow morning at her arraignment? "Sorry, Judge. I was trying to be a Good Samaritan after I broke the man's nose." No judge in his or her right mind would believe that story. *On the other hand,* she smiled to herself, *it would be tremendously original. It might just smack of the truth.*

Marissa bit down on her inner cheek.

The silly fairy tale replayed itself in her mind.

Marissa sighed.

If she really believed God was behind this. . .what was her fear?

She snickered. "I must be dreaming this up out of guilt. There's no way God would be asking me to do this.

"Oh, for pity's sake, girl. You won't know until you try." Marissa punched in the code and turned the key.

Chapter 4

Cameron woke early the next morning. His nose throbbed. He moistened his dried lips with his tongue and grabbed the lip balm from the medicine cabinet, applying it liberally to his lips. A deep shade of purple raccooned his eyes. He thought about camouflaging them with a pair of sunglasses, but with the huge white bandage on his nose, what would it matter?

A swirl of dizziness swept over him when he bent over to reach for his shoes. "Okay, I can't do that."

How was he going to make up for the lost hours and try to get some of those long-overdue orders out? Energy and money were in short supply. Maybe he shouldn't have bought the business so soon. Maybe he should have stayed on with Mr. Perrione a few more years. Cameron rubbed the knotted muscles on the back of his neck.

It was too late for *maybe*s. If the business went under, he'd have given it all he could. He'd just have to accept it and move on. Bankruptcy wasn't that bad, was it? Slowly he trudged toward the kitchen.

"Good morning, Mother, did you sleep well?" Cameron bent over slowly and gave her a tender kiss on her left cheek. Her blue eyes sparkled with love.

No matter what, the Lord would honor him for doing the right thing by taking care of his mother. That might mean simply being allowed to get out of debt with his self-esteem still intact—or perhaps some miracle would happen. Miracles did still happen, right? Of course he believed in them, he reassured himself. On the other hand. . . had he ever seen any real miracles?

Then he lifted his gaze from his plate to his mother's eyes as she sat crumpled in a wheelchair. His heart pounded in his chest. An overwhelming sense of conviction over his self-pity swept through him. She was a miracle. God had spared her life, and with His help she would walk again. "I love you, Mom."

"I love you, too, dear." Jean sipped her morning tea. "How are you feeling?"

"Not too bad. Did you reschedule your therapy for today?" Cameron grabbed a toasted English muffin and some red raspberry jam.

"Yes, but Marcia is going to take me."

"Marcia?" Which nurse was she? He mentally did a check over all the visiting nurses who had come over the past two months.

"She's a lady from church." Jean placed her teacup back in its saucer.

"That's great, Mom, but I'd be more than happy to take you."

"I know you would, dear. But didn't the doctor say you couldn't drive for twenty-four hours?"

Cameron groaned, "Yes," and bit off a huge chunk of his muffin. If he had food in his mouth, he wouldn't say something he might regret later.

"I'm getting better about traveling in cars. And Marcia

has a van with a wheelchair lift. Her middle son has MS."

At least he didn't have to worry about the woman being able to assist Jean into her car. "I'm sorry to hear about Marcia's son."

"It's a tragedy, but they have the best outlook about it. Please understand how I'm saying this, but if I were never to walk again, I know I would be at peace with it after a while. I'm not going to fool myself into thinking I'd accept it with no muss, no fuss, but in getting to know Marcia and her son Derrick Jr., I've come to see God can and will work through anything. It's all a matter of us allowing Him to do it."

Cameron licked the jam off his thumb and gulped down the last of his coffee. "I think you might be right, Mom. Well, I've got to run. I really need to catch up on some orders."

"Be careful, and don't push yourself too hard."

"I promise. Have a good day, and I'll have my cell phone with me at all times in case you need me."

"Thanks, but I'm sure I'll be fine."

Cameron said his good-bye and waited outside for the cab he had arranged for yesterday.

Marissa slapped the snooze button on her alarm clock for the third or fourth time and rolled over, pulling the soft covers up to her chin. "Just another five minutes," she mumbled to herself.

She'd worked in the shop until three in the morning. Tools, she'd discovered, were basically kept in the same place. It was a bit messier than she remembered it. Shoe repair shops were always dusty. Without a woman's touch, Mr. Flynn seemed to let the dust pile up really thick before he swept it up.

Her good deed was done. Thankfully, she wouldn't have to do that again.

She tried to force her eyes open. The bright sunlight streaming into her bedroom compelled their immediate closure.

"Work, get up," she mumbled to herself and rolled her legs off the side of the bed and sat up. She fought the urge to lie back down. A cold shower promised the only answer to her extreme fatigue. If it hadn't been such an emotional day, she would have been tired, but not this bone weary, she figured.

The cool water of the shower shot her eyes open and raised her senses to full alert. Next she would need coffee. Good strong Cuban coffee would be in order, and not one shot, but two. She'd be buzzing for hours.

Dressed for work, she skipped breakfast and stopped by La Minuta for her caffeine boost. The shop was a small one, but it served some of the best Cuban coffee in all of Miami. As she brought the cup to her mouth, she noticed her fingernails. "Yuck. I can't go in looking like this." She downed the first cup and took the second with her.

A quick stop by the drugstore was in order. Marissa dashed in, snatched up a bottle of nail polish remover and a bag of cotton balls, and hustled over to the counter.

The cashier, a thin older woman with silver-gray hair, looked at her purchase and glanced at her nails. Marissa tried to curl her fingers into a fist, but it was too late.

"Nervous?" she asked.

"I was, but it's all under control now."

"Good," she said with a wink.

Marissa relaxed. The woman was just making pleasant

conversation. How would she know she was guilty of breaking and entering? Of course, she hadn't stolen anything, and she did have a key that worked. She had, in fact, repaired ten pairs of shoes, cut the leather for a couple of the handmade shoes that were on order, and done a few other little things that take up time but weren't large income makers. But they were the kinds of things that brought customers back, time and time again. They were probably the same people who were doing all the complaining about the work not getting done.

"Have a good day." Marissa waved as she grabbed her bag and left the store.

As much as she wanted to take care of her nails right there in the parking lot. She was already late and decided to fix her nails at her office. If she attempted it in the car while driving, she'd probably dump the remover on her suit and ruin it.

At the office she slipped into her room without notice. Or at least she hoped without notice. In her "in basket" were tons of morning messages. *I'm late by thirty minutes and the whole world senses it?* She grabbed the top message and slowly began to work her way through the pile.

"Marissa, call on line one," Muriel's tinny voice rang over the intercom.

Tapping the button for the speakerphone, she answered, "Hello, this is Marissa Jones, how can I help you?"

Something's wrong. Cameron stood pensively still in the doorway. Someone had been, or still was, in the shop. He could smell it, feel it, sense it. He grabbed the broom handle that was by the door and slowly walked in, his eyes adjusting to the dark room.

"Hello, anyone here?" he called out. Not that he was expecting a thief to answer, but at least the intruder would know he was aware of his presence. Then again, maybe that wasn't the wisest thing to do. A surprise attack might have been better. Too late now. He stepped forward with one bold giant step.

Nothing, not a sound.

Again, he took a step and paused.

Nothing.

Now he walked briskly through the back work area, opened the bathroom door, the closet, then went to the front room where the customers came in.

Nothing. No one.

Maybe it was nothing. Maybe it was his own weary imagination. Maybe it was simply some weird side effect of the concussion. Who knew? Obviously no one was in the room. He placed the broom against the counter and went to the back of the shop to lock the rear door, then turned on the lights.

Cameron's eyes blinked.

Someone *had* been in there; he felt it more than witnessing any proof to his assumption. All the large tools—the nibbler, sander, shoe jacks—were in place. Of course, it would take a couple strong men to move the sander. He looked at the workbench. The hammer and awl seemed out of place.

But that was foolishness. He had simply laid it on top of his workbench the day before. He hadn't paid attention as to where he'd placed them.

The brass bell over the door rang as the first customer came in. "Good morning, Mr. Flynn." A cheerful mother with a toddler strapped around her hip marched in.

"Morning. How can I help you?"

"What on earth happened to you?" she implored with compassion, her eyes fixed on the protruding bandage on his nose.

"I was hit by a surfboard."

"Surfboard? I suppose so, you're right on the beach. You'd think people would be more careful."

"I agree. So, what can I do for you this morning?"

"I've come to pick up my husband's work boots. You said they'd be ready last week, but I just didn't have a chance to get here before now."

Cameron feared that he still hadn't finished her husband's boots. He took the ticket and went to the shelves where the finished orders were kept.

"That's odd." Cameron rubbed the back of his neck.

"What?" she asked.

"Sorry, I was speaking to myself." He grabbed the brown leather boots and looked them over. The repair was for a set of new soles. They were done, and done well, but he couldn't for the life of him remember doing this job. Maybe he'd been hit harder than he thought and was experiencing some form of amnesia.

"Here they are, good as new." He smiled, still not sure how or when he'd done the work.

The woman grabbed the boots and turned them over to inspect the job. Satisfied, she smiled. "These look like new. Thanks."

"You're welcome. They're good boots. You can replace the soles a few times before the top leather will wear out." So many products today were made with vinyl, it was nice to work with good leather shoes. *You'd think I'd remember working with those, Lord.*

"How much do I owe you?" she asked, retrieving her purse.

"Fifteen."

The money was exchanged, and she left. He went into the back room and discovered the leather cut and tooled for the special handmade shoes he was doing for Joseph Browning.

He collapsed on the stool. He was certain he hadn't worked on those. *I couldn't have—could I?*

"I better call the doctor and ask about amnesia."

The bell jangled again. "Morning, Cameron. How ya feelin' today?"

"Fine, Bud, I think." Bud was an elderly man who often spent some of his mornings drinking a cup of coffee and shooting the breeze with Cameron. When he purchased the business from Sam, Sam had warned and encouraged him to be friendly and patient with some of the elderly who just stopped by. And much to Cameron's surprise, he found he enjoyed talking with Bud and the others, too.

"I heard Marissa knocked you good." Bud peered over his wire-rimmed glasses and looked intently at Cameron's bruises. He let out a long whistle through his teeth. "Guess she got you real good. Broken, I take it?"

"Afraid so. And I think I'm having a little trouble with my memory. Things are done that I don't recall doing."

"Head wounds are peculiar things." Bud sat down on the old bench and lifted the plastic lid off his cup of coffee. "So, whatcha workin' on this morning?" he asked.

"A couple pairs of shoes for Joseph Browning. The leather's all cut; I just need to assemble them."

"He flying into town again?" Bud sipped his coffee

and peered out the large-pane glass window.

Cameron chuckled. "Must be, if he placed his standard order."

"Sam said he got to the place where he almost knew when Mr. Browning would be coming to town and would start on the shoes before he got the call."

"Well, I'm afraid I'm not Sam. Not sure I'll ever be."

"Course not. You're Cameron Flynn, and Cameron does a fine job all on his own." Bud got up and walked behind the counter to the back room. "Look, son, I know it's been tough for you since your mom got injured, but it will work out. Trust the Lord."

"I'm trying. I just don't like disappointing so many of the customers. And the business is slowing. I can't blame folks, but. . ."

"I know. I pray for you regularly." Bud placed his leathery hand on Cameron's shoulder.

"Thanks."

Bud slapped him on the back. "I'll go sit down so you can work on Mr. Browning's shoes."

"You're welcome to sit back here."

"No, thanks. Can't watch for the pretty women." Bud grinned.

Cameron chuckled out loud and went to work. After putting the ribbing on the insole, he assembled the soles. First he placed the outer sole on the counter. Next, he grabbed the cork filler, flipped the inner sole over with rib side down, and slipped the shank between the two layers. Lightly gluing the pieces in place, he clamped them and greeted the next customer.

Again he found an order done that he couldn't remember doing. After the customer left, he discovered there were maybe ten repair jobs on the shelves that he had absolutely no memory of. Did he have some memory loss?

He went through the order book to see if he had written any orders he didn't recall.

"That's odd."

"What?" Bud asked, raising his head from the paper.

"My memory loss. I recall every one of these orders, but I don't recall working on at least ten finished orders."

"Probably some selective thing the brain does, but you ought to tell your doctor."

"Yeah, I guess I should."

Bud focused on a "pretty woman" who walked past the store. Cameron grinned. Bud's idea of a pretty woman was someone over fifty who had a very conservative dress. He didn't take to the young ones who wore next to nothing, as Bud often put it. But give him a lady in a cotton dress and the man was in love, at least for a moment. "I think you know that one," Cameron teased.

"Yes, sir. Took her to dinner once. She's a mighty fine lady, but boy can she talk a man's ear off. Never got the nerve to ask her out again."

Cameron roared and went back to his workbench. It seemed most of his memory was intact. Apart from a few orders he didn't recall working on, he remembered everything else. At least he thought it was everything else. His laughter was interrupted by the ringing of the shop phone. "Miami Soles, can I help you?"

"Possibly, my boy." The man chuckled on the other end of the line. "This is Sam, Sam Jones."

"Hey, Sam, how's it going?"

"Good, thanks. Let me get right down to why I'm

calling. I heard you've been having some troubles. Your mother had a bad car accident, right?"

"Yes, she's recovering well. How did you hear about that?" He knew he hadn't spoken a word about it with Marissa, hadn't even given her the time of day, much less a chance to talk about anything personal.

"Marissa called. She said she'd heard about problems meeting orders and such."

Cameron cleared his throat. "I'm catching up." *Of course, I don't recall doing half the things in the store. . . .*

"Son, I'm not trying to give you a hard time. Life happens, and sometimes situations come up. What Alana and I are wondering is, if you didn't pay rent for three months, would that give you a little extra to hire someone on part-time?"

Cameron couldn't believe his ears. It was an answer to his prayer. It would give him that little breathing space he needed to still be able to take care of his mother, as well as meet the demands of the shop. "I don't know what to say."

"Thank you works well." Sam chuckled.

"Thanks. I'll pay it back."

"Consider it a gift. And if you can turn around some day in your life and give it to someone else in need, that would truly bless me."

"If you're certain, Sam."

"I am. The Lord wouldn't want it any other way. So, tell me about your mother. What happened?"

Cameron spent the next few minutes explaining about his mother's accident, her fear of traveling in another car, her restrictions of being in a wheelchair, and the toll it had taken on him and the business.

"We'll be praying for her complete recovery. Just remember one thing. God honors an honorable man."

Was he an honorable man? Most days he would probably say yes, but the anger and resentment he'd been building up toward Marissa for the accident. . . No, he wasn't honorable. He was just bellyaching about his life and the misfortunes that had come into it and not the blessings.

Cameron looked at the curled photo of him and Mike Perrione. He still had a lot to learn from his mentor. Making things right with Marissa Jones was in order. But how?

Chapter 5

Marissa's concentration was shot. She hadn't allowed herself to do anything but return phone calls and follow up on assignments to the graphic artists at work. New clients, or even tracking down new clients, took creative energy she lacked. The entire day she spent watching the clock sluggishly tick down the hours until closing time. Relief flooded over her as she drove up the driveway of her home, praying Aunt Rosa wouldn't spot her return. Tonight she needed rest and lots of it. A simple sandwich and she was off to bed.

Inside the house she plopped her bag by the door and dropped her keys right next to it. The ringing of the phone jangled her haggard nerves. She decided to let the answering machine take the call. Within seconds she heard the beep and a distinctive male voice. "Ms. Jones, this is Cameron Flynn."

Marissa froze. Did he know?

"I received a call from your father today and well. . . goodness I hate talking to these machines. Basically, I wanted to say thanks. I admit I was angry at first, but after some prayer I realized you were just trying to be helpful. Have a good day."

The machine clicked. *Daddy told him? But how'd he know?* Marissa began to pace. *I suppose Mr. Flynn could have called him and asked who had keys and the security code.*

She began to chew on her left thumbnail. Thankfully, she hadn't repainted them. *Just trying to be helpful?* "All that work last night was 'just trying'?" Marissa hissed out in frustration. Concern for Cameron Flynn did not make sense. The man had barely spoken to her and probably hadn't forgiven her for the accident yet.

"Enough!" She marched into her bedroom. That man, his business, and the accident had been taking too much of her attention the past two days. Enough was enough.

Marissa filled the tub with warm water and her sea breeze-scented bubbles and slipped in, closing her eyes. Tonight's plans were early to bed and relaxing, nothing else.

The water chilled. Marissa woke up and looked out the window. It was dark. How long had she slept? She dried off, wrapped herself in her large, fluffy, terry bathrobe, slipped her feet into her fluffy pink bunny slippers, and made her way to the kitchen. Inside the freezer she found some frozen French bread pizzas for her dinner.

The doorbell rang. "Tia Rosa," she said with a smile. The woman truly cared about her, but, honestly, she didn't need to check up on her every day like when she was a teenager.

Without looking through the peephole, she opened the door. "Tia Ro—aaaack!" she screamed and shut the door.

"Ms. Jones, it's me, Cameron Flynn."

What did the man think she was, an idiot? Of course she knew who he was. "What do you want?" she asked through the solid oak door.

"I wanted to thank you personally. I'm not a fan of answering machines."

"I'm not dressed for company. I, I. . ." *What do you say to a man who wants to thank you for breaking into his store?* "You're welcome," she offered weakly.

"Ms. Jones, I think we got off on the wrong foot. May I. . .I mean, could we. . . Oh, for pity's sake, could you get dressed so we could talk like normal human beings?"

"I suppose so," she mumbled, praying he couldn't hear her through the closed door. "Go around the house and sit on the patio. I'll be out there shortly."

"Thank you."

Marissa listened to his disappearing footfalls. *Dressed . . .I need to get dressed.* In her room she assembled a casual outfit of jean shorts and a nice jersey.

Out her window she saw the sensor lights go on in the backyard. Cameron Flynn had made his way around the house.

She brushed out the damp ends of her hair and let it drape freely over her shoulders. There was no time for makeup, just a quick check to make sure all traces of her daytime makeup were gone.

As she exited her room and progressed to the patio, she smelled the French bread pizza. Her stomach gurgled. When she approached the slider, she saw him standing very still, facing the pool with his hands tucked behind his back. *Tall, lean, and very strong shoulders,* she observed.

"Mr. Flynn, may I get you something to drink?"

He turned, and her stomach flip-flopped as the bandaged nose and massive black eyes came into view. She gasped. "I'm so sorry."

"I'm sorry, too. It was an accident. I shouldn't have been so rude to you."

"Forgiven. And it was completely understandable. I don't know if I would have been sweet if someone had just clobbered me. . . ."

Cameron raised his hand. "All's forgiven."

"I was about to eat dinner. Have you eaten?" she offered.

"Not yet, but my mother is expecting me. I won't keep you. I just wanted to thank you for talking with your father about. . ."

He shuffled his feet and looked down at the white coral patio floor, clearing his throat again. "About my mother's accident and getting behind on the orders."

The accident. . . He doesn't know about last night or, at the very least, he doesn't know it was me.

"No problem."

"Your father is a very gracious man. He's given me three months rent free."

Ahh, so that's it. But what about last night? Did she want to ask him? "Daddy is a sweetheart. How are you feeling?"

"Pretty good. It's hard to breathe, but other than that I'm doing well. And I'm allowed to drive again." He grinned.

"That's helpful."

The kitchen buzzer went off.

"Well, I've got to run. I just wanted to thank you in person. It means a lot to me. My mom has a lot of recovery still ahead."

"You're welcome. You may walk through the house to leave." Marissa pointed behind her.

"Thank you." Cameron stepped past her. She could

smell his cologne. The memory of holding his head when he had passed out washed over her. Bandaged, banged up, and looking like he'd been through a war did not stop the sudden attraction she felt for him. But how? Why? Was it a guilt-driven attraction?

And what did it matter anyway? He wouldn't be interested in a woman who had knocked him out. Would he?

Marissa walked past him and turned off the annoying whine of the oven timer. If anything, it was warning her to rein in her feelings. After all, she was exhausted. *You can't trust feelings when you're worn out,* she reminded herself before entering the living room.

"Pizza?" he asked. Marissa had to have the largest set of brown eyes he'd ever seen.

"Good nose. . . ." Her words drifted off, and a look of horror swept over her.

"Glad it's still working." He chuckled. "Marissa, please, it was an accident."

"I know, but it doesn't stop the images of you in my lap."

"Your lap?"

"I caught your head just before it hit the ground." She diverted her eyes from his own.

She must not have forgiven herself, he decided. "Ah, I see. Thank you. I'd have ended up with another bump, and possibly worse."

"It was the least I could do." She winked.

Was she flirting with him? Did he want her to? Cameron pulled at the collar of his shirt. The house was getting warmer. Perhaps because the slider hadn't been shut yet.

She was beautiful but. . . No, she was Sam Jones's

daughter. He already owed the man a ton of gratitude. He wouldn't risk going into a relationship with the man's daughter and have it blow up in his face. It was best to leave his feelings, and possibly hers, in some remote, dark corner. They would fade away.

"Well, I really must be going. Mother is holding dinner for me."

"No problem. I understand." She led him to the front door. She was a gracious, as well as attractive, host. Five-foot-six, he guessed. She'd fit right into his shoulder, if he were to embrace her.

Embrace her? Whoa, slow down, boy. "Good night, Marissa."

"Good night, Cameron."

The evening breeze hit his face like a refreshing balm as the door shut quietly behind him. What had happened in there? Whatever it was, it wasn't about to happen again. No sirree, not if he could help it. And he could help it, no question about that.

And it wouldn't be that difficult, he surmised. After all, he had no reason to see her ever again.

Marissa finished her dinner and tried to pray. Her mind kept going to Cameron Flynn, wondering what he really looked like under all those bruises. He seemed a decent man. Hadn't he controlled his temper when she first hit him? Of course, he passed out right away, so how could she judge? On the other hand, he had just apologized for getting angry with her.

He didn't mention her work in the shop, though. Maybe he was so far behind, that what she'd done wasn't enough to make a dent.

Marissa worried her fingernails, starting with her forefinger and working her way to the pinky.

Should she go there again? Should she risk it? Did she really need to be acknowledged for doing something in secret?

The very idea challenged her as a Christian, of being a living sacrifice, giving a sacrifice of praise. If she was looking for accolades, then all she'd done last night smacked of worthless actions, done for the approval of men, not for God's approval. Should she go back?

"Is that what You want, Lord?" She listened pensively for a divine revelation. Granted, no one knew she had been in there except for Cameron. And if he knew it was her, he hadn't said anything. In fact, he didn't even hint around looking for answers.

So, did she need to go again? Or was one night enough?

Do not forget to do good, echoed through her thoughts as part of Hebrews 13:16 came to mind. Helping Cameron certainly qualified as "good deeds."

He spoke so tenderly about his mother. Rosa had filled her in about the accident. Jean Flynn was very blessed, a miracle in fact. It was hard to believe she came out of that rumpled metal alive. Marissa remembered having seen that accident on the news several months before.

What could it hurt if you did a little more for him? Just don't stay up too late. Pace yourself. If you're careful, you could put in a couple hours each evening and still get to bed at a reasonable time.

Marissa grabbed her keys and headed back to Cameron's shop. Once there she examined Joseph Browning's shoes. Cameron did good work, she had to admit. She reached into the drawer with the orders and proceeded to work. Several pairs of ladies' heels needed repairing. Marissa took all of the pairs that simply needed new soles on the heels, removed the old rubber and reglued the new soles. She then took them to the nibbler and let it chop off most of the excess. After she worked the nibbler on all the heels, she brought the lot of them to the sander and sanded them down, finishing with a final quick swipe from the polisher.

It was midnight when she was done. It wasn't much, but it would be some help. She set the shoes on the finished rack along with their proper tags. Marissa smiled. It felt good to work with her hands again. She loved her job, but it wasn't the same as working in this shop.

The next morning Cameron noticed the finished ladies' heels and quickly punched up his doctor's phone number. Something was definitely wrong with his memory. He was certain he hadn't done those heels. . .well, almost confident. *What do you do for brain disorders?* he wondered.

"Hi, this is Cameron Flynn. I need to speak with Dr. McIntyre."

The secretary put him on hold. It was early; perhaps he would catch the doctor before he went on rounds at the hospital.

"Dr. Mac, here. How can I help you?"

"Doctor, this is Cameron Flynn. I suffered a mild concussion the other day, and well, I'm having trouble with my memory."

"What kind of trouble?"

"I don't recall working on some of the orders for my customers. Obviously I did, 'cause they're sitting on my shelf done, but I can't recall it. The same thing happened the day before."

"Hmm, why don't you meet me at Adventura Hospital and we'll do some X-rays, make sure there wasn't any other damage."

"Apart from my broken nose, they didn't find anything."

"Broken nose? Right, I remember reading the X-ray report."

"Yeah, a surfboard."

"Ouch. Tell me about it when I meet you at the hospital."

"No problem." Cameron said good-bye and locked up the shop. Going to the hospital would mean another morning's work lost. But he had no choice. He had to know if he had a more serious brain injury than what had been diagnosed.

Three hours later the prognosis was the same. He had suffered a minor concussion, but no other damage showed up on any of the tests.

"There's so much about the brain we don't understand, Cameron. I think you'll be fine, and your memory shouldn't have any more lapses. Tell me again, what's your occupation?"

"Cobbler, shoe repair."

"Are you working with any different glues?"

"No."

"Got any elves running around?" Dr. McIntyre grinned.

"What?"

"You know, the old fairy tale about the elves and the shoemaker."

Cameron groaned. "No elves, Doc."

"Seriously, I believe this will just disappear in a day or

two. If your memory lapses start occurring in other areas, let me know right away. But try to relax. Your mother was in a serious accident, right?"

"Yeah, about two months ago."

"It's probably stress related." Dr. McIntyre applied a new, much lighter dressing to Cameron's nose. "This dressing should be more comfortable. Just try to relax; that's my best advice."

"Thanks, Doc."

"No problem. I'll bill you in the morning."

"Very funny," Cameron snickered. He had a full day of work waiting for him at the shop. Hopefully, not too many folks had tried to come in this morning.

When he arrived, he discovered Bud behind the counter waiting on customers.

"Bud?"

"Afternoon, Cameron. Thought I'd try out for that job you're offering."

"But how'd you get in here?"

"With my key." Bud winked at a middle-aged lady as he handed her a bag and wished her a good day.

"What key?" Cameron asked, once the woman left the store.

Bud pulled a brass key out of his pocket and waved it in the air. "This one."

"I never gave you a key."

"No, but Sam did. And when I saw you went to the doctor's this morning, I decided to see if the key still worked. It did, so I opened the store for you."

I should have changed the locks, he inwardly grumbled. How many others still had keys to Sam's shop? "What about the security code?"

"Now that I didn't know, but when the police responded to the alarm and saw you were at the hospital, they called the security company and told them to turn it off. I'll be needing the code when I open up the shop again for you." Bud grinned.

Bud had just hired himself, and what could Cameron do? The man wouldn't be able to work on orders, but he certainly would be good with the customers, waiting on them, taking their orders, yakking with them the way Sam used to do. Maybe Bud working for him wasn't a bad idea after all.

"The code's the same, too." Cameron smiled.

"Never thought of that. Shoulda tried. But the thing just kept blaring in my ears. A man can't think straight with all that racket going on."

"That's the point of having an alarm."

"I suppose so." Bud set himself on the stool behind the counter. "So, you hiring me?"

Chapter 6

S ure. Can't afford much," Cameron offered.
"Don't need much. I can't earn more than a certain amount in a year, or I'll mess up my social security benefits."

"Thanks for helping this morning, Bud." Why not give the man a try? He was there just about every day anyway, and it would give him something to do with his free time.

"Welcome."

Cameron spent the rest of the day working on orders, applied another coat of wax and polish to Joseph Browning's shoes, and even had a little time to write some notes on the pair of sandals he was developing. Something practical, something comfortable and affordable for the tourist.

Work was definitely easier today than the day before. There was nothing like a good night's rest to help a person recover. Getting to bed at 1:00 a.m. wasn't great, but it was a lot better than three. Those two hours made all the difference in the world.

Tonight she'd planned to attend a concert with a couple of friends. She'd been looking forward to this contemporary Christian concert for months. But a desire to go to

Cameron's shop rather than the concert grew with each passing moment. All day she thought of the pile of orders, especially the various custom shoe orders that had come in. Those would make some serious money for Cameron. But it was the nickel-and-dime, everyday regular customers who kept the business afloat.

In the end she decided the concert and commitment to her friends won out. Not to mention the next morning's schedule would demand an alert mind.

When the concert began with the singing of the chorus "We Bring a Sacrifice of Praise," Marissa smiled. She knew she had made the right choice. After all, it was this week's spiritual lesson from the Lord.

The intermission came, and her friends scurried out of their seats for the rest rooms or vending areas. Marissa stayed put, closed her eyes, and tried to meditate on the Lord. In spite of how wonderful the concert was, she kept thinking about Cameron. Her eyes drifted to a man two sections over and several rows down who seemed to have his same build and hair coloring.

These delusions were getting her nowhere. Maybe she shouldn't help him out in his shop anymore. Maybe she was just becoming attached to a man and not on the secret mission God had for her.

"Marissa?" a honey-smooth male voice whispered in her ear.

Without thinking, she let out a pleasurable moan. The voice almost sounded like. . . Marissa's eyes flew open. "Cameron?"

"Hi. I didn't mean to interrupt." His grin reached the now greening bruises around his eyes.

"No problem." What was he doing there?

"Great concert, huh?"

"Wonderful. You like Christian contemporary music?" she asked.

"Yes, and lots of other styles as well," he offered.

She noticed a new, much smaller bandage. "How's your nose?"

"It's doing well. Saw my doctor today, and he put on this new bandage. Of course, I have to be more careful without that clodhopper of a bandage. It was so large I could barely see around it." He grinned again.

He has a wonderful smile. She shook herself to the present, to reality. *But what do you say to a man whose nose you broke and whose store you're breaking into? "Hello, find anything strange at your store lately?"*

"I won't keep you. I saw you sitting here and thought I'd come over."

"It's nice seeing you again." She smiled and tried to rub the sweat from the palm of her hands without him noticing.

"Good to see you, too. Well, my mother will be wondering where I wandered off to."

"Your mother is here?"

"Yeah, she's the woman in the wheelchair over to your left, down in the lower section."

"I see her, but is it okay for her to come out to such a crowded place so soon after her accident?"

"Yes, but admittedly this is the first time I managed to get her out. She's met a woman at church who has a son in a wheelchair. He's the boy next to my mom. His mother, Marcia, has done more for my mom in a couple of weeks than the two months of therapy combined."

"That's wonderful."

"How'd you know about the accident?"

"My neighbor. She's a sweetheart, but I swear she knows just about anything that happens in greater Miami."

"Wow."

"Exactly; it isn't a small city."

Cameron chuckled. "Oh, by the way, my mom told me a secret."

"What's that?"

"My name, Cameron, means bent or crooked nose."

"You're kidding." Marissa giggled.

"Nope, 'tis true. So you could possibly say I was destined to have a broken nose at least once in my life."

"Oh my. And why did your mother name you this?" Marissa looked into his joyful blue eyes.

"She said she liked the name. I told her it was her fault that my nose was broken."

"Ha! I wish it was." Marissa wanted to reach out to him. . .to establish some physical contact. But that would be too forward.

Cameron placed his hand on her shoulder. "Forgive yourself, Marissa. It's the only way."

Her shoulder instantly warmed from his touch, and in another instant her shoulder chilled when he removed his hand. "Thanks. I'll try."

"Enjoy the rest of the concert." He waved as he headed back to his seat.

"You, too." She couldn't help but follow him, watching how he bent down and whispered in his mother's ear. He was equally attentive to the young boy beside his mother. Cameron Flynn had a tender heart. *Any woman would be honored to have him as a husband,* she thought.

Husband? "Oh Lord, I've got it bad, don't I?"

"Got what bad?" Sally, with her flaming red hair, said as she sashayed to her seat.

"An overwhelming desire to flee before the entire mass of concert-goers decides to leave." She had thought that, but it was when they first sat down. How could she tell Sally about Cameron, Mr. "Bent Nose," himself?

Cameron watched as Marissa's friends came back with arms full of food and drinks. Every so often he caught her glancing over at him.

For a man who'd sworn he wouldn't see the lady again, his conviction proved to be worthless sentiment. Seeing her sitting there so beautiful, so content in her prayer time, he hardly wanted to interrupt, but found he couldn't stop himself. He was drawn to her like a moth drawn to a flame. *And you know where that gets the moth,* he reminded himself. But the more he watched her, the more intrigued he was with her.

"So who is she?" Jean asked.

"Marissa Jones."

"Of surfboard fame?" She grinned.

"The one and the same." Cameron groaned and faced the stage.

"Oh my, she's a pretty thing, isn't she?" His mother stole another glance at Marissa.

Cameron wagged his head. "I hadn't noticed."

"Nonsense. You can't keep your eyes off of her. And I see that dimple of yours every time you get a glimpse of her. Cameron James, don't you try to fool me. You're smitten by the woman whether you want to admit it or not."

"She is pretty, but she's also dangerous." Cameron

pointed to his nose for effect.

"Dangerous there as well," she said, pointing to his heart.

Cameron rolled his eyes.

"I won't say another word." Jean crossed her arms and looked back toward the stage where the band members reassembled.

Yeah right, he thought, knowing his mother would bring her up in conversation again. Of that he had little doubt.

If he was wise, he'd keep his eyes on that stage as well.

The rest of the evening was a continuous struggle not to look over at Marissa. After the concert, they waited for most people to leave the stadium before making their way to the parking area.

"It was hard not to look back at her, wasn't it?" His mother's wicked grin spoke volumes.

How'd she know? On the other hand, how did she always know about everything? When he was little she always knew what he had gotten into without him ever saying or doing a thing. Why did God give mothers that sixth sense? And if it was so useful in raising children, why didn't He remove it once the children were grown? He'd have to take that one up with his heavenly Father someday.

"You've made your point, Mother."

"Good, now maybe you'll stop being so foolish and ask the girl out on a date."

"Not tonight. I already have a date with one of the finest looking ladies in all of Miami." Cameron bent down and kissed the top of his mother's head.

She flushed, and it warmed him that he could bring some joy in his mother's life. He knew she missed his father terribly, but she was going on with her life. The accident, on top of losing her husband a few months earlier, would have been enough to make a lot of people just give up. "I'm proud of you, Mom."

"I'm trying, son. Now, maybe you can try to find me a daughter-in-law so you can give me some grandbabies." Jean wiggled her eyebrows.

"Not today, mom. But I'll look into it."

"That's all I ask, sweetheart." Jean crossed her hands in her lap as Cameron pushed her wheelchair through the aisle and out to the parking area.

Grandchildren? Would the woman ever quit? Of course, working long, hard hours for the past four years had left him no time to pursue a relationship with anyone. If his mother hadn't had the accident, he certainly wouldn't have spent as much time with her as he had during the past couple of months. And she was right, if he was going to get married someday, he would have to make the time.

Cameron pulled the wheelchair beside the car. He opened the door, lifted his mother out of the chair, and placed her in the passenger seat. *I'll need to buy a wheelchair-equipped van if she doesn't start. . .*

Breaking into his own thoughts, he spoke gently to his mother. "Thanks for coming with me tonight."

"I had fun, and I'm not nearly as afraid as I was before. I'm healing, son. Everything will be all right."

Cameron patted her hand, closed the door, and placed her chair into his trunk. Thankfully, his classic convertible's trunk had more than enough room. And when he had the top down, he could place it in the backseat.

❖

The next morning Cameron arrived at his shop and was

greatly relieved to see that he had not forgotten anything. Everything was as he had left it the day before. "Thank You, Lord. My mind is finally healing."

That same Saturday morning, Marissa breezed through her morning appointment. More than once throughout the day she had to push down the desire to go by the shop. The question was, was it the shop or Cameron she wanted or, rather, needed to see? If she was honest with herself, it was Cameron. She longed to see him with his stitches removed, bruises gone, and nose back to its normal state. On the two evenings she had worked in the shop, she found herself staring at a photograph with Cameron and an older, portly man with a very sweet face. There was no question about the source of Cameron's good looks and handsome features.

She'd looked up Cameron's name, and sure enough, it meant "bent" or "crooked nose." She liked the name. But how on earth had it ever come to mean that? she wondered. Were all Camerons destined to have their noses broken at some point in their lives? She certainly hoped not. But her own name meant "of the sea," and she loved the water. Did God inspire parents with the name to give their children? Since He knew who they were while He knitted them together in their mother's womb, certainly made it a possibility she supposed. On the other hand, she'd never been a mother and had never gone through the naming process of her unborn child, so she didn't have a clue. But it was a rather intriguing thought.

She spent the afternoon cleaning the house. As soon as she was certain Cameron would have closed the shop for the day, she was off. Tomorrow being Sunday, she didn't want to spend it working, so she intended to get a lot done tonight. She cut the leather, glued the soles, resoled, stained, and even dyed some shoes a funky purple for a wedding.

On Cameron's workbench she found the plans for a new sandal. She followed his pattern and made a test copy for herself and slipped it on. She found it comfortable, but lacking a little bit in style. On a separate piece of paper, she sketched out some alternative straps.

What am I doing? she asked herself. *If Cameron sees this he'll. . .he'll. . .what? Know someone was in his shop? He already knows that.* He had to, with all the work she'd been doing. But still it wasn't right. These were his designs of a new sandal, not hers. She crumpled up the paper and tossed it in the trash. Slipping off the new sandal, she placed it on the workbench next to his sketches.

She left the shop around midnight with the back orders nearly all caught up. She probably wouldn't have to help again. Her heart saddened at the realization. She loved coming to the shop and helping out.

The drive home seemed longer, her body seemed more tired. Could it be that she wouldn't be helping Cameron out any longer?

Back inside the house, she trudged upstairs and took a long, hot shower. She felt completely drained. Maybe she'd just pushed herself harder than she should have tonight.

She emerged from the bathroom and looked at her nightstand clock. "Three? No way. I left the store at midnight."

Marissa realized she'd unplugged the shop's clock when she plugged in the drill. "Ugh."

Collapsing on her bed, she prayed. "Father, You know I like helping Cameron, but if I've done all that I'm supposed to have done, give me peace to leave and not return. And please, give me a clear mind at church tomorrow—I mean today."

She had not intended to work so late. In just about six hours her Sunday school class was performing for the entire church.

Wrestling a dozen preschoolers was enough to make a person swear off having children, Marissa decided. All morning they squirmed and fussed and tried to be so big and grown-up. *They are adorable, though,* she admitted with a smile.

Finally, their turn came in the morning service. Marissa led them up to the chancel. She stayed on the floor level. Behind her, the morning offering was being collected while the children lined up.

Marissa nodded to the soundman. A moment later, the taped music floated through the sanctuary. Bobby, her most talkative child, froze. He stood like a stiff toy soldier with his dark brown eyes focused straight ahead. It would be impossible to get his attention. Vanessa twirled her fluffy carnation pink dress, and a grin exploded on Megan's chubby freckled cheeks, eager to begin.

Marissa raised her hands and cued the children to start singing.

"Jesus," Marissa sang, and all twelve began at different points, singing "Jesus Loves the Little Children." Megan belted out the song. Vanessa danced, even though that wasn't a part of the program, and Bobby moved his lips—but nothing more, the poor dear.

Marissa fought giggles as the congregation chuckled behind her.

When the song ended, little Carlos, dressed in khakis, a white shirt, and colorful tie, smoothed his rich, dark hair and walked proudly to the mike, right on cue. "Moms and dads and everyone else. Remember, Jesus loves you, too."

The congregation broke into a round of applause, and the pastor asked the children to sing it again to lead the congregation. The children were so proud. Even Bobby relaxed his stance and let his arms fall freely to his side.

After the encore performance, she led the children off the chancel and out of the sanctuary, since it was now time for children's church. They went to the classroom where Betty Green stood holding the door open to them, telling each child how proud she was of them.

"Great job, Marissa."

"Thanks. But the kids did all the work."

Betty's green eyes sparkled as she let out a small giggle. "They were adorable. I better get them settled. They're going to be wound up now."

"See ya later." Marissa stepped out of the doorway and headed back to the sanctuary.

"Marissa?"

Chapter 7

C ameron couldn't believe his eyes when he saw Marissa up front with the children. He'd been invited by Bud to see his great-granddaughter, Vanessa, perform.

"Cameron?"

"Hi," he lamely responded to her questioning gaze.

"What—"

Cutting her off, he explained. "I'm visiting with Bud this morning."

"Ahh." Marissa continued to walk back toward the sanctuary.

"I was wondering. . ."

She paused.

"Would you care to sit with Bud and me?"

"Sure," she hesitantly responded.

Maybe she wasn't as interested in him as he was in her. Why he popped up out of the pew and followed her, he'd never know.

"If you have other plans or someone else you're sitting with, I understand," he fumbled.

She knitted her eyebrows and scrutinized him. Without so much as a blink, she reached over to him and looped her arm around his. "Come on. The pastor's already started his message."

A whisper of excitement flitted through his veins. Did she feel it also? He followed her lead back to the sanctuary, then he led her to the pew he shared with Bud.

Bud nodded as they sat down beside him and raised his eyebrows slightly, noticing the hand-to-hand connection between the two of them. *When did I slip my hand around hers?* Cameron wondered, savoring the one-on-one contact. It felt so right, so comfortable. He caressed the back of her hand with the ball of his thumb.

Marissa squeezed his hand, and then slipped her hand from his, neatly folding her hands on her lap. Marissa focused on the pastor. Cameron glanced over, too. He was animated in his discussion about Moses, or possibly Abraham. He wasn't quite sure. He hadn't heard a single word the man had spoken.

She glanced back at him and smiled, then tilted her head toward the preacher. She was right, they were in church and he ought to pay attention. Cameron closed down his emotions and focused on the pastor. It was Moses and the parting of the Red Sea.

The preacher, a middle-aged man with brown hair, a youthful face, and wire-rimmed glasses, spoke with passion, but did not yell. His words and thoughts were clear, and when he applied Moses and the Red Sea to present, everyday life, he asked, "What is your Red Sea?"

Cameron thought for a moment. The easy answer was his business. The harder one was the care and treatment of his mother.

"And how is God supplying the passageway through your Red Sea?

155

"People, please note here," the pastor continued, "they did have to travel by faith through the sea. Are you trusting God? Do you have faith to travel through your Red Seas?"

Cameron thought long and hard. Was he trusting God with the day-to-day care of his mother? Cameron had overseen every aspect of her treatment and care. And she had needed him. But was he really comfortable with Marcia? There were definite advantages to her helping his mother get to and from the doctor's office. Was Jean's fear of traveling in cars, other than his own, his fault? Had he encouraged her to think that only he could protect her, when in fact he couldn't protect her at all?

The congregation stood for the final hymn. Marissa shared the hymnal with him. She smelled heavenly. What was that scent? He had noticed it on her before when he visited her the other night at her home. It left a fresh air impression, but he didn't have a clue what it was. It wasn't a floral bouquet he recognized. Just one more intriguing facet of this incredible woman, he noted.

As the congregation made its way out of the sanctuary, Bud turned toward Marissa. "Wonderful job with those young'ens."

"Thanks, Bud."

"But I must say, my Vanessa stole the show." Bud's wide grin spoke volumes.

Marissa giggled. "Either that, or she had a fly up her dress."

Bud roared. They obviously knew each other from way back, Cameron realized. And why wouldn't they? He inherited Bud with the purchase of Sam's shop.

"Hear you've been knocking my boss around with

a surfboard." Bud winked.

Marissa blushed.

"Easier ways to catch a man than knocking 'm out." Bud winked again.

Cameron blushed now.

"Believe me, that was not my intention," Marissa clarified. "If I'd known how handsome he was. . ."

Cameron turned to watch her brown eyes widen, her blush deepen.

"Well, let's just say I wouldn't have used a surfboard as my calling card."

Nicely done, he thought. "Bud, if you'll excuse us, I'd like to speak with Ms. Jones."

Ms. Jones? Hadn't he been holding and caressing her hand moments before? Wasn't there some shared connection between them? Or was she imagining it? No, he had definitely taken her hand. She'd had to pull it away in order to concentrate on the pastor's message.

As Bud walked away, Cameron threaded his fingers through hers. "Marissa, may I take you out to lunch?"

"I'd love to go to lunch with you, but—"

Vanessa ran up and tugged on Marissa's dress. "Mama says we can go with you now."

"Ah, I see you have a previous engagement." Cameron grinned.

Marissa definitely preferred to be with Cameron, but commitments were to be taken seriously and she couldn't disappoint the children. "I'm sorry."

"No problem. Perhaps another time." He released her hand and stepped back, allowing some of the other children closer access.

"I'm free Friday night." She grinned and silently fired off a hopeful prayer.

"I'll call you." Cameron smiled and nodded good-bye.

Call me? That man, she huffed. *How could he be so warm one minute and so standoffish the next?*

"Ms. Jones!" Maika whined.

"I'm ready. Let's get this show on the road." Marissa embraced several of her young students but silently admitted she'd much rather have been in Cameron's arms.

The next morning Cameron couldn't believe his eyes. Someone had been in the shop, he was certain of it. He wasn't having a problem with his memory; he had an elf on the loose, just as Dr. McIntyre suggested. But why? And who?

Neon purple wedding shoes seemed to be a pulsating testimony of an intruder. He walked over to his workbench and noticed a sample of his special sandal beside his plans. "It's a woman." He held a woman's size seven sandals in his hand. "And she's good," he murmured.

"But why would anyone come into my store and do my work, Lord?" he prayed while making his morning rounds, turning on lights, unlocking the front door. "Why?"

He slipped the pair of sandals in his back pocket and opened the cash drawer. Everything was there, just as he left it.

"Be serious, Cameron," he reprimanded himself. "If the woman wanted to rob you, she wouldn't have done the work. She would have emptied the entire store and no one would have been the wiser."

The bell jangled over the front door.

"Morning, Cameron."

"Morning, Bud. Look at this!" He pulled the sandals from his back pocket.

"Looks like a pair of sandals, like the ones you've been drawing back there."

"It is." Cameron sighed.

"Great, so you decided to make a pair, huh?" Bud asked.

"Not exactly."

"Huh?" Bud pivoted around and faced him.

"Bud, who besides you has a key to this shop?"

"Couldn't tell ya. Best I know, I was the only one. But I reckon Sam could have given someone else a key. Why, something missing?"

"No, we seem to have an elf." Cameron handed the sandal to Bud.

Bud roared. "You mean like in that old fairy tale?"

"Appears so. Since my accident, I've been finding work done that I have no memory of doing. I thought it was memory loss. The doc even said it was possible with the concussion. And when I came in Saturday morning, everything was just as I left it. But today, there's a ton of stuff done—shoes cut out and ready for sewing, some dyed shoes, and these." He pointed to the sandals in Bud's hand.

"This here elf looks like she knows her stuff," Bud mumbled, then his eyes went wide. "You don't suppose..."

"Suppose what?" Cameron stepped forward, examining the sandals in Bud's hand.

"Nah, couldn't be." Bud handed the sandals back to Cameron. "I'm wondering if you needed me this morning. I've got some things that need doing."

"No problem. Our mystery elf did a fair amount."

Bud nodded and silently walked out the door.

Cameron had the distinct impression that Bud had a

pretty good idea who the elf might be. *Whoever it was had to come at night*, he reasoned. *Tonight*, he determined, *I'll come back and see if she'll return.*

The brass bell rang again.

Cameron looked up. "Good morning, Mrs. Arce, what can I do for you this morning?"

"Marissa Jones, may I help you?" Marissa answered, using the speakerphone on her desk.

"Marissa, it's me, Bud Finley."

"Good morning, Bud. What can I do for you?"

"Marissa, have you been in Cameron's shop lately?"

Oh, goodness. Bud figured it out. "Bud, I. . ." She clicked off the speakerphone and held the receiver to her ear.

"Look," Bud interrupted. "I still had a key to your dad's shop, and this morning Cameron asked me if I knew of anyone else. Plus he told me about the things being done in the shop. And, well, I thought of you. You always loved workin' with your dad."

"You didn't tell him, did you?" Marissa wrapped the phone cord around her finger.

"No. But I don't think you should keep it a secret."

"It's complicated, Bud. I don't know how to explain it."

"Penance?" Bud asked.

"No, not really. It's something I believe God wanted me to do."

"Look, Marissa, I saw you two in church. You both have some feelings for each other. But you've gotta know that a relationship needs to be based on honesty."

"I know." Bud was right. She couldn't keep sneaking around in Cameron's shop.

"I didn't say anything this morning, but if he asks me

again, I don't feel right lying to him."

"I understand. Thanks for calling, Bud."

"No problem, but be careful."

Careful? She wasn't going within a hundred miles of Cameron's shop ever again. Well, a hundred miles was a slight exaggeration. Maybe a hundred feet. "Bye, Bud. Thanks." She hung up the phone and walked over to her office window. The clear blue sky was salted with wisps of white clouds on the horizon.

How had she grown to care so much for a man she hardly knew? And if they were to have a relationship, she couldn't be going behind his back. Marissa gnawed on her fingernail, realized what she was doing, and pulled it out of her mouth. At her desk she removed the now-chipped fingernail polish and repainted the nail. She really had to stop this nervous habit.

She was blowing it dry when her noon appointment walked through her door.

"Good morning." She collected herself and reached for the hand of a thin, brown-haired, professionally dressed woman. "I'm Marissa Jones."

Chapter 8

The afternoon had been hectic. Cameron couldn't wait to close the doors at five. Did he place an ad on television or something? People had come in with armfuls of shoes and handbags, all needing repair. He was happy for the business but uncertain how he was going to meet all the orders. If he worked late, he could probably manage. Maybe his elf would come in tonight and help, too.

It wasn't so bad having an elf. She obviously knew what she was doing. Now, with the doors locked, he sat in back at his workbench and went over the plans for the new sandals. He wondered if his elf thought they were comfortable.

Maybe they weren't—she had left them behind.

He thought back on what he could recall of the old fairy tale. The shoemaker and his wife had waited up one evening and discovered who their helpers were. And the couple made gifts for their elves.

A gift! That would be perfect. He'd make a gift for his mystery elf. He knew her shoe size from the sandal she left behind. He pulled out a clean sheet of paper and began to sketch a thinner, more suitable strap design.

Remembering the unplugged clock on his workbench,

he decided to return around midnight and catch his little elf.

The phone rang. "Miami Soles, may I help you?"

"Cameron?"

The sweet lilt of Marissa's voice caressed his ear. "Marissa?"

"Hi, I was wondering if we could get together tonight. I know I indicated I was busy, but I managed to cancel my evening plans."

"I'd love to but. . ." He didn't want to ruin an opportunity to get together with Marissa. A relationship with her was something he wanted to pursue. "I had a mess of orders come in today, and I'll be working tons of overtime to get them done."

"I understand." Marissa hesitated. "Cameron, I, well I think we need to talk."

"Yes, I'd like that very much." Cameron tossed the pencil down on the desk and rolled the paper with the sketch and threw it into the trash. "I missed."

"What?" she asked.

"Sorry. I was throwing something away and missed the can."

"Ahh, I understand."

Cameron bent down to retrieve the balled paper and noticed another already lying in the trash can. He pulled it out. It was a sketch of his sandals, with a different design on the straps.

"Marissa, what do you do for a living?" he asked. He examined the design more closely.

"I'm a commercial artist, and I work for an advertising company."

"Artist, huh?" Cameron looked at the smooth lines

163

drawn on the sketch by his elf, his female elf. "Marissa?"

She didn't answer.

Could Marissa be his elf? She was the one who broke his nose. Could she be doing this work out of guilt? "You're not feeling guilty about my nose any longer, are you?"

"No, I've forgiven myself."

"Good." *Scratch Marissa then.* She'd been the one with motive and opportunity. So who could his mystery elf be?

"I've got to get back to work or I'll be here till midnight. Can I call you when I get home tonight?" he asked, half listening and half trying to figure out the mystery elf's identity.

"What time?"

"Say around ten?" He placed the sketch on his workbench.

"Ten is fine. I will wait for your call. Good night, Cameron."

"Good night, Marissa."

Why didn't you just tell him? Because she needed to see him when she told him. How he reacted was crucial to her heart. She would wait for his call.

At home, she paced all evening. When the clock hit eleven and still no call, she decided he must be really backed up with these new orders.

Tonight she wanted to help Cameron, not because the Lord was encouraging her to, but because she needed to help him. A desire to be his helper stirred deep within her. Giving in to the temptation, she drove the dark streets to his shop. *Odd,* she wondered. When had she made the transition from her dad's shop to Cameron's?

The lights were out. Nervously, she made her way to

the back door, slipped in her key, and punched in the code.

She clicked on the lights and placed her purse on the workbench opposite from Cameron's. She bent behind the counter and scooped up the work orders that had come in today. He wasn't kidding, there was a ton.

Methodically, she worked her way through one order, then the next. Around twelve she looked at the sketches for the new sandals he was designing.

"Oh my!" Marissa smiled. Cameron had taken her plans for the new strap designs, made a pair, and left them on his workbench.

She lightly fingered the delicate pink rose pattern he etched in the leather strap. He had stained the straps white and hand painted the rose petals. "You do excellent work, Cameron," she whispered.

Marissa, his little elf. Cameron grinned.

After the phone call with Marissa, he'd felt pretty certain that it was her. Who else could it have been? The more he thought about it, the more it made sense. Finally, he had tracked down Bud, who confirmed it.

"Thank you, Marissa," Cameron spoke softly, trying not to spook her.

Her dark brown eyes widened as he removed himself from the shadows. "Cameron, I. . .I'm sorry."

"Shhh, my sweet. Thank you."

"You're not mad?"

She was mere inches away from him. He wanted to scoop her up into his arms and squeeze her, showing her how much love he had for this self-sacrificing lady. "No, silly, I'm not mad. You didn't need to do this."

"I know, but I really did. God was asking me to."

He couldn't believe how beautiful she was, standing there in a shop apron, hands stained, her hair falling out of the bands that held it in place. "You're beautiful, Marissa, and I think I'm falling in love with you."

She blushed and looked down at her feet. "I think I'm falling in love with you, too."

He couldn't resist any longer and scooped her into his arms. "My little elf, my shoemaker's daughter. . . . You're incredible, Marissa."

She wrapped her arms around him. His chest was solid where she laid her head. "I wanted to tell you in person."

"Shh. It doesn't matter. I'm thankful for all your help."

"Where do we go from here?" she asked, quelling her own desires.

"I think we take this one step further and see if the Lord is saying what our hearts have been saying since you banged that surfboard into my head."

"Will I be reminded of that every day for the rest of our lives?" She cast her gaze down from his ocean blue eyes.

Cameron traced her nose with his finger and moved down to her lips. Desire to have Cameron replace his finger with his lips stirred within. She sought his deep blue eyes, now full of passion, and quickly closed her own. He was going to kiss her. She knew it, and she wanted it. There was a bond between them that was more than physical. They were two souls looking for their God-given mates, and at that moment Marissa knew, as his lips touched hers ever so gently, he was the man God intended for her.

When he pulled away, his eyes fluttered open. "Just think, my love. It will be a great story to tell our children."

Marissa laughed. "I think we better start with the next step, not the tenth. I'd like to get to know you some, and

I'd like to have a wedding photo without your nose bandaged up."

Cameron held her tighter. "I know we don't know each other very well, but I believe God is in this."

"I agree. But God wants us to be wise, and wisdom comes with time."

"Agreed. So, what would you like to know about me?" Cameron released her and stepped away from her.

He was wise. If he had held her a moment longer, she would have flown off and eloped. "Everything. Why did you become a cobbler?"

"While I was in college, I got a job working with Mike Perrione, the man in the photo, and. . ."

Marissa sat on top of the stool next to Cameron's bench. They stayed for hours, talking in the shop.

Around three someone pounded on the back door, hollering, "Open up!"

"Who are you?" Cameron asked.

"Marcia's husband, Derrick Evans. Your mother is out of her mind with worry. Why haven't you called her?"

"Mother?" Cameron looked at his watch as he opened the door. "Oh my. I'll call her right away. I'm sorry, Derrick, I just got carried away talking with. . ."

"No problem." The man with silver-streaked hair looked from Cameron to Marissa. "Apparently you have an answering service, and she couldn't get through on your cell phone."

"I appreciate you coming by, but let me call her so she'll stop worrying."

"Glad to help. Good night, Cameron. Night, miss." Derrick slipped back into the shadows of the parking lot and worked his way back to his van.

"Excuse me for a moment while I call my mother." Cameron placed his hand on the small of her back. "I didn't notice the time."

"Neither did I. Your mother must be going crazy with worry."

"I told her I'd be late but. . ." Cameron punched in his home phone number. "Mom, sorry. I'm fine.

"No, no, nothing like that.

"Seriously, Mom, I'm okay. In fact I'm better than okay." Cameron laughed. "No, Mom, I'm just happy. I'm working on finding that lady to get you those grandbabies you were talking about."

Cameron winked at Marissa.

Marissa heard his mother's screech across the phone lines.

"Yes, it's Marissa. How'd you guess? Never mind, don't answer. I already know.

"Good night, Mom. I'll be home shortly." He hung up the phone.

"Been pressured to get married and have kids, huh?" Marissa winked.

"You might say that. I'm twenty-six and my mother's only hope."

"Well I'm only twenty-three. Do you think we could put off having kids for at least a year?" Marissa smiled.

Cameron chuckled. "Oh, I think a year is good. Mom will just have to be patient. It will be a sacrifice, but I think it will be worth it."

Marissa had told Cameron about the verse from Hebrews and her motivation to sacrifice for God, not for her own guilt, or even for praise from Cameron, but to sacrifice for God's pleasure.

Cameron took her hands into his. "Pray with me, love."

And with clasped hands they prayed together for the first time, asking the Lord to guide them in the precious gift of love He had given them.

Before they left, Cameron slipped the handcrafted sandals he'd made for her on her feet. Marissa wiggled her toes in the soft leather. The sandals he designed for others would have a rubber sole, durable for the sun and surf of Miami. But for Marissa, he created a delicate leather treat, a gift of grace, a gift for his little elf.

LYNN A. COLEMAN

Raised on Martha's Vineyard, Lynn now calls the tropics of Miami, Florida, home. She is a minister's wife who writes to the Lord's glory through the various means of articles, short stories, and a web site. She has three grown children and six grandchildren. She also hosts an inspirational romance writing workshop on the Internet, manages an inspirational romance web site, edits an inspirational romance electronic newsletter, and serves as president of the American Christian Romance Writers organization.

Lily's Plight

Yvonne Lehman

Chapter 1

Apprehension flowed through Lily White's veins like water rushing over boulders in a creek. Her pulse kept time with the tumultuous current. She prayed that when she arrived, she wouldn't babble like a brook.

Vince Harmen had invited her to an informal cookout at his home so she could meet her prospective employer and fellow workers to discover if they were compatible. She took that as a polite way of saying, "We want to evaluate you before hiring you." She had this one chance to impress them or run back home as a failure.

She mustn't fail. This was her first, and only, offer of a *real* job.

What is Vince Harmen and his home like? she wondered, driving up Castlerock Mountain, looking for road signs.

A man's home is his castle.

That's what Lily's dad often said. He would add, "And don't you two forget who's the king."

Lily's mother would joke then, make a fist and say something like, "Yes, and don't you forget who will crown the king if he misbehaves."

They would laugh as her dad pulled her mom into his

arms. Lily had liked that, basking in the love, protection, and security of her parents. A part of her wanted to always be their "little princess." Another part of her anticipated the inevitable reaching out for a life of her own.

When that day came to leave Jensen, Tennessee, 125 miles from Castlerock, North Carolina, her mom shed tears and her dad said, "Don't forget who's the King."

Lily knew he wasn't talking about himself. He was reminding her of the King of kings and Lord of lords— Jesus Christ. Being away from home for the first time meant she'd need to lean on the security of the Lord more than ever.

Following the map that had been sent along with her invitation, Lily slowed to catch a glimpse of the road signs for her turnoff. She'd left the motel near the interstate, off which she'd taken the exit to Biltmore Avenue, then turned onto Mountain Street.

That rose higher yet. Tree limbs reached over the winding mountain road, bordered by lush foliage. The map indicated she'd come to High Top Road after traveling up the incline for about two miles.

Yes! She saw the sign on the left.

After turning onto High Top, she glimpsed a two-story, round house first, then a larger contemporary with a wraparound deck. Beyond were fantastic mountain vistas. Shortly, she came to a fork in the road. Stopping to study the map, she realized the road curved downward at that point. The right lane should be Vince Harmen's driveway.

She turned her economy car to the right and followed the curving drive, bordered by immaculate flower beds flanked by the thick growth of shrubs and trees. Suddenly, she found herself perched on top of the mountain, with a house on her left and a parking area on her right. Without taking time to absorb the surroundings, she turned into one of two vacant spaces, beside a white European sports coupe, in a line of about seven or eight cars.

Lily stepped out of the car, aware of birds chattering in varying tones. One called with a single note. Others trilled. A forest of trees surrounded the property, obscuring any other view, except for the house that sat against a background of clear blue sky and hazy mountain peaks as far as her eye could see.

Apparently, everyone else had already arrived. What a way to start. They'd think if she couldn't be on time for a cookout at five o'clock in the afternoon, how could she be expected to be on time for work? However, her car clock read 4:55.

Taking a deep breath, she decided to focus on the house. Nature's materials, stone and wood, came together in an organized fashion to create this beautiful, but unpretentious home. The light gray roof tiles did not dominate, but blended with its surroundings. Bordering the stepping-stone walkway were summer flowers—golden, orange, and yellow marigolds; red, yellow, white, purple, and candy-striped pansies interspersed with leafy green plants, hedged by low Japanese boxwoods on the outer edges.

Perfect! popped into her mind.

What else? came her immediate response. What else could she expect of the home of the owner of a design firm?

She walked up two stone steps onto a narrow stone porch surrounded by a rustic wooden railing. Standing at the front screen door, but hearing no voices, she wondered if she should ring the bell or walk right in. Of course, she wouldn't walk right in. How could she have considered such a thing? She had noticed the driveway curved around to the side, probably to the back.

A male voice intruded into her thoughts. "Oh, hello there." Turning back to the screen, she saw a shadowy image walking toward her, saying, "You must be the guest of honor."

"I'm Lily White," she said, as he opened the screen door. She returned the smile of the tall young man. "Come in," he invited, and she stepped inside a small foyer.

"Ben Tripp here." He extended his hand. As her eyes adjusted to the dimness of the foyer, she saw that he was a nice-looking young man, about nineteen or twenty, she'd guess, with his sandy-colored hair cut short around the sides and sticking up at the front. She breathed easier, noting his blue jeans and knit shirt. Maybe she hadn't dressed too casually in doeskin pants and a yellow cotton shirt. He gestured toward the arched entryway. "Everybody's out back," he said. "We'll just go through the house."

Upon entering the next room, her eyes were immediately drawn to the far wall, made entirely of glass, beyond which lay mountain peaks and sky.

"If you like, I can put your bag up there on the bed. That's what the other women did." His friendly smile dimpled both cheeks. "Feel free to look around."

Lily removed the shoulder strap of her small denim purse and handed it to him. He bounded up several steps that lay along the side of a wall of bookshelves. When he opened the door, she saw a bed with a high curved headboard and lower matching footboard, in a rich mahogany color.

Turning back toward the living room, her quick perusal

revealed a large stone fireplace along the front wall. In the center of the room two couches faced each other, separated by a rectangular oak table. A whirling fan hung by a long gold chain from the open-beamed ceiling. Wood-paneled walls lent a cozy aura to the room.

Hearing the door close, she glanced over her shoulder as Ben strode toward her. "Thank you," she said.

"No problem," he said, giving her another of those appealing smiles that she thought would melt a lot of younger girls' hearts. She followed him across the room, grateful that he'd made her feel at ease.

Ben shoved open a glass door and they stepped out onto the enclosed deck, its windows shoved aside to let in the mountain air. Laughter and talking drifted in from below. Just as she was taking in the incredible beauty of the scene before her, Ben said, "By the way, I'm the one you'll replace."

Lily turned to face him. She couldn't read his expression. He stood looking at the panoramic view, but she didn't think he saw it. The blank stare could be just a reflection of the blue against his brown eyes. Or could he resent her if he'd been fired? If that were so, why was he here?

Rather than ask questions, she stated a fact. "I'm not hired yet."

With a short laugh, he glanced at her. "No problem there. They put up with me all summer. But that's nepotism for you." He laughed again. "I'm the son of the manager. If I can do it, anybody can. If you don't believe that, just ask my ol' man." He scowled. "Oh well, you don't need to hear this." He shook his head as if to clear it. The dimpled cheeks reappeared, but the eyes remained distant.

He shrugged. "Anyway, don't worry about it. All you have to do is answer the phone and switch the call to whomever they ask for."

If Ben meant that to encourage her, he'd failed miserably. She didn't like to think she might be hired because the job was so menial that "anybody" could do it. She wanted to contribute to a job—even if it was "only" a receptionist/secretary job.

This young man had built up her confidence, then destroyed it in a matter of a couple of minutes. But, Vince Harmen must seriously be considering her—even sight unseen—since he had invited her to come meet the employees, then come to the office the next morning to look over the agency and get an idea of the working conditions. The agency was paying her travel and motel expenses.

Perhaps Ben was right. Maybe "anybody" could do the job. But she had additional goals. She considered this a stepping-stone to her plans.

"We'll go down over here," he said, leading her to a side glass door and steps along one side of the house. Glancing down at the group, she saw people of all ages, including several children, and she felt apprehensive again. She was not outgoing like Ben. She was out of place in surroundings like this, and they all would know it.

As she descended the stairs, she realized there was a whole other story to this house.

Like people! she thought.

She'd just witnessed two different sides to Ben. He'd greeted her as a friendly, happy extrovert. A few minutes later he'd revealed a dissatisfaction within himself, although she didn't know if it was because of her, his dad, or himself.

Like advertising. First impressions of attraction attention were of utmost importance. But, then, one needed to inspire the consumer with the quality of the product. She would attract attention just by descending the steps. Would they think her nondescript enough to fill a position that "anyone" could handle?

And could she tell, by looking, which one was king of this castle—Vince Harmen?

Vince Harmen looked up from slathering more barbeque sauce on the ribs and chicken. *Oh, please tell me that's a girlfriend of Ben's and not Miss Lily White,* he thought. But any girl he'd seen with Ben had been much younger and wearing clothes that advertised, "Look at me." This one wore modest attire.

He feared this was, indeed, the applicant.

He knew her résumé by heart. He'd looked it over long enough.

Name: Lily Ann White
Age: 24
Marital Status: Single
Education: BA Degree in Advertising/Interior
    Design
Work Experience: Two years as secretary at
    White's Furniture Store, Jensen, Tennessee
References: Mr. John D. White
Next of Kin: Mr. & Mrs. John D. White, parents
Religious Affiliation: Christian
Expected Salary: Negotiable

Each time he and Dick Tripp went over applications,

they always returned to Miss White. The other applicants were too young, too experienced, or requested too large a salary. He'd had enough of the younger ones. His first secretary worked a year and a half, then decided she deserved more money than he thought she was worth, so she left. The second stayed six months, then married and moved away. He hired a married woman who became pregnant and decided to be a stay-at-home mom. Then, desperate, he'd hired Ben for the summer. Now Ben wanted to take a couple of weeks off and go to the beach before returning to college.

Vince and Dick determined that Miss White might be the right choice. Her "negotiable" response meant she'd take what they offered in salary. Having been a secretary for two years for her dad implied she hadn't been able to get a job in advertising or design. He understood that— no experience, no job!

Her willingness to move to another state indicated she wasn't seriously attached to a man. And being twenty-four indicated something about her had prevented that.

He needed someone presentable enough to greet his clients when they came into the office and competent enough to answer the telephone. The duties weren't overwhelming. And if she needed a little work on her personal appearance, he knew just the person to help with that— Grace Grant.

He didn't need a second look to realize Grace's expertise wouldn't be needed.

Chapter 2

The moment her sandals touched the patio, Ben shouted, "Okay, everybody. The guest of honor is here." With a mock bow and sweeping gesture of his outstretched arm, he presented her like one might some royal personage. "Miss Lily White."

What could the group do but applaud? They did, as they laughed or smiled and made mild exclamations of welcome.

"Since she's taking my place, may I do the honors of introducing her?"

The chef, his tall white hat askew, raised his scepter, dripping with barbecue sauce, and nodded his permission. With his hand at the small of her back, Ben led her around the group. The men who were seated politely stood. Lily knew that remembering their names would take awhile—*IF she were hired.*

They all made her feel right at home. Friendly smiles and handshakes abounded. A slight discomfort raced through her when introduced to the chef, who turned out to be Vince Harmen. Below the edge of the hat, damp blond hair lay over his forehead above vivid blue eyes in a lightly tanned, handsome face. He could be an advertisement in a top magazine with that mussed, everyday look combined with an unreadable aloofness in his eyes.

He said the right things, welcomed her, and told her to make herself at home. The barrier she detected was nothing more than his paying attention to his grilling. The guarded look in his eyes was caused by the heat of the grill, or the smoke, or something.

I'm just self-conscious, she chided herself. *I'm an inexperienced applicant trying to make it into the big leagues.*

Be yourself, she remembered her dad saying. *They'll love you.*

Realizing her dad was a mite biased, she nevertheless felt better. Soon, she forgot her apprehension and enjoyed the fellowship. She tried remembering names by word association.

Robert, the reserved.

Hap, the happy-go-lucky. After Ben introduced him, Hap gestured toward the very pregnant woman in a chaise lounge. "That's my wife, Nina—as in 'We're lucky to get our little monsters to bed by nine a'clock.' "

He laughed, then ran off to chase his two year old, Billy "the kid," who was running too close to the grill, and his four year old, Barney "the dinosaur," who was leaning too far over the side of the water fountain watching the goldfish.

The only one introduced with "Dr." before his name was Dr. Paul Harmen, the uncle of Vince Harmen. He preached at a local church. Paul, the preacher! Now, if she could just remember his wife as "Pearl" and not "Jewel."

She could remember Ben's dad as the office manager, but not his first name, nor his wife's. Both wore eyeglasses. Maybe Ben had introduced them as "Mom and

Dad" or "Mr. and Mrs. Tripp."

Next came Grady the grouch, who smacked his hands together and shouted, "Didn't I tell you to stay out of there!" Billy and Barney scampered out and rushed to their mommy with flowers from a manicured flower bed.

"Don't pay any attention to him," his wife said.

"Well, if she plans to work in the office with me, she'd better pay attention." He turned then and hastened toward the grill. "Hey, don't overcook my meat. I don't like to put anything in my mouth I can't chew."

His wife shook her head, looked toward the sky as if pleading for help, and then resumed a conversation with Mrs. Tripp. Ben led Lily to another woman, who stood from where she'd been sitting in a chair talking with. . . "nine a'clock Nina."

Lily doubted anyone could forget Grace Grant, whose parents could have been such lookers as Grace Kelly and Cary Grant. The tall, beautiful woman had expressive cat-like green eyes emphasized by her green silk blouse. She wore shorts that displayed long, shapely legs. A jeweled comb adorned her golden hair, smoothed back into a French twist. Her long brown lashes almost touched her high cheekbones when she spread her beautiful smile over perfect white teeth and greeted Lily. Like Vince Harmen, she looked to be in her early thirties and could have stepped from the pages of a fashion magazine.

Lily flashed Ben a grateful smile when he asked if she'd like to walk over to the fountain. Robert joined Hap in trying to get the boys to toss a ball to each other. She dared not ask personal questions. Sitting on the side of the stone fountain, she realized that everyone seemed paired off except Robert, Vince, and Grace and that each of the men had been introduced as working for the agency except Dr. Paul. She asked Ben if Grace worked there.

"No, she's a prospective client." After a short laugh, he spoke out of the side of his mouth. "I have a feeling she's prospecting for more than her business, if you get my drift."

Suddenly, the big red rubber ball landed in the fountain, splashing her, Ben, and the nearby Grady. Ben and Lily jumped up, looked at their spattered clothing, and Lily began to laugh.

"Go tell them you're sorry," Hap said to Barney.

The little boy sauntered over, looked up with big doleful eyes. "Sowwy," he said.

Grady grumbled, "If you're gonna give me a shower, at least furnish a towel." Ben laughed and flicked some water into the little boy's face, making him laugh.

"I'm fine," Lily said. "That just cooled me off. But, maybe we'd better check on the fish. You might have to tell them you're sorry." He climbed up and she held him around the waist while they put their fingers in to see if any fish were hurt.

The two year old wanted in on it, too. Robert brought him over and held him while the four of them spent the next ten or fifteen minutes trying to tickle the fish, giving Hap a break.

"Come and get it," called Vince. Lily looked around to see one of the long tables laden with food and drink.

❖

During the meal, Lily often forgot that she was being evaluated and felt an easy camaraderie with the friendly people. The conversations were light—about food, Tennessee, and Castlerock. She joined the group in gales of laughter as Hap kept them entertained.

After the meal, Ben stood, thanked Vince, and said he had to go. He needed to check with his buddies about what time they'd leave for the beach in the morning. Several said good-bye and bade him a good trip. Lily returned his smile when he looked her way. As he passed his dad, Mr. Tripp got up and the two walked over to a secluded spot. She dared not look, but out of the corner of her eye she had the impression they were disagreeing about something.

Vince told the group not to worry about the dishes. That would be taken care of. Next to leave were Hap, Nina, Billy, and Barney. The two year old had begun to fuss. Hap pulled his wife out of the chair so she could waddle over and tell the others good-bye.

"Let us know if anything happens," several said.

"If it's a girl, the whole world will know," Hap promised. "If it's another boy, I'm gonna put 'im back."

"Eeeeww," the women groaned while the men laughed.

Nina shook her head, then looked at Lily. "We already know she's a girl. He's such a nut."

Just as Lily began to wonder if she should leave, Grady announced he had to get home to see a TV program that he wasn't going to miss for anybody.

He said "good-bye" once, encompassing everyone, then glanced at Lily. "Lily of the valley, huh?" he said.

She didn't know what that meant. Her part of Tennessee did look like a valley compared with these high mountains. Was he implying that she wouldn't fit in with the people of this resort area? Before she could think of an appropriate reply, he grunted and walked away. His wife ignored him, as she'd done most of the evening, then expressed her delight in having met Lily.

As the sky began to turn orange and pink, Lily again wondered if she should leave. But Mrs. Tripp gestured for her to come over and sit in a chair near her and Pearl. They talked briefly about Lily's family in Tennessee, and Mrs. Tripp said this must be hard for Lily, having to spend an evening with those characters and not having been told whether she had a job.

Pearl patted Lily's hand. "But I can't imagine you have a thing to worry about."

"Thanks," Lily said and smiled.

They both looked up as the four remaining men and Grace approached.

"I want to thank you personally for joining us this evening," Vince said directly to Lily, who stood, thinking this was her cue to leave.

"Now that you've seen us in action, I hope you won't hightail it back to Tennessee," Mr. Harmen said.

"Oh, no," Lily said. "This was wonderful. Thank you so much for inviting me." As a touch of gold tinged the sky over the mountain ranges, she had to say, "I've never seen a more beautiful setting."

His blue eyes scanned the sky then searched the group. "How about joining me in a look at my most valued asset?"

Lily returned his smile and nodded, "I'd love to." Maybe he wanted to give her a tour of his house.

"It's worth seeing," Mr. Tripp said, "but Marjorie and I need to go."

Dr. Paul said he and Pearl wanted to stop by and see a couple who had visited the church on Sunday.

"Robert?" Grace asked.

Robert's quick glance moved from Grace to Lily, who

couldn't imagine why this seemed like such a difficult decision for him. Did he blush, or was that just the reflection of the pink sky? "I. . .I need to g—go."

Lily felt as uncomfortable as Robert sounded. Was he reluctant because only the four of them remained and he didn't want to be in a situation that looked as if he were paired up with the prospective secretary? His good-bye to her was quite warm and friendly, though.

She watched Robert walk away, mentally kicking herself for accepting Vince's invitation without first waiting to see what everyone else would do. Grace hadn't said she would stay. Apparently that was taken for granted—by both Vince and Grace. Was it her imagination or Grace's green glance that labeled Lily an intruder? What could she do now but try to make the best of this awkward situation?

Vince led Lily and Grace—not toward the house— but across the flagstone path through the manicured gardens, onto a dirt path through the shadowed woods, and into a glade where the mountaintop sloped down, presenting the most spectacular view Lily had ever seen.

She noticed the benches when they came into the glade, but no *way* could she sit while looking at God's magnificent creation. She felt more like raising her arms in praise or even lying prone on the ground in awe.

"Oh," Lily whispered in awe. "God is so great."

She didn't even try to hide the moisture that welled up in her eyes.

"How could anyone look at something like this and deny there's a God?" Vince said quietly.

Lily couldn't reply. But she figured that was a rhetorical question. It didn't need an answer. She couldn't imagine that anyone could believe such grandeur "just happened."

As if knowing a person could stand only so much splendor, the sun allowed its rays to fade, closed its eyes, and, having served God in such a glorious fashion, modestly made its exit from the sky.

Not until Grace said, "That was so beautiful, Vince," did Lily brush away an errant tear with her fingers. She and Vince turned from the still-magnificent view in impressive shades of gray as Grace rose from a bench.

What a way to end an evening, Lily thought. Even if she didn't get the job, she could never forget a man of means who spoke of his most prized asset as—not what he had fashioned—but what God had created.

Chapter 3

Dick placed his hands on the edge of Vince's desk, glaring at him through his dark-rimmed glasses. "Vince, you're a Christian man. How can you even consider sending that girl back home after she drove 125 miles, came to the cookout last evening, and will be here this morning to check out the workplace?"

Vince shook his head, causing a wavy lock of honey-blond hair to fall over his forehead, giving him the appearance of a boy with unruly curls. Sighing, he leaned back against the swivel chair, trying to escape Dick's scathing remarks. Sometimes the "Christian thing to do" seemed as clear as a mud hole after a cloudburst.

Suddenly, like a spring uncoiling, Vince moved to the edge of his chair. "You're the office manager. You tell her."

Dick stepped back, straight as a soldier at attention. He pushed his glasses farther up his nose. "Vince, if Ben deserved it, I would fire my own son if you asked. But surely you're not asking me to do something you know is unethical."

"Unethical, Dick?" Vince stood, facing him. "You know she's not going to work out. We discussed this fully before she arrived."

"I didn't sneeze, Vince. Not once."

Vince snorted. "Dick, we can't hire somebody just because you're not allergic to her."

Dick spread his hands wearily. "She hasn't even seen the offices yet. We've only observed her for a few hours at your place last night."

"Yes, and that was long enough to know she won't last more than three months, if that long."

Vince knew Dick's nod indicated acquiescence. He knew the truth when it stared him in the face. They'd wanted to avoid this kind of situation.

"Let me think," Dick said. He began to pace.

Vince walked over to the front window where store owners began turning CLOSED signs to OPEN. Lily White would arrive at any moment. What would it accomplish to have temporary help again? He might as well contact the temporary help service and get an employee who might come in for two months, two weeks, or two days.

Oh, no. The car coming down the street was unfamiliar. The driver wasn't, however. She'd spent three hours at his home last night. As she passed, he saw the Tennessee license plate and the directional signal that indicated a right turn that would take her alongside the building. Another turn and she'd drive into his parking lot behind the building.

"She's here," Vince said, casting a worried glance toward Dick.

"Don't panic, Vince," Dick said. "I have an idea. Now let's go through this like any decent employer should do with a prospective employee. If it turns out like I expect, our problems may be over. We'll do the right thing." He sounded confident, even when he said, "After all, we're professionals."

"Professionals," Vince mumbled. "In over five years we haven't even been able to keep a secretary."

Lily parked her economy car in a reserved spot, as she'd been told she could do, again next to the white sports coupe. Her stomach felt like it had wiggle-worms in it. She hadn't even been able to eat half the breakfast she'd ordered in the motel restaurant. And, too, she couldn't even remember where she'd spent a twenty-dollar bill she thought she'd had in her change purse.

She'd prayed about the job numerous times. Now she needed to sit and realize God was in control and gain perspective. She sat for a moment, thanking God for this wonderful opportunity. She remembered her fascination piqued when she'd arrived yesterday afternoon in this small, quaint resort town surrounded by lush tree-laden mountain peaks. Then, this morning she'd driven straight up Main Street from the motel, several blocks into town, and saw the stone and glass building taking up half a block. Black awnings with a gold fringe draped elegantly over long windows. Above the awnings, in gilded bold letters, glistened the name: CASTLEROCK ADVERTISING AGENCY. Each window displayed in artistic script the gold initials—CAA—inside a black circle.

Her watch and car clock indicated she had ten minutes before the agency opened. The door might be locked. She wouldn't want to appear overly anxious. But she felt good about it last night. At first, she'd wondered about being invited to a cookout. Now, she delighted in having seen "the boss" in an apron over casual slacks and a knit shirt. Ben and Robert had worn jeans.

Lily felt sure they'd wear suits to the office. Yes, Grady

pulled into another reserved spot a couple of spaces away. When he stepped out, she saw that he wore a sport coat that matched the gray color of his beard, giving him a distinguished appearance. He looked like somebody's nice old grandfather—if he just wasn't so negative.

She stared when Robert parked beside her in a red convertible sports car. She'd expect someone like Grace to drive a car like that—but not the reserved man she'd associated with last night. There must be a daring side to him she hadn't detected. She found that a pleasant surprise.

She stepped out of her car when he did.

"Good morning," he said, with warmth in his gray eyes. He looked the part of a successful businessman in his gray suit that matched the color of his eyes. He wore a white shirt and conservative gray and maroon silk tie and a maroon silk pocket square. His neatly trimmed, dark, straight hair complemented his handsome face. She hadn't thought about his looks last night, except for his being tall. She shouldn't be surprised that a handsome man, working for an advertising agency, would dress in such an attractive manner.

She hoped her own dress would be suitable. She had an eye for fashion but decided she should dress conservatively for her interview. She'd chosen a crinkle, small-check dress of khaki and ivory. It boasted a round collar at the throat, short sleeves, buttoned front, and stitched-down pleats to below the waist. The skirt reached to midway between her calves and ankles. With it, she wore three-inch khaki-colored slings. She carried a handbag she'd designed herself—khaki-colored with ivory buttons of various sizes and a drawstring closure.

Perhaps her attire was too nondescript, she thought,

considering how distinguished Grady and Robert looked. But at least no one could say she'd dressed too conspicuously—and she'd never paid such a high price for any other dress.

Walking past Robert, who held the door open for her, she approached the big oaken reception desk that dominated the room. That would be hers. . .if they hired her.

The phone rang—three times. No one answered. The machine came on, informing the caller to punch in the correct extension for the person to whom they wished to speak. The caller listened to all the instructions, then the phone beeped. Then Grady peeked around the doorway of another room. "Robert, it's for you." Robert hurried through another doorway. Lily readily saw this place needed a receptionist.

Seeing a movement on her left, Lily looked at a doorway and felt her heart stop at the sight of Vince Harmen. Then it began making up for lost time with rapid beats. She should not be so mesmerized by an incredibly handsome man whose eyes turned her world into a blur of blue.

A lock of blond hair fell over his forehead. A dark blue silk tie hung loosely down the front of his light blue shirt, open at the neck. An ivory-colored silk thread ran through the lightweight summer suit. The jacket was pushed back, his hands sunk deep into his pockets.

I must stop this, she warned herself. *Just because this man holds the key to my future—No!* came a more sensible thought—*God holds the key to my future. But. . .I really do want this job.*

Vince Harmen stepped into the outer office. "Good morning, Miss White," he said. He pulled one hand from his pocket and extended it.

Oh dear, why so formal? That didn't sound like a good sign. But if memory served her correctly, he hadn't addressed her by name last night. And besides, that had been pleasure—this was business. She noticed the furrow between his brows.

"Good morning," she said.

He stepped farther into the room, allowing the smiling Mr. Tripp to come in. He addressed her as Lily.

The phone rang again.

Grady's voice rang out, "That thing's driving me crazy. Let that little girl answer it, and we'll find out what she can do."

Vince and Mr. Tripp both headed for it, and Lily asked, "May I?"

Vince's gesture indicated, "Why not, could it be any worse?"

She picked up on the third ring, turning away from the two men staring at her. "Good morning. You've reached Castlerock Advertising Agency. May I help you, please?"

She paused, wondering how she'd ever become so nervy. But this was her do-or-die day, so to speak. "Yes, ma'am. I will connect you. If he's on another line, I'll come back on and take a message. You're quite welcome. Enjoy your day, ma'am."

Lily wasn't about to ask which button to push. She turned the phone to face her, punched the intercom button, and saw a G. Bullock's name with an extension number. She pushed the button. "Bullock here," he said. She'd recognize that voice anywhere. "Mr. Bullock, you have a call on line two."

"It's about time they got you on that desk," he exclaimed loudly.

Was that a compliment? When she turned toward the two men near her, Vince had his back to her, his hands again in his pockets. Mr. Tripp nodded. "You certainly know how to answer a phone, Lily. But I can show you a faster way. You don't have to talk so much, and you can just buzz in without telling each person he has a call."

"Oh, I enjoy talking with clients. That personal touch is—" She stopped talking when Vince turned toward her again with that questioning look in his eyes. *I'm talking too much again,* she warned herself. "But," she said quickly, "I will. . . I mean. . .I would do it your way, of course."

"No, no," Mr. Tripp said. "Our way is just 'a' way. Not necessarily 'the' way."

Vince said nothing about it. He just said that Mr. Tripp would explain what her duties would be and take her around the offices to give her an understanding of the workers' jobs, how they differed and how they related. Then he would bring her into his office and they would talk.

Before ten o'clock, Lily had a mini-course in what Mr. Tripp, Robert, Grady, and Hap did. When she walked into Hap's office, he said, "Do you know why the orange kissed the apple?"

Lily shrugged, having no idea.

"Because it had a peel."

She and Hap laughed. Mr. Tripp groaned and led her into the outer office. She answered the phone when it rang, much to the men's great pleasure. Mr. Tripp asked her to call him Dick.

"Think you're ready to talk with Vince now?" Dick asked.

She drew in a deep breath. "Ready as I'll ever be."

When they were midway in the outer office, he stopped and turned toward her. "I'm glad you don't wear those overbearing perfumes. They drive my sinuses crazy."

Lily didn't bother to tell him that she'd neglected to pack her perfume. She made a mental note to forget it forever—*if they hired her.*

"Uh-oh," he said.

Lily followed his glance. Right outside on the sidewalk stood Grace Grant, who smoothed back her hair, straightened her shoulders, and patted her flat stomach. Lily realized the door was a perfect mirror.

Dick strode to Vince's doorway. "Lily's ready to talk with you, and Grace is here," he said.

Grace entered the room like she owned it. She spoke to both Lily and Dick. He already had the handkerchief out of his back pocket and sneezed as she neared him. Her countenance brightened perceptibly when Vince came to the doorway.

Her green eyes narrowed. "Oh, Vince," she said, pursing her lips and shaking her head as if he were a naughty child. She walked right up to him, reached out, and pushed his stray lock of hair back into place.

Vince took a step back and looked at Lily. "Would you mind waiting, Miss White?"

"That's fine," she said, as Grace led him back into his office.

"She's a client," Dick explained, as if apologizing that she had to wait. "She's owner of the Mirror Image Modeling Agency and considering going national." He turned away as he sneezed again.

"I'll just sit here and answer the phone," Lily told him.

Dick went into his office, located behind her.

Of course I should wait. A client outranks a secretary any day. And Grace Grant is obviously someone very special to Vince Harmen. Lily had thought Vince Harmen looked perfectly wonderful just the way he was. But she heard Grace's light musical laughter and her teasing words when she said, "Vince, you're a total wreck. Here, let me straighten your tie," just before she closed the door behind them.

Lily sighed. She didn't think Grace Grant would be an easy act to follow. But what choice did she have? And anyway, the phone began to ring.

Chapter 4

Vince heard Grace say, "Toodles," to Lily. She lifted her hand to him again then gracefully placed one foot in front of the other and exited the building. How a woman could walk like that in high heels, he'd never understand. Nor could he understand how ballerinas danced on their toes. And he couldn't understand how he was supposed to tell this girl she couldn't work for his agency.

"Come into my office, please," he said to Lily.

He motioned to a chair near his desk and seated himself behind the desk. Seeing the hopeful look in her eyes, Vince looked mainly at his desk instead of at them. "Do you have any questions, Miss White?"

"Not concerning the job. Mr. Tripp explained that to me. It's all within my range of experience. And he said I could ask him when someone calls but is unsure to whom they should speak. After a short while, I should be able to figure that out for myself."

Vince nodded in time with the ballpoint pen he tapped on his desk calendar. "He mentioned the salary?"

"Yes."

Vince tried to keep his voice level when he asked,

"And that's satisfactory?"

"Yes," she said immediately. "I understand that someone like myself, who's had only one job that wasn't in advertising, could not expect a huge salary. But, Mr. Harmen, making money is not my only goal, although I have to make a living. You see, I want to learn about the advertising business. That's what I studied in college. Working here would be. . ." She paused and took a deep breath. "Would be beyond my wildest dreams."

He swallowed hard. "You are aware, Miss White, that you're not our only applicant."

He heard her quick intake of breath—then only the clicking of his pen.

Click. Click. Click.

That made him nervous. Or rather, he clicked the pen because he was nervous. *What kind of man am I?* His lack of businesslike manner irritated him.

He cleared his throat and sat as straight as she. But he didn't look down at clasped hands like she was now doing. He stood. "I appreciate your coming in. All the way from Tennessee. Would it be all right to call you within the hour?"

She stood. "Yes, thank you," she said, but her eyes didn't meet his. She knew. He'd said as much as "Don't call us, we'll call you," which basically meant "Forget it!"

Why couldn't he have said all that without sounding as if he had regrets? And what good would it do to tell her of his regrets? None! That would just rub salt into the wound.

She left the building without going into the offices to tell the others good-bye. Of course she knew. She was no dummy.

He resisted the urge to look as she passed by his window. Instead, he visualized her shoulders slumped and her head bent. This time her tears would not be from joy, but from disappointment. And he had just prolonged her agony for another hour.

Vince went into Dick's office. He had an hour to figure out how to convince Dick to do the dirty work of making the final call to Lily White. Or get some insight on how to do it himself.

As Vince stepped into the outer office, a prospective client came in. He directed him to Robert then answered the ringing telephone before going in to see Dick. Time was passing. He pictured Lily sitting by the phone, waiting for the axe to fall.

"You let her go?" Dick boomed.

"Not exactly," Vince said. "I thought you could do that better than I." He walked farther into the room and took a seat near the desk.

Dick sneezed, took out his hanky, and exhibited a look of exasperation, as if Vince shouldn't go near Grace's perfume. Vince stood and walked away from the desk. Dick's sneezing could be as nerve-racking as the telephone monologue.

Vince shook his head. "Dick, you saw how she looked. And you saw how she behaved at the cookout."

He watched Dick push his glasses farther up his nose, a gesture he used when trying to think of a solution to a problem. But Vince could take this even farther. "You witnessed the efficient and personable way she answered the telephone. She must have responded as intelligently with you as she did with me. And she wants this job. But you know as well as I do, the minute word got around that someone like her worked here, the guys would swarm in here like bees to honey. She'd be snatched away from us before you could say boo."

Vince shook his head helplessly. "I don't know how to tell Lily White that we can't hire her because she's too. . . perfect."

"Let's analyze this and see what we can come up with," Dick said. "There may be a way."

Vince started to walk closer to Dick but thought better of it. Grace's perfume still hovered on his shirt. He didn't want to interrupt any solution Dick might have by causing another sneezing fit.

"I see your point perfectly, Vince," Dick agreed. "We've discussed this before. And you're right. Any man in his right mind can see Lily's outstanding qualities. She's uncommonly pretty. Any single eligible man is going to pursue her." He pushed his glasses farther up his nose. "Now where is the closest eligible bachelor you know?"

Before Vince could reply, Dick took it farther. "And who did she spend some time with at the cookout?"

Robert?

Why not? Robert was a couple of years older than Vince. He'd never married. Apparently, like Vince, he'd been busy in his career and the right girl had never come along. But maybe Dick was right.

They didn't come any finer than Robert Newman. If Robert and Miss White got together, that could work in the agency's favor. Robert knew the trouble they'd had keeping a secretary. He wouldn't be taking Lily off somewhere else. He'd encourage her to stay on as office help. That could work.

Yes, Lily would be blessed to have a man like Robert—

a fine Christian, a good worker, a reliable, responsible, respectable man. And, if his instincts were right, Robert wouldn't be able to find a better woman than Lily.

She was as pretty as the lilies described in Solomon's Song in the Bible—*behold the lilies of the field, how they grow.* How could Robert not be taken with her attractive figure, fair skin, big brown eyes that seemed flecked with gold when she turned them toward you? She'd been well-received at his cookout. Everyone liked her. How could Robert resist a Christian girl who became teary when she looked at a sunset?

"Yes," Vince said. "If those two get together, we just may be able to keep her." He nodded. "We do indeed have an eligible bachelor right here in the office."

Such relief swept over him that Vince hurried from the room, concerned with calling Lily White instead of allowing Dick's last remark to register.

"I may not be the world's greatest mathematician," Dick had said, "but using all my fingers and toes, it seems to me that in this office we have *two* eligible bachelors."

As soon as she arrived at the motel, Lily checked out. She'd packed everything and put it in the car, ready to return to Tennessee as soon as she got official word from the agency. Time crawled toward 10:45. She couldn't stay in the room beyond 11:00 a.m.

She stood staring at the phone, willing it to ring, although she dreaded getting the call. Vince Harmen had to know whether or not he wanted to hire her. Suddenly, she jumped at the shrill sound.

She picked up on the second ring, but a weak "Hello" was all she could manage.

"Miss White?"

"Yes."

"Vince Harmen here. If you're still interested, you have a job at Castlerock Advertising Agency."

After a quick intake of breath, she managed to say, "Oh."

"How soon could you start to work?"

She cleared her throat. "In, um, t–ten minutes?"

Was that a laugh? Or surprised breathing? Oh dear, she'd messed up already by being too eager. She should have said "Monday."

He must have thought it all right. After the moment of silence, he did laugh lightly and sounded as if he might be joking when he said, "Don't be late."

Lily arrived at the agency a couple of minutes before eleven o'clock. Dick explained how she should direct calls and how to consolidate individual appointment calendars. She'd never felt so appreciated in all her life—except when Grady passed by her desk. Stroking his beard, he stared at her for a long moment and growled, "Well it's about time you got back. That was a long coffee break, young lady." He humphed as he continued across the room. "You didn't even ask if you could bring me a cup."

Hap came in with his perpetual smile and asked, "Hey Lily, why didn't the skeleton cross the road?"

She couldn't think of a thing.

Hap waved the air with his hands. "He didn't have the guts."

About eleven thirty, a thin, elderly man came in and introduced himself as "Nico, the night janitor." He looked into her trash can and shook his head. "You're gonna have to do better than that, or I'm going to be out of a job."

She promised to do better but feared he might lose his job, because he apparently had his days and nights mixed up. After he left, however, Dick came in and explained that Nico had narcolepsy. Due to his condition, he couldn't hold down just any job. Vince tried to help him out by having him keep the offices clean, and he worked at his convenience.

"Just be warned," Dick said. "He might be talking to you and all of a sudden crumple before your eyes and fall into a deep sleep."

After working for an hour and a half, Dick said she could put the phone on the answering machine while she went to lunch. The others went when they could get away, but Lily's hour would be 12:30 to 1:30.

As if on cue, Robert came in and asked if she'd go to lunch with him. A couple of minutes later, she and Robert walked out into the bright afternoon sunshine, around the corner of the agency, and down the street for a couple of blocks. Across the street a furniture store took up an entire block. After they passed a hardware store and a souvenir shop, he led her beneath a royal blue awning on which H&H was printed in bold white. Printed in smaller letters on the glass door were the words "From Health to Happiness Sandwich Shop."

Since the booths and tables were full, mainly due to tourists, Robert said, they went out back. Small, round white tables for four, with blue and white umbrellas in the center, stood on the flagstone patio. A high white fence obscured a view of other buildings but allowed a distant view of trees and mountain peaks.

Lily looked at the design of the menu before she even considered what she might order. The royal blue sketch of the shop front against a white background drew her attention. But the scripture verse beneath it made her think.

"Blessed is the man who does not walk in the counsel of the wicked or stand in the way of sinners or sit in the seat of mockers. But his delight is in the law of the Lord, and on his law he meditates day and night" (Psalm 1:1–2 NIV).

On the inside, royal blue letters listed the calorie count, along with choices of food. She was not surprised to find her favorite scripture, printed as the last entry on the back.

" 'For God so loved the world that he gave his one and only son, that whoever believes in him shall not perish but have eternal life' " (John 3:16 NIV).

"I like this menu," Lily said.

At Robert's "thank you," she returned his smile. "You designed it?"

"The H&H logo and the menu," he said. "But I can't take credit for the initial idea of including scripture. Vince encourages all the Christian business owners to remember they are the light of the world and to reflect that somehow in their advertising whenever possible."

Lily thought she might have been mistaken about Robert's reserve last evening. Now he appeared completely comfortable, and he invited her to go with him to hear Dr. Paul preach on Sunday.

A dark shadow passed over Grace's mind when she called the advertising agency a little past eleven to invite Vince to lunch. A female voice answered the phone. In her heart, she knew it had to be none other than Lily White.

Grace had been wary from the moment she saw Lily, who looked about eight or ten years younger than she.

The mental picture of Rajni flashed before her eyes. Before Rajni, Grace had experienced the saying, "Gentlemen prefer blonds."

She'd had to remind herself that just because Lily had dark hair and dark eyes, in addition to being young and pretty, she was nothing like Rajni, whose pretended innocence had caught Grace off guard. Grace would never be naïve again about another woman. Grace had an eye for unusually attractive girls. Her business depended upon that expertise. But she shouldn't give Lily another thought—she was no princess nor did she have exotic beauty.

Although Robert's working at the agency often gave her a self-conscious feeling, she determined not to let that disturb her. He was as uncomfortable around her as she with him. His presence reminded her of where she came from and who she used to be. But that was in the past. People grew up. *I am no longer little "Gracie" that Robert Newman knew in grade school and junior high. I am Grace Grant, former internationally famous runway model, owner of the Mirror Image Modeling Agency, and considering expanding into other cities and states.*

She planned never to be like other women—letting their hair turn gray or looking like a zeppelin. How could one live happily like that? What secret did these happy, contented people have that she didn't have? Was she really missing out on life like her parents indicated? How could anyone even think such a thing? She'd had a wonderful career. She had a bank account bigger than most people in town. She'd set her sights on Vince Harmen. She'd seen too much of the world and men who had nothing on their minds but self-gratification and money.

Vince had integrity. Before he took her as a client,

he had her read the company's policy. Two things stood out in her mind. One, he encouraged clients to include Christian principles in their advertising when appropriate. Two, none of his employees fraternized with clients on a personal basis while planning the client's advertising campaign.

Grace had found a way out of that. She'd told him that since his agency had no women employees, she would like to get some female opinions about her campaign. The wives of his employees might be the perfect ones to peruse the plans. After all, those whom she must impress were not male agents but the general public, mainly females.

Vince agreed and said the cookout would be an ideal time for that. It had seemed so, until the intrusive Lily White appeared on the scene.

For Pete's sake, Grace, she'd told herself. *You're concerned about a mere secretary?*

How ridiculous.

Ridiculous? Then why on the morning the mere secretary was to have been interviewed did she answer the telephone?

"Who's speaking, please?" Grace asked.

"Lily White."

"Oh, I met you at the cookout. This is Grace Grant. I take it you've been hired."

"Yes, I believe so," answered Lily White. "They're rather desperate here."

Apparently!

"Put me through to Vince, please."

"He's on another line right now."

Grace laughed. "Miss White. Vince always takes my

calls, even if he has to put another caller on hold."

"Just one moment, please."

The next voice Grace heard was Vince's. Ah, mission accomplished—even though Vince did say he was on another line and would return her call.

During her afternoon coffee break, Lily sat in Robert's office and looked at advertising the agency had done. CAA's own included the scripture from Matthew 5:14–15. " 'You are the light of the world. A city on a hill cannot be hidden. Neither do people light a lamp and put it under a bowl. Instead they put it on its stand, and it gives light to everyone in the house.' "

A short while later, she sat at her desk taking notes while Dick explained which employee handled design layout, artwork, market research, media selection, promotional strategies, budgeting, and other aspects of a design agency.

She and Dick looked up as Vince walked in the office. *A shining light*, she thought when he came through the front door. Her thoughts, however, were not entirely spiritual, although that aspect of him impressed her. The sunlight turned his hair to gold, his smile brightened his face, and his blue eyes shone with a glow that warmed her heart. How a man could so light up a room just by entering it, she didn't know. She'd never experienced that while working at her dad's furniture store. No one had affected her quite so emotionally since Sammy Ellison had given her a soft-centered lollipop in the third grade.

The mesmerizing quality dimmed as he walked farther into the room. Dick began to sneeze, leaving no doubt in Lily's mind about with whom Vince Harmen had spent the afternoon.

"You had several calls," she managed to say.

"Thank you," he said, still smiling. But Lily had no illusions that she was the one who put that smile on his face. He went into his office but quickly turned around. "Miss White," he asked, "did you check out of the motel?"

"Yes, I had to be out by eleven."

"Then you don't have a place to go. This is tourist season. There won't be a room available anywhere."

Before she could say a word, his distress turned to what looked like pure delight. "You'll just have to come home with me and stay at my place."

Chapter 5

Lily had heard her mother say, "When it rains, it pours." The scripture stated, "It rains on the just and unjust." A line of poetry read, "Into every life a little rain must fall."

That particular day in mid-August, when the clouds drenched the area in a much-needed rain, she had no idea that scenario would happen within her own heart before the middle of the morning. A quick review reminded her of how wonderful the past weeks had been.

Since the agency closed on weekends, she'd gone back to Tennessee for her clothes, although she'd been tempted to take Vince Harmen up on his invitation to stay at his place. Pearl had called Lily to say she could stay with her and Paul until she found a place, so she'd gone there on Sunday evening when she returned to Castlerock.

With Robert's help she'd found the perfect rental—a one-bedroom log cottage, in a group of seven others, located off the main road and only two miles from the agency. Her cottage sat below a cluster of oaks, maples, dogwoods, and rhododendrons near a narrow creek, making a picturesque setting.

At first she thought she couldn't afford the furnished

cottage, but the owner said rent was higher during tourist season. She'd pay two hundred dollars less after October. She could handle that, even if it meant getting into her meager savings account.

Yes, her days had been sunny, and she caught on to her office responsibilities quickly. Now, on this rainy day, she arrived shortly before nine o'clock, as usual. She'd been given a key in case she arrived before the others. Standing underneath the awning, she shook the rain off her umbrella, unlocked the front door, went inside, and plunked her umbrella into the large earthen urn set there for that purpose.

She hadn't yet seen Nico fall asleep, but there he sat, slumped in her chair, sound asleep.

She smiled while making coffee and hearing the men in the front office. She loved having them come in to the aroma of fresh coffee permeating the offices. Grady reached the lounge, grumbling about the weather, and said the coffee looked too weak.

Dick appeared and suggested he make it himself. Grady shook his head. "Nope. Drinking inferior coffee keeps me humble. Anyway, making coffee is a woman's job."

"That reminds me," Hap said, "when women's lib first came along, a million women declared, 'I will not be dictated to.' Then they promptly went out and became secretaries."

Lily didn't mind Grady's grumbles nor Hap's kidding. She loved the job. She'd begun to suspect the reason for Robert's reserve and prayed about that matter. Vince called her "Lily" except when addressing her in front of clients. She respected Dick's management of the office. Another thing she prayed about was her attitude when Vince returned from a long meeting and Dick would sneeze. That meant Vince had been with Grace again.

Lily told herself that her heartstrings were playing off-key notes. That was not sweet music when she thought of Vince. She saw no special gleam in his eyes when he looked at her. She should not allow herself that slightly breathless feeling when he was near. She should not allow her admiration and respect to turn into anything stronger.

Nico awakened, and she got her chair back. Everything went fine for the next thirty minutes. Then, shortly before ten o'clock, everything turned upside down. Lily lost the respect of everyone in the office. Her credibility came into question. She could be fired.

A tall, dark, well-dressed, middle-aged man hurried out of the rain and into the office. Lily rushed to get paper towels for his wet hair. He thanked her, smiled, and wiped his head, face, hands, and the shoulders of his suit coat.

Handing the towel back to her, he said in a musical-sounding accent, "I'm here for my appointment with Mr. Harmen."

Lily quickly went to her desk, threw the towel in the trash can, and looked at the appointment calendar. Nothing! "Your name, please?" she asked.

"Luciano Calabria," he said, his dark eyes boring into hers, as if she should know without asking.

"Excuse me," she said and went into Vince's office. No appointment was written on his calendar either. She returned to the front office. "I'm sorry, sir. I don't have a record of your appointment."

His eyes widened. "Just tell Mr. Harmen I'm here."

"He hasn't yet come in."

"Hasn't come in?" the man blared, jerking his arm out, then toward himself to look at his watch. "What kind of place is this? I travel all the way from Italy, stop off here on my way to Atlanta, Georgia, specifically to see Mr. Harmen, and you tell me he's not here? And I have no appointment? Are you the one who answers the phone?"

His voice had risen with every word. She could not recall taking a call from anyone with his kind of accent. Northerners, Southerners, and one from Boston, yes. But she could not be mistaken about talking with someone with an Italian accent. And she always made a note when anyone called, even if it were only an inquiry and said they would call back later.

"I am the one who answers the phone," she admitted. "When did you call, Mr. Calabria?"

His dark gaze rolled around the ceiling. Apparently he wasn't accustomed to being questioned by secretaries. Then the piercing eyes met hers again. "A week ago, last Friday. I told you that I would stop by around ten o'clock, Eastern Standard Time, on Monday, this day of August. That, I don't believe, is too difficult to understand."

Lily couldn't come right out and accuse him of lying. "Are you sure—," she began.

He interrupted. "I'm sure I talked with a female. Is there another in the office? Such inefficiency should be dealt with—harshly. Believe me, I can take my account to another agency."

By this time, his irate tone of voice had brought the others to their doors. While she said, "I'm sorry," to the man who didn't care to listen, Dick came into the room, asking if he could be of assistance.

Lily shrank into her chair, staring while the man loudly

voiced his irritation, threatened again to remove his account, and reiterated that this inefficiency called for action. He had taken his valuable time to stop off in North Carolina when he could have flown directly to Atlanta. He'd rented a car and risked his life to drive around mountain roads in a storm. Now he had wasted at least half a day for nothing.

Lily didn't think it would help matters if she tried to defend herself and say she didn't take the call. She was the only female in the office. She could only whisper once again, "I'm so sorry."

After he stormed out the door, Grady, Robert, Hap, and Dick looked at her. She thought of the scripture that stated, "It rains on the just and the unjust." The way all the men in the office stared at her gave her the very distinct impression she had taken root among the unjust.

Covering her face with her hands, she sobbed.

"I'll handle it," Dick said, and the other men returned to their offices.

Between gulps and bitter tears, Lily insisted she had not taken the call. By the time Dick had her calmed down, Vince walked in. "What's going on?" he asked. Dick told him and it all started again.

"Lily, how could you let this happen?" Vince blared. "The biggest account we've ever had!" His hands lifted as if he were Atlas holding up a glass world but about to drop it and his world would shatter into a trillion pieces. "This client has international connections."

Lily could only shake her head. "I did not talk to that man. I would remember."

"Miss White," Vince said, with his hands on her desk, leaning toward her. "When we make mistakes, we admit it and do all we can to correct it. But we don't lie about it. Tell me, what other female answers the phone around here?"

As soon as he said it, his face paled. He straightened and exchanged a long look with Dick, who offered a suggestion. "Lily hasn't missed a day of taking her lunch hour from 12:30 to 1:30. If we can discover the exact time of his call, then we can know for certain."

"He's gone," Vince said helplessly.

"He's in a rental car, heading for the airport."

Vince pondered what he should do as he drove to the airport. What he must say to Lily wouldn't be easy. How could he be tactful, yet honest, but not go overboard? That same question ran through his mind every time he met with Grace Grant to discuss her Mirror Image Modeling Agency plans or took her out on a business luncheon or dinner.

When Grace first came into the office, he'd been vulnerable to her physical appearance, her charm, and he admired her plans to go national. Heads turned when they went out together, and he had to admit that was quite an ego trip for him. He analyzed the situation, told himself that the years of total dedication to building his business had ended. He had a well-established agency now. He could think about settling down with a wife and maybe even children. Was Grace the one God had in mind for him?

The longer he associated with Grace, however, the more he realized she did not have a strong commitment to the Lord. She didn't care to mingle with the singles at church, saying she had nothing in common with them.

Vince had dismissed the thought that they all had in common the most important thing—a commitment to the Lord Jesus Christ as personal Savior.

He excused her reasoning by telling himself that if they fell in love and married, then the two of them would have more in common with married couples than with young singles, divorced persons, and older widows. After all, she did occasionally attend the worship service at church, and she claimed to be a believer. He knew people were at varying levels in their faith and expressed it differently.

As Lily became more a part of the agency and his everyday life, he stopped making excuses for Grace. He faced the fact that Grace was a beautiful woman with much about her to be admired. But it was Lily who crept into his thoughts and ultimately into his heart. He'd often wondered what lay beneath the made-up façade of Grace. He never wondered that about Lily. He felt she was exactly as she appeared—a lovely young woman trying to live each day to the best of her ability and give a good day's work. On Sundays she attended the singles' Sunday school class and made friends immediately.

Vince had to admit that if his intentions about Grace had been serious, he would not have reacted to Lily so strongly the first time he saw her. When she walked down those back stairs, he felt like someone had begun to chip away at his carefully guarded heart.

By the time Vince admitted his feelings for Lily, she and Robert appeared to be an item. Besides sitting together in church, they had lunch together almost every day. He assumed they went out on dates. He should have let it penetrate that first day when Dick had said there were two eligible bachelors in the office. Now how could he attempt to stab his friend Robert in the back by admitting his personal interest in Lily? With friends like that, who needed enemies?

But he had to talk with Lily.

When he walked up to the doorway of CAA at closing time, Vince stepped aside then held the door open to allow one of their local clients to leave. They talked for a couple of minutes about how the newspaper ads were making a world of difference in her midsummer sale. After a grateful smile, she walked on down the sidewalk to her apparel shop.

That short interim, nor the fact that the rain had stopped, did nothing to alleviate his uneasiness on how to handle the situation with Lily. He walked right up to her desk as Dick walked in, grabbed for his handkerchief, and began to sneeze. Vince gave Dick a glance that meant, *Yes, I've been to see Grace, and what of it?*

Vince had to get this over with. "Lily, we need to talk. Could you stay after the others leave?"

At her single nod, he breathed more easily. "Thanks," he said and headed for Dick's office, bracing himself for an onslaught of sneezing.

Lily felt the tears threaten again and tried to force them back. For the umpteenth time, she grabbed her bag and headed for the rest room to pat her eyes with a wet paper towel and try to reduce the swelling. Each time she thought about Mr. Calabria's anger and Vince's disappointment in her, it brought on another onslaught of uncontrollable tears. Grady, Hap, and Robert kept to their offices all day, and Dick had tried to reassure her that everything would be all right—they'd get to the bottom of this.

Fighting back the tears, while holding the towel on her eyes, she knew she couldn't work where she wasn't trusted to do the job. She couldn't explain this mix-up to herself, except either she or Mr. Calabria had lost their minds. But up against an important man like him, her word didn't stand a chance.

Pray.

She'd prayed and begged all day. She'd asked God to work this out in some reasonable way. But she kept seeing Mr. Calabria's face, then Vince's. Oh, he would never look at her again with that warm glow in his eyes. He'd never smile and tell her again how grateful he was that she worked with him. He never said "for" him but "with" him. That had given her a feeling of importance. Those special moments were over.

Again, she felt the hot tears sting her eyes. *Pray. Yes! Lord, help me realize this is not the end of the world. Lord, help me realize that in a life, a little rain must fall.*

Little? There'd been storms all day long—and the greatest portion had streamed down her face. If she didn't get those waterworks turned off, she'd end up in the hospital as a victim of dehydration. A realization slowly dawned. *Lord, You brought me here for a reason. I need to exercise my faith and believe You can work this out, like Dick said. You're in control. My life is in Your hands, and You know best. I'm going to hang on to that.*

With that determination, she patted powder on her face, applied lip gloss, straightened her shoulders, and left the rest room. Despite her resolve, her feet didn't take her any farther than the small lounge set at the back of the offices between the two rest rooms.

She walked over to the back window, vaguely aware of moving vehicles and her fellow workers—or former fellow workers—hurrying to their cars. Viewing the world outside through the venetian blinds, she felt it had turned into gloomy slices, like paper pushed through a shredder.

She tried counting her blessings. She'd had a wonderful month. Everything had been perfect. Now it was a blur.

How long she stood there, she didn't know. She was waiting. Waiting for Vince. Waiting for Vince to tell her this was all over. She was fired.

Then she heard him say her name. "Lily?" The soft patter of rain against the windows shut out every other sound but his footsteps and her name in the quietness of the room.

She'd never heard her name sound so special as it did when Vince said it. Earlier, when he believed she'd ruined his business, he'd reverted to formally calling her "Miss White." Now, he quietly said, "Lily." She detected relief in his voice when he said, "I was afraid you had left us."

Oh, she wished she had. How could she bear hearing him say she must go?

She didn't turn until she felt his hand lay gently on her shoulder. "Lily," he said again, and it sounded like a raspy whisper she'd detected in her dad when he'd had to spank her and he'd said, "This is going to hurt me more than it's going to hurt you." No, Vince was not the kind of man who would take any pleasure in firing anyone—no matter what the reason.

Then, thinking of his unpleasant chore, instead of

herself, she turned her face toward him. The blue of his eyes was the only spot of color in this longest dull-gray day of her life. Their gazes held. Her mind entreated, *Oh, please, tell me my fairy-tale life isn't over.*

Chapter 6

L ily," he said, both hands now on her shoulders, turning her to face him. "Luciano Calabria no longer blames you. We got this whole thing straightened out. It's all a big misunderstanding that's over."

Over? Oh, it would never be over. Yes, she could believe they all could forgive her, but they'd never trust her again. Things would never be the same. They wouldn't be able to forget. Nor would she.

Vince's hand moved from her shoulder to gently wipe away an errant tear sliding down her cheek. "Stop your crying," he said gently. His voice was kind, his gaze warm. His fingers trembled against her cheek. Or maybe that was her own being that trembled. Her knees felt weak.

"I know you didn't take Mr. Calabria's call, Lily," Vince said.

Her lips parted in surprise and her eyes widened. "How can you know?"

"Have dinner with me, and I'll explain," he said. "That's the least I can do to try to make up for my rude behavior. I am so very sorry."

"You don't need to—"

Interrupting, with a trace of a grin, he asked, "Who's the boss here?"

She hoped he was still her boss, despite the heaviness in her heart. He headed toward the hallway, glancing over his shoulder, so she followed a few paces behind.

The phone rang. Lily started toward it, but he caught hold of her hand. "It's after hours. The machine can get it." He kept talking, even when the answering machine began its spiel. "I told Dick what I'd learned and asked him to tell Robert, Hap, and Grady before they left. So, they all know you're not to blame."

"Please leave your message after the beep," the machine said.

The unmistakable voice of Grace Grant sounded. "Vince? Vince? Are you still there?" He stopped talking then and stared at the phone. Lily walked to the door while Grace continued. "If you're there, pick up. If not, and you get this later, give me a call please. I have so much to make up for."

Vince hurried to the door, pushed it open, and held it for Lily to exit. Just as he locked the door, Lily realized she forgot to get her umbrella. Oh, well, she wouldn't bother him about that. The rain had stopped.

On the way to the restaurant, all the rain in Lily's heart dried up as Vince described what had happened. That morning, Vince arrived at the airport before Mr. Calabria and was waiting for him at the car rental section.

Calabria's surprise and pleasure that the trip hadn't been completely in vain overshadowed his earlier anger, and he agreed that Vince could take him to lunch and show him the plans that he'd put in his briefcase before leaving the agency. His flight wouldn't leave until 3:24 p.m. Vince took him to the country club, where they ate, looked out over a golf course which pleased the Italian, and spent a couple of hours discussing marketing goals and implementation.

"Did he admit he hadn't called?" Lily asked.

"Oh, he called all right." Vince glanced over. "A week ago Friday, around four o'clock."

After a thoughtful moment, the light dawned in Lily's brain like the late afternoon ray of sun peeking through a break in the clouds. She remembered that day well.

Until about 3:45, the day had been calm. All the workers had stayed in their offices working on projects. Even the phone had been relatively quiet. Grace had come in to talk with Vince. Nina stopped by the agency with Billy and Barney. She commented that she was so tired of waiting for the baby to be born; she'd just keep busy and forget about it.

About that time, the baby decided she wasn't about to be forgotten. Nina made a strange strangled sound, bent over holding her stomach, and grabbed hold of the desk for support. "The hospital—now!" she said. "I have quick deliveries."

The office became an uproar. Hap went crazy. Lily thought after having two boys he would be more calm. But Hap wasn't a calm kind of man. "Call. . .call. . . ," he said, then threw up his hands. "Call somebody!"

"Call my parents," his wife ground out between grimaces.

"I can keep the boys," Lily offered, "if that would help."

"I'll call Nina's parents," Dick offered. Grady mumbled and returned to his office. Robert paled and did the same.

After Hap left with his wife, they discussed what to do. Lily said she could keep the boys all evening if Nina's parents wanted to be at the hospital. Dick called and told them that. Vince told Lily to take the rest of the day off and gave her the keys dangling from Nina's abandoned purse and directions to Hap's house.

Later, Marjorie joined Lily at Hap's house. Later still, Vince came by to tell them the baby had been born, a six-pound, two-ounce perfect little girl. Mom and Dad were doing fine, except Hap was running around the hospital giving pink candy cigars to everyone he saw and telling every baby joke he'd ever heard.

Now Lily wondered if she had gotten a call during that turmoil when trying to keep track of two active little boys and just didn't remember.

But that's not what Vince began telling her. "Mr. Calabria says he called a little past four o'clock. You and the boys had gone by then. That's when everything broke loose. Grady had to go and talk with a client. A client came in at four to see Hap. I took the man to my office. Grace and I were going out at five. Dick couldn't stay in the office with her because all he'd do is sneeze. So when Grace said she'd like to help and could answer the phone, we had little choice. Robert said he could show her how to switch calls and she could ring his office if she had a question."

"So Grace talked to Mr. Calabria?" Lily asked.

Vince nodded. "I figured that the moment he told me when he called. So, after Mr. Calabria got on his plane, I came back and stopped by to see Grace. At first she didn't remember. Then she remembered that she took the call, but before she could write down the message, another call came in. Then Hap's client and I came out of my office."

Lily listened to the excuses Vince made for Grace. "She's not a secretary," he said. "She's never worked except on her dad's apple orchard in early years, then as a model. She doesn't realize the necessity of writing down such things immediately. I shouldn't have allowed her to answer the phone."

"She doesn't answer the phone at her agency?" Lily asked, hoping she didn't sound sarcastic.

"She has a secretary." After a thoughtful moment, he added, "And she has only one assistant."

Neither said anything for a while. Vince seemed to be concentrating on finding a parking place at the restaurant. Lily wondered if he were thinking the same thing as she. Almost anyone would need instruction and practice for even the most simple telephone system. But how could a person—who ran her own business—forget or neglect the importance of writing down a message—particularly one that came all the way from Italy?

But, as Vince said, Grace was not a. . .secretary.

Suddenly, Lily felt self-conscious. A chill ran up her spine just as a cloud obscured that errant ray of sun.

Lily's mood changed the moment she stepped from the car. The view was breathtaking. Mountain peaks ascended above low-hanging clouds. A mist rose from the forested hillsides. They were seated by a window before another awe-inspiring view.

"When I see something like this," she said, as Vince sat opposite her, "reminding me of the greatness of God, I feel ashamed of allowing myself to become overwhelmed with petty things."

"You're referring to today?" he asked.

He smiled. "Your integrity was called into question. Attacked, really. You had every right to be upset. That's why I must apologize. Please forgive me."

"Apology accepted," Lily said.

"But there's something else I want you to know," he said. "When I discovered Grace had taken that call, I didn't yell at her like I did at you. I didn't jump down her throat as if she'd torn my world apart. I wasn't as angry with her as I was with you."

That's because you love her, Lily was thinking. *And you want to make sure I know it.* Oh, did Vince suspect. . . ?

"I've analyzed that," Vince said, and Lily braced herself for the rest.

"I think it's like reading about an accident in the newspaper. It doesn't have the same effect as if the accident happens to your own family or your friends. I would never say harsh words to my clients the way I have to my own parents, friends, and coworkers. Why is that?"

He began to answer the question himself. "I think it's because we care more deeply about the actions of those closest to us. Maybe this is a protective defense. But what I'm trying to say, Lily, is that you're not just an employee to me."

More than an employee to him? Could he mean that? If the storms had ended, then why was her heart thundering so?

"You're part of my family, Lily. Like Paul, Grady, Robert, Hap, Dick, and their families. You're one of us. You're their friend, too. You baby-sat with Billy and Barney. Paul and Pearl enjoyed your stay at their home while you looked for your own place. You're one of us,

Lily. And as bad as this may sound, that means you're subject to our emotional outbursts. Does that make sense?"

She nodded. It made perfect sense. She'd been promoted from employee to. . .family. She could think of nothing more to say than "thank you" before the waiter set their plates in front of them.

Vince reached across for her hands. "Shall we say grace?"

He said the blessing but didn't let go of her hands for a moment after he finished. "Don't quit, Lily. Give us—give me another chance."

Chapter 7

The following morning, Lily got the distinct impression that all the men had come a little earlier than usual. They were all in the lounge before the coffee finished dripping.

"Good to see you've dried out," Dick said, with a big smile.

"Well, if you see any Italians headed this way, just lock the door," Hap said then snapped his fingers. "That reminds me. Why did the frog say 'Meow'?"

Without giving anyone time to speak, Grady poured himself a cup of coffee, stared at it, then said, "Looks mighty weak to me." He stirred in cream and said, "Speaking of yesterday, I think we just might have a fox in the henhouse."

Lily felt the tension and noticed the glances that the men passed around to each other. What did Grady mean? Was he inferring that he still thought Lily might be incompetent? But Vince had said he asked Dick to tell the others that Grace had taken the call from Mr. Calabria. Did he mean that Grace had some ulterior motive for not mentioning the appointment?

What motive could she have?

A shadow passed over Robert's face, as if the remark greatly disturbed him. Vince sighed then said, "Okay, Hap, tell us why the frog said 'Meow.'"

Hap grinned. "He was learning a foreign language."

"Okay," Vince said, "now that we've had our morning laugh—"

"You didn't hear me laugh," Grady interrupted.

"I was trying to be kind," Vince said. "Anyway, I'd like to make a suggestion."

Lily felt the conversation was turning toward business, so she started to walk away. Vince called her back. "This involves you," he said. Then he began to tell the men that since Lily wanted to learn more about the advertising business, they might give her a few pointers from time to time, and he thought she might like to sit in on their viewing meeting that morning.

The others looked as surprised as she felt. "I don't want to cause anybody extra work."

"You won't," Grady said. He took his coffee and left the lounge.

She supposed that meant he wasn't going to be involved in it. She couldn't blame him. They didn't owe her any favors.

"Frankly, Lily," Dick said, "you've saved us a lot of time with your efficiency and understanding of advertising."

"And, as you all know, the viewing this morning is Paul's advertising for the living Christmas tree program to be held at the church in mid-December. I asked Paul and he said he'd be delighted for Lily to join us."

Thank You, God, Lily prayed silently, *for turning such a devastating experience into such a surprisingly wonderful one.*

After Dr. Paul arrived, they started toward the conference room. When the phone rang, Lily turned back, but Vince said to let the answering machine get it. She felt totally out of place, although Dr. Paul made a special effort to talk with her. Before the meeting began, he said he'd be glad to have a woman's perspective on the advertising.

However, she felt self-conscious until she walked in and witnessed Nico growing limp as he stepped away from the trash can and eased into a lump on the carpeted floor like a rag doll. Robert and Vince got on each side of him and dragged him over to a big chair in the corner, where he looked as limp as a wet noodle but sounded like a pig snorting.

With Nico sprawled and snoring, Lily didn't feel so much out of place. In fact, she rather liked the way they included her in the discussion, and she was able to ask a few questions and offer a few changes. She suggested the word "man" be changed to "mankind" or "man and woman." She noticed the earrings on the women in the living Christmas tree brochure and questioned it. Should the brochure chance anyone focusing on women's jewelry instead of the musical program? They agreed to think about that.

Dick sneezed while Nico snored. Lily looked around the table and almost burst into laughter at the irony of it all. She felt kind of like Snow White must have felt when surrounded by the protective seven dwarfs. Nico was a perfect Sleepy. Dr. Paul could be Doc—and she hoped her thoughts weren't sacrilegious. Grady certainly filled the bill of Grumpy, although she'd learned he barked but never bit. Dick was Sneezy, around Grace's perfume. Hap, she'd learned, had been given his nickname long ago because he always seemed so Happy. And Robert, if she stretched it, could be called Bashful, although she'd come to realize he wasn't really timid, just reserved at times.

Vince Harmen had as much appeal as any Prince Charming, she felt sure. The analogy ended there. Although these men made her feel rather like a princess, she wasn't one. And she knew neither a Dopey nor a Wicked Witch.

Lily tried not to revise that opinion when she returned to her desk and answered a call for Vince from Grace Grant.

During lunch hour, Lily and Robert sat out on the patio of H&H Sandwich Shop beneath the much-needed shade of the umbrella on such a hot August afternoon.

"You don't think Grace deliberately neglected to mention Mr. Calabria's call, do you, Robert?"

After a long moment, he admitted, "It's possible."

"But why? I mean, is she trying to hurt the agency?"

"Oh no. She wouldn't do that while she has her eyes set on Vince Harmen. No. Not that."

"Then. . .what? Who?"

His lengthy gaze indicated she should guess again. Lily didn't want to think what had crept into her mind many times. She wasn't fond of Grace. Lily had felt a dread each time the woman came in or called. But she'd stacked that up to her own feelings of how fortunate Grace was to have gained the special attention of Vince Harmen.

But. . .why wouldn't Grace like Lily? Would she dislike her enough to want to deliberately threaten her credibility? She asked Robert that question.

"It's not really about you, Lily," he said with a furrowed brow. "Grace feels threatened by you. She might very well try to get you fired."

That seemed unbelievable. "Why would she feel threat-ened by. . .me?"

The smile that crossed his lips was not a happy one. "Because of her own insecurities. You're young, beauti-ful, and just beginning your career. Her career as a model has ended. I understand Grace," he said. "I knew her in grade school."

Their sandwiches lay untouched for the next twenty minutes while Robert lost his reserve and shared with Lily a part of his heart.

Robert and Grace had grown up together. They'd gone to the same church. At age ten, at a church camp, they'd both given their hearts to the Lord and vowed eter-nal allegiance to Jesus and to each other.

At age twelve, she lost her mother.

At age thirteen, she felt she'd lost her dad when he remarried.

She became a model at age fourteen—by fifteen she had a contract with a New York agent and by age seven-teen was a model on the runway and her picture appeared in major fashion magazines. For a couple of years she cor-responded with several people in the area and came home at Christmastime. After she had gigs in Europe, she no longer came home for Christmas. No one he knew heard from her. After several years, tabloids ran pictures of her and the fashion designer for whom she modeled. Later, the headlines were of a sensational nature about the man dumping her for a younger model.

"We lost touch," Robert said. "When she returned, she had changed. She no longer shared anything about her life with the few of us she knew who are still around here. But I remember the sweet young girl that. . ." His voice trailed off.

Lily's heart ached for him. Apparently, he'd never lost those deep feelings he had for Grace years ago. That would account for the impression he gave of being timid around her. But he had so much to offer a woman. How it must hurt Robert to see Grace with Vince almost daily. But he had to face facts, just as she did.

"Robert," Lily said quietly, "she's not a little girl anymore."

"I know, Lily. And I'm a grown man. I've done things I'm not proud of. Haven't always lived as closely to the Lord as I should. But deep inside, that little innocent, trusting boy lives there. I can't get away from the belief and faith in Jesus Christ that I accepted way back then."

His eyes brightened, and hope tinged his voice. "I believe that little girl I knew, named Grace Grant, is still inside her. She can't hide her forever. This grown-up Grace is a façade. It isn't real life. She's going to realize that someday. And I intend to be around at that time, in case she needs me."

Chapter 8

Lily could hardly believe all that had happened to her during the past months. She truly had become an accepted member of the agency's extended family. Each day, a few words from her fellow workers, a brief explanation of a project, or a longer meeting with one of them became building blocks on her foundation of advertising and design courses she'd had in college.

She really was learning the business from the ground up. In the evenings she made sketches and outlines of how her handbag project might be marketed. She mentioned her progress to Vince one day in mid-October. He asked her to bring the material into his office.

After looking it over, he said, "If you'd like to meet after we close, I can suggest how you might be ready to take this a step farther."

"Oh, yes," she readily agreed. Later she told her hand, her whole being in fact, to stop shaking with joy. He probably had a few hours to kill. Grace had taken several of her students to a modeling show in Atlanta.

After five o'clock and the others had gone, she took her project into Vince's office. "We could do this another time if you had other plans," he said.

"Laundry can wait," she said.

"Laundry? What about Robert?"

"What. . .do you mean?"

"I know you two are seeing each other. I mean, you take your lunch breaks together, and I see you sitting with him in church, and you're always together at the singles' meetings."

"Robert is a wonderful man," she said, "but we're good friends, that's all. That's all we can ever be."

"I wanted to make sure," he said, then his glance fell to the folder in front of him. He looked over the colored pictures and sketches, then they went to work on design, layout, and artwork. "You've done some good work here," he said. "We need to get some of these on a web page or video." His warm blue gaze, beautiful smile, lock of hair falling over his forehead, and wonderful praise sent shivers of joy down her spine and into her heart.

Like many times before, she had the feeling he thought her special, more than just a member of his extended family. But then, he revealed that his mind was on Grace. "I think you might be the perfect one to help Grace. She's getting closer to being ready to launch her all-out campaign, but we disagree on much of it. She has asked for a woman's opinion before. Would you mind taking a look?"

For the next half hour, they looked at Grace's campaign. "Do you agree with me or her on the graphic design?"

Lily studied it for a long moment, reluctant to respond. But he had asked. "Well, you both have some good ideas, but I'd do it differently."

Lily stepped back when he suddenly stood. Had that offended him? But a light came into his eyes, and he smiled.

"Let's go eat and discuss it."

With that, he put the materials together, and she got her own. Almost before she knew it they were striding down the sidewalk, surrounded by the most glorious colors she'd ever seen. The fall colors had reached their peak. Varying shades of gold, red, orange, yellow, brown, and green mountainsides turned the town into the most picturesque setting she'd ever seen. She loved it. She loved. . . everything.

A few moments later, behind the H&H, she hardly noticed the vivid colors of her surroundings. Suddenly her world seemed to be encompassed in the blue of Vince Harmen's eyes. When they held hands to pray, she didn't know what he said. She only knew that the warmth of his hands had lingered, long after he said, "Amen."

She had done this many times with Robert. But never before, even while talking about Grace's campaign, had she felt like. . .this.

Grace felt cold. She'd had a virus and fever for days, and now she couldn't get warm enough. The world seemed bleak. The leaves had fallen. The autumn rains had come and gone. Now November wind whistled around her big house.

This was one of those rare occasions when she asked herself what she had that really counted—except that she had lived to be thirty-four years old today. In six years she'd be forty. Forty! How could she stand it? She had dark circles under her eyes and crow's feet at the corners of them. She was getting old. Maybe she should have a face lift.

Her assistant had taken over her classes. Classes for little girls, some of them half her age, others not even one-third her age. Sometimes she wanted to throw up her hands and let it all go. But what would she do? She knew nothing but modeling.

Several days later, she chalked up her melancholy to the medication she'd been on. Having survived her middle-aged birthday, she regained some of her old confidence after carefully grooming herself to look like a human being again. She called Vince to tell him she'd recovered. He came to Mirror Image, and they looked over the campaign strategy.

She loved the changes and told him so. "This is really terrific, Vince," she complimented. "Maybe I should get ill more often. You could get more work done."

"No, it's not that," he said. "It's just that these new ideas are really clicking. On some projects, we at the agency have a viewing and everyone tosses in their opinions. So, I'm inviting the team and their families to the house for Thanksgiving dinner. We can review the campaign and view the video. Are you free that day?"

Of course she'd be there. Grace Grant, who once had the world at her feet, now had no man in her life but Vince Harmen. She mustn't lose him, too.

Thanksgiving with Vince and the "extended family" sounded wonderful to Lily. But Grace was invited, too. She felt uncomfortable around her. "I should spend the holiday with my family," Lily told Vince. "I've never missed being with them on Thanksgiving."

"Invite them here if you must," he said, "but you can't miss this. I have a surprise, just for you."

She knew her parents wouldn't mind if she delayed her visit until Friday and then spent the weekend with them. They were proud of her working with the agency, and everything was going so well.

Lily couldn't imagine life getting any better during the days Grace had been sick and didn't come around. Lily and Vince worked on the Mirror Image campaign and her own handbag project. On the nights they worked late, he either had supper brought in or they went to H&H or another local food place.

They'd begun to talk personally, about their likes and dislikes, their upbringing, and their goals. She cared so much for him, she had to constantly remind herself that his interest in her was the same way she felt about Robert—as a friend. She mustn't allow her heart to rule her head. And if a fine Christian man like Vince believed God chose Grace for him, then she should not yearn for anything different.

She should not.

Each time that thought came, it was accompanied by a verse of scripture where Paul wrote something like, "I want to do what is right, but I inevitably do what is wrong." Not that she was "doing" anything wrong. But the Bible taught that whatever is in a person's heart is what they're really like.

In her heart, she cared for Vince Harmen. . .too much.

Vince recognized this as a delicate situation. He hadn't meant to mislead Grace Grant. He'd been attracted by her beauty the first time he saw her. She was a good conversationalist, and he enjoyed her company. They liked many of the same things. But the more he learned of her, the more he became concerned about her soul. When he tried to steer the conversation to spiritual matters, she evaded the subject.

His concern increased after the matter with Mr. Calabria. Lily never mentioned Grace's part in it to him, but soon afterward, as they worked together on Grace's campaign and they were discussing Dr. Paul's Sunday sermon, Lily behaved as if a lightbulb had been turned on inside her.

This afternoon, Vince would tell the group about that "lightbulb" and hope in so doing he didn't lose his client. A disgruntled customer could cause great damage to a business.

He prayed about the approach he'd take to the viewing and hoped it would not seem manipulated. Of one thing he was certain, the viewing and the eating would have to be over before the ball game started. That's about all Grady and Dick had talked about for weeks.

Sudie, his head housekeeper and cook, had her helpers readying a long table on the covered deck for the afternoon dinner. The others, including wives and Ben, who was home from college for the holiday, went down to the sitting room where materials could be laid out on a table. The web site and video could be viewed on a large screen. Hap's children were spending the day with grandparents, so the viewing should be without interruptions.

The hard copies were readily approved, with only a few changes suggested. When they came to the video, Vince reminded them it still needed work. He stopped the video at intervals to explain where changes might be.

Grace was the client who had to be pleased. "Grace," he said, "we want to feature you more and the younger models less. This is where the campaign theme comes in. Young hopefuls would like the video the way it is. They would compare themselves with the models and want to be like them. However, the parents will make the decisions about whether they should send these young people to you. They need to see the mature person in charge, one who can promote their child while protecting them. Most of all, the parents must feel they can trust the one in charge of Mirror Image."

Vince knew his enthusiasm showed. The agency often struggled to find the perfect phrase, the idea to inspire the public. When it happened, it was like a blind man beginning to see. That enlightenment is what made the struggle worthwhile.

Applause and favorable comments followed his statements. The women added their opinions. Grace would be the deciding factor, however. "What do you think, Grace?" he asked.

"I had thought primarily about the product—models. It hadn't occurred that we should focus on reaching the parents to such an extent." Her thoughtful expression quickly changed to enthusiasm. She nodded. "You told me when I first came to you that we needed a theme or a motto that would catch the attention of the audience. You said it would surface in time. It appears the time has come. I agree—the perfect word is 'trust.' "

Yes! He had the client's enthusiastic endorsement.

Now, for the next step. Vince cautioned himself, *Tread carefully.* Just then, he heard a bell tinkle and looked over his shoulder to see Sudie at the top of the stairs. He nodded, acknowledging her summons to dinner, then turned to the group again.

"We can continue the discussion during dinner if you have other comments or suggestions. But before we go up, I want to give credit where credit is due. Since Grace wanted female input, we obtained that. The member of our agency who gave us this theme is. . ." He spread his hand toward her. "Miss Lily White."

Grace's face registered surprise. Ben had no reaction as if it mattered not to him, but everyone else appeared delighted.

Later, in private, Vince would tell Lily that since his client and his coworkers had endorsed her ideas, she would be working, not as a volunteer, but as a paid apprentice-designer when helping with Grace's campaign video.

While the group applauded Vince's announcement and Lily's contribution, Vince thrilled at the look in Lily's eyes as their gaze held and her eyes became watery. For a long moment he couldn't tear his eyes away, even when she lowered her gaze and modestly accepted congratulations from everyone. *Almost everyone*, he realized as the group expressed their pleasure and congratulations. Robert shot glances at Grace, while Grace stared at Vince as if she couldn't believe it.

Why were those two concerned? Grace's expression became stony as her green eyes narrowed. Was she concerned about an inexperienced apprentice working with her campaign?

Or was it something else? Were Robert's feelings for Lily deeper than he'd let on? Grace and Robert were astute persons. Had they both detected what lay in his heart when he had gazed at Lily?

Grace didn't like the fact that Robert lagged behind while others ascended the stairs for dinner. He began to tell her how effective her campaign would be.

Effective?

She'd lost to a mere secretary. Vince and Lily had worked nights together. Lily was promoted. A younger girl had won—again! Yes, Lily White had great ideas—on how to steal another woman's man. *She waited until I became sick—and moved in!* Grace, who once had international men falling at her feet, now couldn't even hold on to a small-town mountain man.

Effective, ha! She felt as effective as the day Salitori replaced her with Rajni.

She looked straight ahead and saw Hap poke Ben in the arm. "Hey, you know what is green green green green green?"

Ben guessed. "Grass?"

"Nope. A frog rolling down a hill."

Grace didn't find that funny at all. She could identify. Her runway of life had tilted, and she was spiraling downhill—fast.

At the top of the stairs, she watched Marjorie lead Lily toward the front of the house, instead of the back deck, saying, "You can wash your hands in the bathroom at the top of the steps. Just turn left when you reach the bedroom. I'll use the one near the kitchen."

Grace deliberately lagged behind as several went out to the table on the deck, in case Lily had also replaced her at Vince's right—as his honored guest. "Has Lily worked on other accounts, Robert?" she asked as an excuse to linger.

Robert's quick glance held surprise—no doubt that she spoke to him. She saw the slight change of color come onto his face and he swallowed. "N—no, Grace. Let's step over here." They moved a few feet away. He assured her, in no uncertain terms, with only a couple of stutters, that

Lily only made a few suggestions from a woman's point of view, but Grace could reject any of it. "Your opinion is what counts in the f–final analysis, Grace."

Grace appreciated that vote of confidence. And she disregarded the knowledge that handsome, successful, articulate Robert stuttered only when near her. She didn't want to acknowledge the reason. She even looked beyond him instead of into his eyes that revealed a kind of warmth he'd exhibited years ago.

Not wanting to be reminded of when she'd been that young, innocent girl who had long ago vanished, she watched as others took their seats. Lily and Marjorie returned and sat beside each other. Robert led Grace to the vacant seat on Vince's right.

Where I should be, she reminded herself. *I am the client here—if nothing else.*

During dinner, the conversation turned to food, which Grace hardly tasted, and to prior Thanksgivings, which reminded her of having been replaced in her dad's affection by a stepmother. Now, at least, Vince had the courtesy to include her in conversation.

When Sudie served dessert, Ben stood and said Sudie promised him a batch of brownies to take with him. He planned to watch the ball game with his buddies. They all expressed their good-byes, and Ben left the table.

Grace refused dessert. The owner of Mirror Image had to keep her figure.

But Lily got two desserts. One was pecan pie; the other was Vince's declaration when he brought up the subject of her handbag project. He casually mentioned that, unknown to Lily, he'd sent a few of her handbag designs to Mr. Calabria, who was impressed and even mentioned the possibility of using her idea but replacing cloth flowers and plastic buttons with real jewels.

The look that passed between Vince and Lily was anything but casual.

Anyone could see it. Grace felt like all eyes were on her—not in admiration, but pity. Her dad, then Salitori, and now Vince had all hurt and abandoned her. "Excuse me," she said as she rose from the table, feeling as awkward as she must have been at age thirteen before she'd learned how to walk properly.

The star of the hour was not Grace, who had brought her business to the agency, but the young twit who came up with one little word—trust!

Grace walked through the living room, up the few steps to the front bedroom, retrieved her purse from the bed, and went into the bathroom. Surprise washed over her when she opened the purse for her lipstick. Her billfold was open with part of a bill sticking out. How did that happen?

She counted her bills. She was missing a fifty-dollar bill!

"I'm so sorry," Grace said when she returned to the deck and stood behind her chair. Conversation died away. Lily wondered if Grace hadn't gotten completely well from the flu. She looked peaked.

"What is it, Grace?" Vince asked and others stared. "Are you ill?"

"No, not physically anyway. I hate to say this, but. . . I'm missing fifty dollars."

All sorts of questions sounded. Was she sure? Where was the last place she'd been before coming to Vince's?

Did she search her purse?

Grace took out her billfold and extracted a fifty. "I had two of these. If I'd stopped and bought anything, there would be change in my purse. There is none. And this is not the first time I've missed money while here." She looked at Vince. "You don't suppose anyone comes in when you have guests, do you, Vince?"

"No," he blurted. "The kitchen staff would notice. But what do you mean, this is not the first time?"

"I missed money on the day of the cookout." She looked around. "Am I the only one?"

"I can't say for sure," Grady's wife said, "but I asked Grady the next day if he took some money out of my purse. I thought I had more."

"I can't be sure either," Lily added, "but after the cook-out I had twenty less than I'd thought."

"Oh, Vince," Grace said, "you don't suppose your household staff—"

"No, I don't," he said immediately, "but I would appreciate you ladies checking your handbags, while I talk to the staff."

Soon, Vince and the women with their handbags returned to the deck. Vince told them that he asked if any of the kitchen help had left the kitchen. Sudie knew for certain they had not. There was no need. They ate in the kitchen and had a bathroom right off the kitchen.

Hap's wife said she didn't bring a handbag. Everything she had of importance was in a diaper bag.

Grady's wife shook her head. "I can't be sure."

Lily held a wad of bills in her hand. She'd gotten cash from the ATM to have while in Tennessee. "I can't say. I went to a couple of stores, but—"

"Lily, you don't need to go into all that," Marjorie said. "This is all some kind of mistake. I keep track of my money and not a cent is gone. It wasn't the day of the cookout and it's not today."

"Oh," Grace said. "I should have kept my mouth shut. I certainly didn't mean to imply that any of you—I mean, my goodness, I don't think any of you have even been to the bedroom since we all came in today."

Lily's discomfort began when Marjorie's face turned toward her. Marjorie, and probably others, knew she had gone through the bedroom to the bathroom. Several had used the downstairs bathroom to wash their hands before dinner. If she said nothing, they would think she had something to hide.

"I was up there before dinner," Lily said and saw the smug gleam in Grace's green eyes before she narrowed them.

"But I certainly didn't take anybody's money."

"Oh, honey," Grace purred, "I didn't mean to imply that anyone here would do such a thing. Marjorie's probably right. I'm mistaken. I must be." Grace sat and put her hand on Vince's, now doubled into a tight fist. "I'm so sorry. Let's forget this."

"Oh boy," Grady ground out. "Here we go again."

"Hush, Grady," his wife said.

Lily looked around the table. Marjorie lowered her eyes to her dessert dish. Dick looked off into space, shaking his head. Hap and his wife stared, and Lily wished he might crack a joke and make everyone laugh. He didn't.

Robert propped an elbow on the table, leaned his head into his fingers, and had his eyes closed as if praying. Vince's face wore such a look of distress Lily thought she couldn't stand it. Things didn't look good for her.

Lily felt like she'd swallowed a bite of poison apple, and it stuck in her throat.

Chapter 9

Vince couldn't believe Lily had anything to do with stolen money. Grace had pulled that telephone trick before. Was she now behaving like a woman scorned since his attentions had obviously switched from her to Lily? Was it his fault? Had he led Grace on? His intentions had always been honorable. Something might have come of that if the Lord hadn't brought Lily into his life.

What should he do? Grace said to forget it. But how could he? If a theft happened in his home, he should get to the bottom of it. But how? Sudie had been with him for years. She trusted her helpers, so he did, too. But one could easily have gone out the side door, come around front, and gone into the bedroom. He doubted it, because it would have been too risky.

His friends tried to regain the earlier camaraderie. Grace had quickly begun to talk about her latest showing in Atlanta, and some of the women asked questions and commented. Except Lily, who looked as if her world had ended. Soon, everyone expressed their pleasure at having been his guest for dinner. He knew some of the men normally would have stayed, and perhaps the women, to watch the game.

He understood when Hap and his wife left to be with their family. Grady decided to watch the game at home. Earlier, Vince had thought it would be nice if he and Dick watched the game. Marjorie and Lily had gotten along so well, he'd hoped they'd want to watch with them or find something to do together.

Dick gave Vince a long stare and opened his mouth as if he wanted to say something, but no words came. He said they needed to leave.

Marjorie protested and glanced toward Lily, who looked as if she might burst into tears any moment. "We need to go," Dick said again, so Marjorie said good-bye to the others and left with him.

Lily said, "Thank you for the dinner."

"Be careful driving to Tennessee. I'll see you Monday morning," Vince said.

She didn't respond to that but walked out behind Dick and Marjorie, with Robert following.

Grace remained behind to again express her regrets. "Vince, you don't think Lily had anything to do with it, do you?"

"No, I don't," he replied immediately. "I don't think anyone else did either—not even the kitchen staff." He added stiffly, "But the fact remains."

"I didn't accuse anyone, you know," she said once again.

"I know," he said. But he was quite aware of implications made without accusations. Grace graciously said all the right things about the day and soon left. He felt lonely. This was going to be a long weekend.

But it didn't have to be. Why not drop Grace's

materials off at the office, then go and talk to Lily? He hadn't trusted her about the phone mix-up with Calabria, but he should have. He should trust her in this. It was she and her ideas on "trust" that had so impressed him. He knew that was part of her character—trusting God and trusting others.

He should tell her. Yes, that's what he'd do. He'd go to her cottage and make it plain how he felt about her. And if she invited him to go to Tennessee for the weekend and meet her parents, he'd go.

Lord, he prayed on the way down the mountain, *thank You that I've come to my senses. The right thing to do is tell Lily, and let everyone else know, how I feel about her. I believe You brought the two of us together. Now, even if it means I lose Grace Grant as a client and take a loss on all the work I've done, I'd rather have Lily and let her know I trust her. Thank You, Lord, for this insight.*

Thirty minutes later, after dropping off the Mirror Image material at the agency, he drove to the cottage. He didn't see Lily's car. When he knocked on the door, no one opened it. When he returned to his car and called her from his cell phone, no one answered. She must have decided to go to Tennessee today. She might never come back. And he couldn't blame her. He should have said in front of everyone that he knew she didn't take the money.

Lord, he asked, *are You on holiday today?* He immediately felt contrite. That was no way to speak to his heavenly Father. *Lord,* he began again, *forgive me for thinking I have all the answers. And for expecting You to work things out according to my desires. I'm turning it over to You. Your will be done.*

And lonely? A man of his means and blessings had no

business being lonely. There were too many places that needed helping hands for him to ever sit around moping because things didn't go his way. If nothing else, he could go home and help with the cleanup so his staff could get home earlier to their families.

Sudie ran out and waved him down as soon as he drove up in front of the house, before he could even park. "Vince. Dick called. Ben's in the hospital."

Lily felt totally helpless. Outside Vince's house, Marjorie put her arms around her shoulders and said, "None of us thinks you took that money, Lily."

"I certainly don't," Dick said with feeling.

Robert asked if she'd like to go somewhere with him and talk or take in a movie or something. She didn't feel like that. "I may go to Tennessee today," she told him.

"But you'll be back?"

She took a deep breath. "Robert, how can I work where my integrity has to be questioned? Grace didn't make it up about money being taken. Grady's wife and I had missing money. But I'm the only one anybody saw go into that bedroom."

"Somebody else had to," Robert stated.

"I know. But who else really knows that? I have to be suspected."

He sighed. "Just go home and enjoy your family, Lily. Come back to us. Give it to the Lord and let Him work it out."

She nodded. But all the way down the mountain, she wasn't able to give it to the Lord. She tried, she gave it, then took it back. For a long time, she drove around and finally remembered the church would be open for anyone who wanted to come and give thanks to God on this day.

She went inside, and instead of going to the sanctuary or even attempting to speak to Dr. Paul, she went into the parlor, closed the door, went over to the couch, and fell on her knees.

God, I'm heartsick. I'm helpless. Your Bible says that all things work for good to them that love the Lord. You know I love You. But I can't see what good can come from this. Her tears started then. *But, okay. I'm giving it to You. But I don't see how I can ever go back to the agency and face those people whom I love and have them be suspicious of me. How can I do it?*

You can do all things through Christ who strengthens you.

But I've been falsely accused.

I know how that feels.

Yes, Lord, I know You understand. You're strong, but I'm weak. What should I do?

Love your enemies. Pray for those who persecute you.

What? Pray for Grace?

Yes.

Lord, if she deliberately tried to place blame on me, forgive her. Forgive me for disliking her. Forgive me for being jealous of her relationship with Vince. You know I want him for myself. But, God, ultimately, deep inside, I want what is best for me. And only You know what that is. She did have missing money. I do look like a suspect. I think I really can give this to You now.

Peace came like a river and Lily felt so full, it spilled over and down her cheeks. *Now what?*

Do good to those who persecute you and do all manner of evil against you.

Do good? What could she do for Grace?

Grace kept telling herself that she had not accused any-one. She simply stated a truth that she had fifty dollars missing. They could draw their own conclusions. And if Lily White decided to seek her fate in Tennessee, then so be it. Like she'd heard her dad say more than once, "If you can't stand the heat, get out of the kitchen." Lily White would discover she was no match for Grace Grant.

For some strange reason, that didn't make her feel too well. Maybe she hadn't completely recovered from that bout of flu. But soon the campaign would be over. She and Vince could relate on a personal rather than "client" basis.

When the phone rang, she thought perhaps Vince might be calling. But Robert said, "I just heard from Vince. Ben is in the hospital."

Chapter 10

"From what we can gather from his friends," Robert told Grace, "they'd been doing drugs while watching the game. We don't have the whole story. Ben's in a coma."

"Oh, Robert. I want to go. Will you come and get me?"

"Be right there," he said.

How easily he said it. She'd deliberately ignored him for years. But he had been there. . .waiting. And she'd known that. It always made her feel guilty. But he never condemned. Maybe. . .it wasn't Robert who made her feel guilty. Maybe it was her own conscience.

As soon as Robert arrived, she jumped into his car. "Have you heard any more?"

"No, the doctors are working with him. We don't know if he's out because of a concussion or because of drugs."

"I'm so sorry," Grace said to Marjorie and Dick when they entered the hospital waiting room. She sat down beside Robert. All of those Vince referred to as his extended family were there to lend their support, except Lily. She'd succeeded in driving Lily away.

A doctor came and said Ben had to sleep it off. He wouldn't be talking before early morning.

"Let's pray about this," Vince said.

Grace wasn't sure what he prayed, but by the time he finished, she realized how far apart she and Vince really were. Then she realized how far she was from all of these good people. She thought back to the Thanksgiving dinner when she'd gone to the bedroom. When she'd started up the steps, the bedroom door had opened and a surprised-looking Ben hurried past her with a mumbled word of good-bye, picked up his plate of brownies, and rushed out the front door.

When she'd noticed her open billfold and thought back to the day of the cookout, she remembered that Ben had been the first one to leave that evening. She had deliberately tried to place suspicion on Lily.

The agony of her actions pained her heart. A boy could die because she'd been concerned only about what she wanted and not what others wanted. She hadn't even considered why a young man like Ben would steal when he had everything money could buy.

"You need to know," she said, unable to look at any of them. "I saw Ben leave the bedroom today right before I found my open billfold. And he was the first to leave the day of the cookout."

"We knew he struggled with drugs for a while," Dick said. "Drugs can make a person do things they've never done before—like steal. Thank you, Grace, for telling us this. On the day of the cookout, Ben and I argued because I wouldn't lend him more money. When you mentioned money being taken, I feared he'd been doing drugs again."

"That's why all the women had missing money, except me," Marjorie added.

"Yes," Dick said. "At least he hasn't gone so far as to

steal from his own mother. But we know he wants to stay clean. We'll see that he gets all the help he needs." He looked around at his friends. "We ask for your prayers."

Prayers? Grace hadn't prayed in years. She'd felt God had abandoned her. A thought she'd learned as a young child crossed her mind, *If you feel you're far from God, just remember it wasn't God who moved.* Yes, she was even farther from God than from these good people in this room. She rose from the chair and left the room.

Robert followed. She tried to shirk him away, but he pursued her to the parking lot and got into the car with her.

"I'm to blame, Robert. That boy could die because of me. Should I have taken Dick or Marjorie aside earlier and told them Ben was in that bedroom?"

"I can't answer that, Grace."

She shook her head. "But I do know I shouldn't have made it sound as if Lily took that money. And if things don't turn out right for Ben, how can I ever face anyone again?"

"Turn it over to God," he said, "and trust Him."

"Trust?" she groaned, then realized she was crying. She hadn't cried in years. She'd hardened her heart. Emotions hurt too much.

"I can't let anyone see me like this." She flipped down the mirror visor. Then she flipped it back up. "Oh, what does it matter. I'm getting older, Robert. I've been jealous of Lily and her fresh young beauty, but I realize I've been a shrew. A real witch. But I'm tired, Robert. Tired of the rat race, of trying to stay young. Maybe I should just try to be me. Oh, I must look a mess."

"No," he said gently. "I've never seen you more beautiful than you are right now, Grace."

She wiped at her wet cheeks with the back of her hand. "If you're willing to attempt to teach me how to be as nice as you, I'm willing to attempt to learn."

He handed her his handkerchief. "It's the Lord who changes us, Grace."

She nodded. "I know that. I just haven't let it be my priority since I first looked into the mirror and realized I had a beautiful face. I never stopped to think that I didn't make my face. I've been so foolish." She laughed suddenly. "Are you serious about helping me?"

"Very serious," he said.

Grace smiled back with her lips and her eyes.

"Let's pray."

Afterward, he asked, "Are you in love with Vince?"

"I've been too much in love with myself. The closest I came to love was with Salitori. But that involved my ego and career more than a matter of the heart. So have my feelings for Vince, except I've come to love the kind of person he is and know he isn't for me."

She caught her breath at the loving look in Robert's eyes. Hadn't it always been there? She must finish her sentence. "Robert, you haven't stuttered once since we've been talking."

He smiled. "That's because I'm relating to the real you, Grace. I knew you when you were a wonderful Christian girl. I believe that girl is still in there."

"Oh, Robert, how I wish we could turn back time and start over."

"In a way, we can, Grace. When we take Jesus as our Lord, we die to our old selves. He grants us the grace to become like newborns. He wants us to grow up in Him."

Grace nodded. "I knew that a long time ago. The

knowledge of it, the urging of it, has lain dormant for many years. But I'm ready, Robert. Ready to die to self and live for the Lord again."

"His Word is the best teacher," Robert said, "but if you could use an assistant. . ."

"Are you serious about improving the inner me?"

"That's God's department," Robert said. "I'm just serious. . .about you."

Vince knew the Lord answered prayer, but he also knew the answer was sometimes "No" or "Wait." He hadn't expected such a turn of events. Grace and Robert were both different people. During the night while Ben slept, they returned to the hospital and they all talked.

Grace had become humble, repentant, and asked them all to forgive her. Vince rejoiced inwardly, seeing the new Grace, more appealing now that her inner beauty shone forth. Robert behaved like a man who had received one of the Lord's choicest blessings.

Vince had one other matter to handle. Hap, Grady, and his wife had left after the doctor came in the early morning, saying that Ben would be fine. He had no broken bones, just some bruises and scratches.

Vince tried calling Lily again, to no avail.

Dick reminded him that her parents' number was in the files in the office.

"I'll go," he said.

"We'll go, too," Grace said. "I need to apologize to her."

As if he hadn't a thought other than staying by Grace's side, Robert took hold of her hand as they left the hospital.

Lily thought and prayed all evening and refused to answer

her telephone. She wanted to hear God's voice but didn't like what she thought He must be saying. Around midnight she fell into an exhausted sleep and awoke in the early morning.

The answer seemed clear concerning what "good" she could do for Grace. She could leave her to Vince. Although her heart ached at the thought, her feelings about Grace had changed from resentment to pity. Maybe God wanted Grace and Vince together so he could influence her spiritually.

But Lily knew she couldn't work under such conditions. She loved Vince. And she could not stay in a place where her honesty and integrity continued to be questioned.

She peeked through the window blinds as morning light began to touch the sky. Then a light snow began to fall. It lay on the trees, covering everything with its blanket of white. A beautiful new day had dawned. God could turn the bleakest day into the most beautiful. How ingenious of Him to have thought of snowflakes.

Peace filled her heart as she drove through the soft snow to the agency. The offices would be closed today, so she had plenty of time to clean out her desk and write a short note of farewell.

When she went inside, she and Nico surprised each other. He explained that he was going to Alabama and wouldn't be back until next Wednesday. So he wanted to make sure the offices were clean before he left later in the morning.

"But what are you doing here?" he asked.

Before she could say anything else, the front door opened and in came Vince, Robert, and Grace, all with their hair sprinkled with snow.

No one asked Lily why she was there. No one reprimanded her. Vince took her by the arm and said, "Let's go into the lounge."

The three of them began telling about the events of the night as they walked down the hallway. She could hardly believe the turn of events. Perhaps she was dreaming. Ben was going to be all right, and Lily had been exonerated. No one thought her a thief. Grace asked forgiveness for her actions and attitudes.

Grace looked different—and she sounded genuinely nice. She and Robert loved each other?

After Grace and Robert left, Vince came up to Lily, who stood staring out the window. She barely registered that Nico came in, mumbling something about the trash can. She had eyes only for Vince as he made clear to her that he hadn't for one moment believed she was a thief. He'd tried to find her last night after his guests left. He'd wanted to tell her that he loved her.

A lock of his hair, still damp from the snow, fell over his forehead—the way she liked it. Lost in his blue gaze, she whispered, "Oh, Vince, I love you, too. But I'm so afraid I must be dreaming."

"Then, let's see if I can awaken you," he said, "with this."

His head bent toward hers, and she lifted her face to his. As she was about to yield to his sweet, gentle kiss, a sudden strangled noise made Lily jump back, and Vince looked over his shoulder.

They gazed at Nico, sitting on the floor, leaned back into the corner, fast asleep, and snoring.

"Let's go out for coffee," Vince said, "and talk."

Outside the snow fell fast and furious, making the

area a wonderland of white. Vince laughed. "Instead of Lily White, you look more like Snow White."

"And you, sir," she said playfully, "are my Prince Charming."

With his arm around her waist, he pulled her close enough to plant a warm kiss on her cold lips. Then Lily lifted her face to the snowflakes. No, she wasn't dreaming. Her Prince Charming had awakened her with a kiss.

YVONNE LEHMAN

As an award-winning novelist from Black Mountain in the heart of North Carolina's Smoky Mountains, Yvonne has written several novels for Barbour Publishing's **Heartsong Presents** line. Her titles include *Southern Gentleman, Mountain Man,* which won a National Reader's Choice Award sponsored by a chapter of Romance Writers of America, *Catch of a Lifetime,* and *Secret Ballot.* Yvonne has published more than two dozen novels, including books in the Bethany House "White Dove" series for young adults. In addition to being an inspirational romance writer, she is also the founder of the Blue Ridge Christian Writers' Conference. She and her husband are the parents of four grown children and grandparents to several dear children.

Better to See You

Gail Gaymer Martin

[A] hireling, and not the shepherd,
. . .seeth the wolf coming,
and leaveth the sheep, and fleeth:
and the wolf catcheth them, and scattereth the sheep. . . .
I am the good shepherd,
and know my sheep, and am known of mine.

JOHN 10:12, 14 KJV

Chapter 1

Hurrying along the puddled sidewalk, Lucy Blake shuddered from the dampness, clutching the hood of her bright red raincoat with one hand and her grandmother's shopping basket with the other. Disappointed by three days of rain, she looked above the slate roofs of Oberammergau, longing to see the Bavarian Alps rising in jagged peaks above her head. Since she'd arrived four days earlier, she'd seen only low clouds and now the persistent downpour.

Though the June weather frustrated her, the lovely mountain town did not. Opposing the drab sky, brightly painted murals covered the front of the town's buildings. Lucy had never seen anything like it before, except in photographs.

Since she'd arrived, she'd not wandered far from her grandmother's home, concerned about the elderly woman's recent illness. Today, seeing the splendor, she longed to have time to wander the lovely gift emporiums and woodcarving shops to purchase items to take back home to Michigan.

The grocery basket weighed on Lucy's arm. She stepped beneath a shop's green awning, shifted her burden, and dropped her hood. At home when she went to the grocery store, she'd stock up for a week or two, but here, small refrigerators and tradition sent the townspeople to the bakery and meat shop almost daily.

While she paused beneath the canvas, the store window display of handmade crafts caught her interest: animals, manger scenes, nutcrackers, but, in particular, she eyed a hand-carved angel. Lucy leaned closer to the window, admiring the intricate design, the pastel shades of flesh and pink that tinted the face and the muted blue of the flowing gown. It would be a perfect gift for her mother's birthday.

Though her mind told her to wait for a more convenient day, Lucy's enthusiasm propelled her forward. She stepped through the archway and pulled open the shop door.

Inside, she faltered, marveling at row after row of lovely handcrafted items. Art pieces, wall carvings, and delicate Christmas ornaments filled the shelves. The pungent aroma of fresh wood rose in the warmth of the shop.

Wandering the aisles, Lucy searched for the angel she had seen in the window. She paused, studying the unusual gifts and novelty wooden toys. A lone salesclerk talked to another customer, and rather than bother her, Lucy headed through a wide archway into another showroom.

Ahead of her, she saw a young man bent over a piece of wood. Curious, she headed toward him. She'd never seen a woodcarver, and the experience excited her. But before she drew near, she faltered, a shiver of familiarity rising up her arms and down her spine.

Ron. The similarity between this man and her college steady took her breath away. *Ron Woodson.* How long had it been? Six, maybe seven years. Standing a few feet away,

Lucy couldn't take her eyes from him as a tender sadness washed over her, remembering their parting.

The bent head raised, and dazzling blue eyes aimed in her direction. The similarity was uncanny. The only change was a look of maturity and a more manly physique. Lucy pulled away her gaze and stared in confusion at a row of carved birds.

"Red?"

Her heart tumbled to her toes then bounced into her throat like a rubber ball. *Red.* Ron always teased her about her straight, unruly red hair. She looked at him in disbelief.

He rose and stepped toward her. "Is it you?"

His face registered the same astonished expression that she felt tugging at her features. "Ron?" With hesitation, she took a mini-step forward.

"Lucy!" He rushed forward, his arms opened in greeting. "What are you doing here?"

As if time and hurt had never happened, Lucy let the basket drop to the floor and ran into his embrace, throwing her arms around his neck, her voice lost in his broad, firm chest.

Lucy felt at home nestled against him, inhaling the faint musky odor of his aftershave mingled with the scent of wood shavings. He seemed taller now, and she pulled her head away from him to speak. "I can't believe this."

"You'll never know how often I've thought of you, Lucy," Ron said, his color heightened by his excitement. "You look exactly the same." He raised his hand and tousled her disheveled hair. "Red hair with a few waves, just like I remember." His fingers slid down her tresses, and he brushed her cheek with his index finger. "You look so good."

"You, too, Ron, but. . ." She hesitated, not wanting to admit the feelings roused in her. "It's only seeing someone familiar. You know, someone from home." It was more than that, but she couldn't say it—not to Ron. Not after their frustrated parting.

"You can call it what you want, Lucy. . .and I know you will. . .but it's more. I've missed you."

"You haven't changed. Still the same old line."

He shook his head. "It's not a line, Red. Trust me."

Trust me. That's what she'd not been able to do back then. Ron wanted so many things she didn't understand, and the one thing she wanted, he didn't. She prayed for him to accept Christ as his Savior.

He hadn't.

His eyes narrowed as if sensing her thoughts.

Shoppers moved past her, stepping around her discarded basket. Lucy bent down and shifted it out of the aisle.

Obviously aware of the empty woodcarver's chair, Ron followed the customers with his eyes as if feeling guilty that he wasn't working. "So, tell me what you're doing here," he said.

"I don't suppose you'd remember, but I've always wanted to see the *Passion of Christ*. You know, the play that's performed here every ten years."

He chuckled. "You can't live in Oberammergau and not know about the play." His lean, handsome face grew serious. "I remember, Lucy. And so you came to make your dream come true?"

She nodded, deep in thought. "But it's more than that. My grandmother lives here and—"

"Yes, I remember that, too."

"She's recuperating from a stroke."

"Stroke. Oh, I'm really sorry." He wrapped his strong arm around her shoulder, giving her a squeeze. "Puts a damper on your trip, I suppose."

"A little." She struggled to reduce the sadness that suddenly filled her. "But I'm glad I can be here for a while anyway."

"Is she hospitalized?"

"No, she's home. I'm grateful that Grandmother has enough finances to care for herself. She's found a handyman who's been wonderful. He runs errands, helps around the place, and seems to ask little in return. I haven't met him yet, but I will, I'm sure."

Ron's arm still hugged her shoulder, and the familiarity warmed her. How long had it been since she'd felt so complete? "So what about you, Ron?"

The arm holding her dropped to his side, and he raised the other, running his fingers through his thick, wavy blond hair. His near-center part tugged at her memory—the way she'd kiss his forehead just below his hairline. . . .

"One thing you probably recall about me," he said, "I might be stubborn, but when I'm wrong, I admit it."

A smile curved her lips. That was the truth. Ron was the most stubborn man she knew, but he wasn't too proud to admit his errors. "That's true, but what does that mean?"

"It means you were right. A vagabond's life wasn't meant for me."

She stepped back, amazed at his words. "But you're sitting here in a woodcarving shop in Germany. How can you say that?"

"I'm in school, doing an internship in woodcarving."

"Internship," she repeated, still not understanding.

He glanced at his wristwatch. "Look, I'd love to talk, but I have to get back to work. When can I see you?"

Her stomach knotted with his question. If she'd used her old wisdom, she'd say "never." Instead, revived memories prodded her to give a different answer. "Are you free tonight?"

"Tonight? Sure."

"Come to my grandmother's. I'll give you the address—and telephone number, just in case." She fumbled in the bottom of her shoulder bag for a pencil and her small notebook. After jotting the information, she tore off the page and handed it to him.

He eyed the address then tucked the paper into his shirt pocket. "I'll come right after work. About six, okay?"

"Six is great." Her heart tripped as she retrieved her basket then stepped backward toward the door. "I'll see you at six."

Not until her hip bumped a shelf of merchandise did Lucy turn and hurry from the shop.

Chapter 2

Unpacking the groceries, Lucy remembered she'd forgotten to purchase the angel, but she was too filled with excitement to worry about it. Another day, she'd go back and take more time selecting a gift for her mother's birthday.

Her mixed emotions rotated back and forth like a weather vane in a cyclone. Seeing Ron pulled her feelings out of hiding. They'd parted with such anger and hurt, yet today she felt comfortable seeing him. Two old friends accidentally meeting in a foreign land—like providence.

With her parcels stored and the grocery basket tucked in the kitchen closet, Lucy hurried into the living room to tell her grandmother about Ron.

"You have troubles?" Gretchen Stein asked her granddaughter in her hesitant English.

"Nein, Oma," Lucy said using the German "no."

Gretchen nodded with a look of pleasure. "Good."

Lucy sank beside her on the sofa. "I saw an American friend in town this afternoon."

"Ja!" her grandmother said, surprise filling her face.

"An old boyfriend, Oma, from college. He's learning woodcarving."

"A fine trade," her grandmother said.

Lucy wasn't sure about that, but she continued. "I liked him so much back then." The breakup, she wouldn't mention. "We haven't seen each other for nearly seven years."

"*Ach*, seven?" Gretchen spread out her seven fingers and presented them to Lucy.

Lucy nodded and laughed. "Uh-huh. That's a long time. I invited him over tonight. I hope you don't mind." She studied her grandmother's face, hoping to catch any discomfort, but the elder woman only smiled and patted her hand.

"*Zu Abendessen?*" Gretchen asked, then corrected herself. "To evening meal?"

Lucy grinned. "If you don't mind. Is it okay?"

"*Ja, ist gut.*"

"Thanks, Oma."

She kissed her grandmother's cheek and jumped from the sofa, hurrying back into the kitchen.

When she reached the doorway, she skidded to a halt, wondering what she could prepare. Her German cooking skills were minimal. If she were truly honest, her cooking skills were minimal. . .period. German or American.

In thought, she pivoted a full circle, then stopped and headed for the refrigerator. Inside, she found four newly purchased bratwurst. If she and Oma ate one each, Ron could have two. She figured that would be enough.

At the bakery, she'd bought a loaf of crusty bread, and she remembered they hadn't eaten all the pork-flavored kraut her grandmother had prepared yesterday. That would do. For dessert, she'd serve the end of the raspberry torte.

While Lucy organized her thoughts, a deep masculine

voice drifted in from the living room. She hadn't heard anyone ring the bell, and with interest, she crept toward the doorway to glimpse at her grandmother's guest.

Lingering in the short hallway, Lucy studied the graying, well-built gentleman in casual attire, standing above her grandmother. In his hand, he held a bouquet, the heads facing downward. But he didn't offer Oma the flowers. Curious, Lucy stepped into the living room.

At her footfall, the man swung around to face her. "Ah, Lucy," he said, opening his arms to greet her.

Lucy hesitated, having no idea who he was.

"Here is Henri Wolfe, Lucy," her grandmother said. "He is the helping man I told to you."

Lucy relaxed. "The handyman," she said, correcting her grandmother's phrase. "How do you do?" She extended her hand to the stranger.

But instead of clasping it, Henri placed the flowers against her palm. "For you," he said with a sweeping bow, then, with his other hand, curved her fingers around the stems. "For Lucy."

She smiled at his gracious greeting and thanked him, but her words sounded muffled in her ears. She felt flustered. Amazed at her reaction, she stared at him, mesmerized by his eyes—large, flashing brown ones. The flesh crinkled around the outer edges when he smiled.

"You know me, yes?" he asked.

"Oma mentioned you, yes," she answered.

"Good. I am here always to help your lovely Oma. I am her. . .how to say it. . .her right-hand man."

"That's how you say it," Lucy said, cradling the flowers against her chest. Their sweet perfume drifted upward, as beguiling as the gentleman who'd given them to her.

He stood in silence as if waiting.

Finally, she remembered her manners. "Please, have a seat." Lucy motioned to an empty chair.

"You first," he said, gesturing like a gallant cavalier.

"But I have the flowers—"

"Only for a minute," he said.

Lucy grinned, understanding why her grandmother was so enchanted by this charming man. She sat first, then he followed.

He chatted for a moment, relating what he planned to do for Gretchen, but despite his conversation with her grandmother, he continued to gaze at Lucy.

She nestled the flowers in her arms, feeling uncomfortable with his admiring look.

Then a look of apology rose to his face. "I am sorry to stare, but you are as pretty as your grandmother, *Liebchen*. Very lovely. Just as Gretchen has told me."

She squirmed, not comfortable with his compliments but finding herself wanting to reciprocate. "If we're sharing flattery, I must mention your eyes. They're intriguing. And huge."

Tilting his head backward, he laughed, then leaned forward. "That makes them all the better to see *you*, Liebchen."

Joining his chuckle, she rose. "I'm afraid you'll have to excuse me. I have company coming for dinner, and besides, I don't want these wonderful flowers to wilt."

Before he could respond, she scurried from the room.

Bending over the rough-carved miniature donkey, Ron faltered, then lay down his carving tool. His shoulders ached. Normally, he enjoyed his work, priding himself in the skill and precision he had learned to make these intricate gift items. He could work for hours without feeling any weariness.

But today his mind was elsewhere, knotted by a head of uncooperative red hair and a generous smile as mischievous as her tresses.

Lucy had taken his breath away—seeing her here in the shop and realizing that he still cared about her after all these years. Though their parting had been tense—horrible was more like it—today, she'd leaped into his arms as if the past had never been.

Time had left her unchanged. She looked the same as she did in his memory: eternally young, petite, slender as a willow, with a smile that could break a heart. And she had.

Thinking back, he remembered her frustration with his career choice. He was an artist, his interests jumping from sculpture, to oil painting, to design. He'd wanted to charge into the world to study his art and live in a garret as a starving artist honing his craft with foolish dreams of being famous one day.

Now he laughed at his own fantasy. Lucy came from a down-to-earth family, tangled in the sturdy threads of Christianity, a faith he couldn't understand. . .then. But he did now. Her parents taught her to keep her feet to the ground, her heart tied to a solid promise, and her soul in God's hands. Ron had been far removed from that.

But as his life changed, he'd so often thought back to Lucy's eagerness for him to know Jesus. When she probed his thinking now, he'd have a surprise for her.

Finally, without a crowd of tourists, Ron sat alone and straightened his spine, stretching back his shoulder blades to reduce the tension that pulled at his muscles. The excitement of seeing Lucy was the motivation for his anxiety. He hadn't asked her if she was married or engaged. He'd asked so little, but then they'd only spoken a few moments.

Was this God's work? He wondered. He'd been such a difficult person back then, not only disbelieving but scorning those who believed. . .except Lucy. She had made her faith so desirable, so sincere that he had a difficult time taunting her. But she'd heard him goad others, and he was sure, along with his career choice, Lucy had given up on his soul and walked away.

Still, her happy heart and open arms had instilled a small seed of question, of wonder about her beliefs. And he'd done the rest, fertilized by memories of her joy in living, he'd stumbled along until one day, alone in a motel room, he'd picked up a Bible. During the evening, he read a few chapters of the New Testament. That day was only the beginning. Lucy would never believe how much he'd changed.

Checking the time, Ron gathered his equipment and rose. The next woodcarver in training would take over soon, and he could be on his way. Things had worked well for him. His other responsibility wasn't until tomorrow. Now, he'd stop at his apartment first to clean up, and then. . .he'd see Lucy again.

Chapter 3

L ucy heard the bell and hurried to the front door. Foolish, she knew. Ron had changed perhaps, but not in a way that was important to her, she was positive. But she couldn't explain that to her heightened pulse.

Swinging open the door, she faltered. He'd gone home—or at least, changed his clothes—because he stood before her in a dark gray, European-style sport coat with a bright blue knit shirt beneath. The color illumined his eyes like a bright July sky. She could never forget those eyes.

From behind his back, Ron withdrew a box of chocolates and presented them to her as he stepped through the door.

"Yummy," she said, seeing that he'd remembered her favorite, almond-filled candies. "Trying to make me fat?"

He slid his arm amiably around her shoulder. "You'll never be fat, Red. Anyway, you can share them with your grandmother." He gave her a wink, like in the old days, that melted her heart like chocolate on a summer's day.

Lucy took his arm and guided him into the living room. "Oma, here's Ron."

Her grandmother smiled and extended her hand.

Ron gave it a squeeze and waited.

"I hope you haven't eaten," Lucy said. "I forgot to mention that we'd have dinner."

His guilty expression let her know he'd hoped for a meal.

"Great," he said. "I hurried right over."

She gestured to his clothing. "*After* you changed, you mean."

With a sly smile, he nodded.

"Dinner's almost ready." She turned to her grandmother and extended the box of chocolates. "Oma, he brought us almond chocolates."

"*Ach, meine* favorite," she said, her sentence a mixture of English and German.

"Tell Grandmother about your work, Ron, while I finish dinner." She gestured to a chair.

As he sank into the cushion, Lucy clasped the chocolates and hurried from the room, struggling to control her silly thoughts. Why? Why was she allowing her heart to rule her head? She knew better. Clinging to the kitchen counter, she bowed her head and asked God for control and guidance. She needed someone far bigger than she was to monitor the emotions sailing through her.

After she poured the sauerkraut into a serving bowl and placed the wurst on a small platter, Lucy checked the table. All looked ready, and she called them from the living room.

When Ron entered with her grandmother on his arm, he'd discarded his jacket. The form-fitting knit shirt clung to his defined brawn and made his already broad shoulders look like a giant's. Chiding herself, she refocused on the seating arrangement and motioned to his chair.

After the blessing, Ron continued to answer her grandmother's faltering, yet probing, questions, and Lucy listened, nibbling on her sausage and wishing she'd left the meat for Ron. Tonight, she had no fondness for her meal. . .only for her guest.

Still, he seemed content with the food, lifting fork-fuls to his mouth between answering her grandmother's questions. On occasion, he gave Lucy a grin of patient understanding.

She loved Ron's smile. His full bottom lip curled upward, so inviting. She'd never forgotten his kisses, gen-tle yet commanding, leaving her yearning for more. Still, she'd tempered her emotion, seeing her faith-witness mak-ing no progress. Coupled with his plan to roam the world, she'd finally planted her feet in her family's teaching and said good-bye. But not without many tears, wishes, and what-ifs.

Today, her "what-if" sat beside her at her grand-mother's table. . .like a miracle. She paused a moment, wondering. Was this how God guided believers? Or could this be Satan's treachery, trying to draw her away from all that she held dear?

Ron pushed back his plate and patted his trim tummy. "That was good. I eat sandwiches so often, home-cooking is a real treat." As if with sudden awareness, he turned to Lucy. "And I thought you couldn't cook."

She was unable to contain her grin. "Oma made the kraut. I cooked the wurst. You can't go wrong with that."

He sent her a coy grin. "Well, it's the best wurst I've ever eaten."

Feeling giddy, Lucy laughed at his silliness while her

grandmother missed the humor with her limited English.

Lucy suggested they move to the living room for dessert. While she made coffee and placed the torte and almond candies on a tray, Ron and her grandmother went on ahead. After the sweets, Gretchen said good night, leaving them alone.

Ron leaned back against the sofa, gazing around the comfy room. So few people afforded their own home in Germany, and Gretchen Stein was one of the few. There were two stories above her, and he'd learned she rented out flats. The handyman that Lucy had mentioned kept them and her property in shipshape condition. She was a blessed woman to have such luxury.

He'd noticed the flowers earlier and was curious. "It looks like your grandmother has an admirer," he said, gesturing toward the lavish bouquet.

Lucy's face broke into a smile as grand as the floral arrangement. "No, *I* do," she said.

His heart sank to his boots. "Oh. . .well, that's nice." He wrestled the frown that tried to reach his brow.

She tilted her head. "Not a *real* admirer," she said, as if his attempt had failed. "The flowers are a gift from Henri. . .the man who works for Grandmother."

"The handyman?" Ron said, amazed that a handyman could afford such an expensive bouquet. "He must not be hurting too bad for bucks if he bought you those."

Lucy shrugged. "He's really nice. Very charming with a capital C."

Her comment didn't set well with Ron. Someone that charming made him nervous. Ashamed, Ron halted the pervading thoughts. Maybe the man was only being kind to Lucy—a guest in his country. Henri cared about Gretchen, so why not her granddaughter?

Pushing back his concern, Ron changed the subject. "Your grandmother looks good in spite of the stroke. You'd never know."

Lucy ran her fingers through her shoulder-length hair and twirled the ends with her index finger. "She does, but now that I've met Henri, I feel better about her being here when I'm gone."

Though he knew he was foolish, a gnawing sense of jealousy rattled through him. Sensing the need for validation, he wiggled his finger, beckoning Lucy to sit beside him on the sofa.

Hesitant at first, she finally rose and plopped beside him, curling her legs beneath her and shifting to face him.

"That's better," he said, wishing she'd nestled closer but still pleased that she'd moved nearer. "So what's happened to you since college? Tell me about your family and career. Everything."

Her face brightened as she gave him a good health report of her parents and her sister, who was happily married and the mother of three children. Then, she detailed her career in a successful business firm, working as an accountant.

"How did you get time off to come here?" Ron asked.

"They have a deal where you can take a leave if you're vacationing out of the U.S. I guess they feel it makes you more cosmopolitan or something. I'd been saving to come, so everything worked out perfect."

His earlier question jolted into his thoughts. "You're a free woman then. . .not married or engaged or anything."

Her eyes widened. "Me? No, I'm unattached." She

leaned over and pressed her palm against his hand. "How about you?"

"As single as a one-dollar bill," he said, embarrassed that he'd even bothered to ask.

She gave him a knowing grin. "I guess that's settled."

An uncomfortable silence stretched between them.

"I heard you telling Oma about your plans to start a business," she said, finally. "That's so exciting. . .but where will you get the money?"

He wanted to laugh at her typical concern. Growing up in a financially comfortable family, she'd asked this kind of question so often, but today he wasn't irritated. Instead, he was pleased at her interest.

"Investors, partially, but I've also been very bles—fortunate," he said, stumbling over his words, "to have made some wise investments myself."

He'd almost given his surprise away. If he'd said "blessed," she'd have known immediately that he'd had a serious change of heart. If he could hold off his revelation, he'd thought of a perfect moment to share his conversion with her.

He rattled on to Lucy about some ideas he'd presented to a furniture design company and the excellent bonus he'd received from them. He'd done well investing the money. God had been good to him. Truly good to one who had been a devout unbeliever, like his family. Now he'd begun to work on his parents, praying that in time, they, too, would come to know the blessings of being a Christian.

"I've dreamed of designing custom-built homes," he said, "but first I thought I'd try my hand with handcrafted furniture. Learning real European woodcarving will give my pieces a unique twist."

Lucy's enthusiasm glowed in her face. That's what she was like—a major support for her family and friends, always delighting in their success rather than being envious of their accomplishments.

Lucy slid her feet to the floor and scooted toward him. "So it seems that the Lo— that things have worked out well for you."

Ron bit his tongue rather than comment on the faltered word "Lord" that he knew had nearly tumbled from her lips. . .her full, sweet lips now bent into a generous smile.

Such a down-to-earth, genuine person, Lucy was. Nothing false. No pretenses. Just like when they were in college. He remembered the perfume of her freshly washed hair, and she wore only a hint of makeup. So natural. Remembering made him smile.

"Why are you grinning?" Lucy asked.

"Looking at you makes me happy, Red," he said, brushing a wayward strand of hair from her forehead. "Life hasn't been the same without you. You broke my heart, you know."

She chuckled, but a serious look shimmered from her eyes. "Men don't have broken hearts, do they? At least, not hard-nosed ones like you."

"Sure they do," he said. "Feel." He lifted her delicate hand and pressed it against his chest, wondering if she could feel the rising pace of his heartbeat.

She only smiled at him, her fingers splayed across his knit shirt.

The tender touch roused his remembrance. He'd tried so hard to move on after she dumped him. He dated other college girls, but they all seemed so false, empty of values. He let his emotions get carried away, but when he found the Lord, he asked for forgiveness. Ashamed of his behavior then, he cringed inside, sensing Lucy's purity.

Unable to contain himself, he drew her hand into his and lifted it to his lips. When he looked into her face, he witnessed a flash of confusion evolving into a shy grin.

"I could try to deny it," she said, "but it's really good to be with you. I'm glad life has been good to you, Ron. Really. I know our parting was bad—"

"More than bad, Lucy. It was horrible. I almost lost it that semester."

She lowered her head, a tremor stirring in her hand. "I dropped two classes."

What could he say to her? When he'd changed and grown, he knew the fault was his. But then, he'd blamed her foolish beliefs. He had cursed the God she loved. Odd how the Lord worked. Her God and Savior had become his.

When Lucy lifted her chin to look at him, a surge of longing washed over him like a rolling tide. Right or wrong, he was drawn to kiss her, but caution constrained him. Instead, he studied Lucy's face. Now that God had brought them together, what would he do if she didn't want to try again?

Chapter 4

Lucy sat in her small bedroom, marveling at the sunshine spilling through the window. Though she could finally see the jagged peaks of the amazing Alps, her heart lay in a deep valley.

Frustration rattled in her head, wondering why she'd allowed herself to get tangled again in Ron's life. Though she sensed a new maturity, a commonsense approach to life that he'd never shown before, he hadn't really changed at all. If he had, she'd have heard from him by now. Three days had passed—and nothing.

Ron had always been like a frog, jumping from one thing to another, and deep in her heart, she'd hoped one day, like the old myth, her kiss would turn him into a fairy-tale prince. Now, here she was in Germany, a land of castles and storybook villages, and Ron was still the same old frog.

Lucy pulled her shoulders back, determined to yank herself up from the doldrums that weighed on her shoulders. Why did she care anyway? She'd come to Germany to visit her grandmother and to see the passion play. Nothing had changed. . .well, not much.

She rose, watching the sunlight spread patterns across

her shoes. With only a feathering of clouds, the sky was bright blue, almost like Ron's eyes. Her spirit lifted as the summer day called to her.

Ron's eyes. She drew in a ragged breath. Why had she entered the shop on that rainy day? She remembered, the angel in the window. She paused, searching frantically for wisdom to waylay a growing plan. She should go back to the store and find that gift for her mother's birthday. The package needed to be in the mail soon, or it would arrive too late.

Stepping into the kitchen, Lucy found her grandmother sitting at the sturdy wooden table. "Good morning, Oma." She leaned down and kissed the older woman's cheek.

"Morgen," her grandmother said in greeting.

"Do you need anything from the market? I'm going out to buy Mom a birthday gift."

Her grandmother mentioned bread, and with only a bakery stop, Lucy waved good-bye and rushed into the morning sunlight. The fresh air filled her lungs as she walked, and nearing the center of town, she faltered, wondering where her good sense had gone. She was setting herself up for disappointment again. Her attitude hadn't changed. She would never again fall in love with an unbeliever. Miracle conversions didn't happen unless God willed them. Without the Lord, her own determination to change Ron meant nothing.

She'd reached the cluster of shops and, again, admired the unique buildings. Gold and silver scrollwork framing windows and fabric draping the doorways were nothing more than elegant paintings. Colorful scenes from the Passion of Christ and the lives of early German forefathers came to life in the gigantic murals that covered the stucco buildings.

She paused for a moment beside a larger-than-life-sized nutcracker, his gold and black cap and red jacket glinting in the bright morning rays. Now, that would be a real surprise birthday gift for her mother. She chuckled at her silliness and continued toward the shop where she had previously spotted Ron.

The building stood ahead of her, colorful flowers spilling over the edges of its wooden window boxes. Her chest tightened as she neared. How would Ron react when she appeared a second time? Confusion shivered in her thoughts.

That last evening at her grandmother's, she was certain that Ron had nearly kissed her, but he'd faltered. For a moment she'd been riddled with disappointment. Now she was grateful. With the days passing and no word from him, she realized his change was only wishful thinking. What excuse would he make this time?

In the window, she spotted the same lovely angel that she'd seen days earlier. Outside the door, she concentrated on her purpose for returning. Yet, guilt nudged her. She had two purposes, if she were honest.

As soon as she entered the shop, Lucy noticed the angels. She focused on her task and studied each one, some with musical instruments, others in prayer. Selecting her favorite, she carried it with her along the aisles until she reached the archway to the next showroom. She took a deep breath and trudged forward, waiting until she reached the spot where she had seen Ron.

Disappointment shrouded her. The head bent over the carver's bench was not blond but had straight, black hair. She ambled down an aisle and up another, again pausing to look at the woodcarver. Still no Ron.

With a sigh, she turned, wending her way back to the salesclerk. She paid for the angel and waited until it was boxed securely for mailing.

Outside, she stood for a moment, deciding what to do next—head for the bakery or stop at the café across the street for coffee and *Brotchen*. Her stomach gave a low rumble, answering her question.

Selecting a window table, Lucy placed her order then stared across the way at the gift shop, wondering about Ron. When her breakfast arrived, she poked her fingers into the crusty roll and tore off a piece, still warm from the baker's oven. A basket of jams and potted meats sat on the table. She selected a berry preserve and slathered it across the bread, then sank her teeth into the tasty morsel.

A rap against the window drew her gaze upward, and her heart skipped, seeing Ron smile at her from the sidewalk. He stepped away, and in moments, he appeared at her side and slid into the adjacent chair.

"I'm glad I saw you," he said. "Are you heading to the shop?"

"I was there already." She pointed to the shopping bag beside her chair leg.

His expression let her see he felt guilty. "Sorry I haven't called, Lucy. I have school and then I work two jobs. . .sort of. One is only temporary. I'm just filling in for a friend who broke his leg. He'll be back there in another three weeks, and then I'm free."

"Oh," she said, wondering why he hadn't told her about this before.

He slid his hand over hers. "Really, I should have

called, but it was always late and I hated to wake your grandmother."

She nodded her head, not knowing how else to respond.

"I'd planned to call you after work today," he said.

"You did?"

She stared at his face, trying to read what he was thinking. His eyes looked as if he were telling the truth. When she thought for a moment, she realized Ron had never lied to her. He was flighty and unpredictable. . .but truthful.

"I'm going to Mittenwald tomorrow," he said. "Ever been there?" His hand still lay against hers.

"No. I haven't been anywhere except here." Was this another excuse? He was calling her tonight to say he would not see her tomorrow either. And maybe the next day.

"Then you'd enjoy yourself," he said. "Would you like to come along? I have a little business at our other shop, and then I'll be finished."

His offer struck her unprepared. She'd set herself up for excuses, and instead, he gave her an invitation. She lingered over his words. "Where is this place?" she asked finally, her finger twirling the ends of her hair.

"Only a few miles, but you'll see some beautiful countryside." He grinned and squeezed her free hand. "And I can arrange a couple of surprises. What do you say?"

What should I say? He'd addled her enough. And for what? "I don't know, Ron." She struggled, wanting to announce a strong "no thank you."

"Please, Red. Let me make it up to you. You'll have a great day, I promise."

When she didn't respond, she watched his face riffle with concern.

"How about this?" he said. "I'll drop by in the morning. . .about nine thirty. It's on the way. You can check with your grandmother first."

His pleading eyes melted her firm resolve. "Okay," she said, her voice a meek whisper.

"You'll love the village. It's twice the size of Oberammergau and every bit as picturesque."

She forced a smile to her face, excited yet concerned that she was making a grave error.

Ron rose. "I have to get to work, Red. I'll see you tomorrow then." With a wave, he darted toward the door.

She looked through the window and watched him dash across the near-empty street and enter the gift shop. She shook her head, wondering if she'd hear anything loose up there. Was she making a mistake? Bowing her head, she asked God to give her direction.

Ron pulled up in front of the white stucco house and collected his thoughts. What would he say if Lucy plied him with questions about his second job? He wanted that to be his surprise. . .that is, if it worked out that way. First, he had to find out when she had tickets for the passion play.

Her disappointed face poked at his conscience. If he were kind, he'd blurt everything out so she would understand. But since the first moment he saw her in the shop, his newfound faith flashed in his mind like a neon sign. He wanted a special moment to tell her.

He stepped from the car and headed for the white wooden gate. Beyond it, a yard of flowers rose as high as the fence. Some he recognized: foxglove, hollyhocks, and blue delphinium.

Before he rang the bell, the door flew open. Filling the

doorway, a tall, graying man studied him with piercing, inquisitive eyes. "You are Ron?"

A small tremor began in Ron's legs. *Lucy?* "Yes, is something wrong with—"

"No. No," he boomed, stepping aside to allow Ron to enter. He stuck out his hand. "I am Henri Wolfe." He motioned toward the living room. "Go in. Lucy is nearly ready."

Confused, Ron went ahead of him and felt relief when he found Gretchen in her easy chair.

"Come, come," she said, pointing to the sofa. "You sit. Lucy will be here."

He backed up and sat, his attention shifting from Lucy's grandmother to the large man. "Are you well, Frau Stein?" Ron asked.

"Ja," she said, nodding her head.

Her eyes shifted toward the archway, and Ron turned his head in that direction. Lucy came through the door-way dressed in a summery skirt and blouse.

"Sorry," she said. "I couldn't decide if I should wear walking shoes or sandals."

His attention shifted to her feet. "Sandals will be fine," he said, assuming she wanted him to say something. He rose, anxious to get away from Henri's penetrating gaze.

She kissed her grandmother and, to his surprise, gave Henri a bear hug. "Thanks for the pretty scatter pin," she said, lifting her hand to a small gold piece attached to her blouse collar.

"You are welcome," he said, his strong accent giving his words a heavy sound.

Turning from Henri, she flashed Ron a beaming smile. "Let's go. Oma said I'll love Mittenwald."

At the doorway, he gave a cursory wave and guided Lucy outside. Heading down the sidewalk, he felt weighted by the man's scrutiny. "Does that guy think he's your father?" Ron asked.

"No, why?" Her smile faded to a scowl. "What did he say?"

"It's his look. I think he has X-ray vision."

"You're being silly," she said, heading off in front of him.

He let it drop. Tension had already wedged between them since his three-day absence, and apparently she was defending this man. Why, he didn't know. He was certainly too young to be her grandmother's boyfriend. . . man-friend. He couldn't find the right word.

Befuddled, he pushed the thoughts out of his head. Today he wanted their time to be fun and special, a day that would ease the pressure he sensed.

Lucy was quiet until they left town. Then, she chattered with excitement each time she spotted a small village nestling in the distance or a castle ruins rising on the mountainside. She didn't ask about his second job, and he steered as clear as he could from the subject.

When the car rolled into town, he parallel parked. "Do you want to come with me, or would you rather explore while I take care of business? I can meet you by the statue at the end of the street." He pointed toward the sculpted figure at the base of the colorful domed steeple. "See the old baroque-style church down there?"

She looked in the direction he pointed. "How long will you be?"

"About an hour." He checked his wristwatch. "Let's meet there at eleven."

She nodded, and tugging her purse strap onto her shoulder, she strode off down the sidewalk without looking back. He prayed that when they met again in an hour, she'd be more relaxed. He had so many nice surprises for her later.

Chapter 5

L ucy marched down the street, confused with her actions. After talking to her grandmother, she'd convinced herself to enjoy the day with Ron. She'd seen so little of Germany, and this seemed a perfect opportunity. But she'd been upset by Ron's attitude toward Henri. Why? He did have strange eyes that seemed to search inside her head. She'd noticed that more and more. Still, he was charming and very thoughtful.

She lifted her fingers, feeling the small gold scatter pin he'd given her. He told her it was a wagtail bird. She'd seen those funny little creatures fluttering around her grandmother's garden, flicking their tails as they strutted along the ground.

She focused ahead of her on the quaint buildings. Like Oberammergau, the shops and pensions were decorated with colorful murals, most depicting the life of Christ. It seemed funny that Ron, an unbeliever, was excited about sharing this town with her.

The church stood ahead of her, its belfry spire adorned with biblical scenes. The clock's face could be seen just under the belfry opening. Ten after ten. She had only fifty minutes to explore the picturesque town before she had to meet Ron.

At the statue, she marveled at the plaque, not a religious figure, but a sculpture of a seventh-century violin maker. But she was drawn beyond the church to a cul-de-sac where brightly painted buildings with flowering window boxes stood forming a private plaza. In the center, an ornate horse trough stood like the square's fountain. With her limited time, she turned and headed back to the main street.

Gazing into the shop windows, Lucy's thoughts drifted to Ron. She wondered about the second job he'd mentioned. Though he never lied, she sensed that he was avoiding something, keeping things from her. An eerie concern edged through her. Could she trust him? He seemed so eager to make her happy. Yet, at times, he was so evasive.

And why had he disliked Henri? She sensed it, saw it in his face. Henri had been nothing but kind to her and, for all she could tell, to Oma. She'd overheard him telling her grandmother about some major repairs she needed, but she hadn't had time to inquire. Major repairs meant money. That worried Lucy.

She stopped again and glanced into another shop window. This time Lucy wandered inside, browsing through the unusual items lining the displays. More than souvenirs, they were wonderful gifts. But time was fleeting, and she'd have to wait for more shopping.

With only ten minutes to spare, she returned to the church. Rather than sit on the bench outside, she tried the door. It opened, and she walked inside. Silence hung in the shadowed corners, but prisms of light spilled down from the crystal chandeliers, washing the ancient pews and beautifully carved altar with rainbows.

Mesmerized by the building's antiquity, Lucy wandered down the aisle, awed by the towering pulpit that rose above the heads of the parishioners where clergy stood proclaiming God's Word. Near the front, she slid into a pew. She needed some solace, and here she felt close to God.

Her first thought was her grandmother, and she lifted the elder woman in prayer, asking God to return her to health. Then, Ron came to mind as he did so often. With her hands clasped and head bowed, she asked the Lord to give her direction, to remove the growing feelings, if it was not His will.

Leaning against the hard seat back, Lucy drew in a breath and felt refreshed. She'd missed church last Sunday, but today, God breathed new strength into her. Glancing at her wristwatch, she rose and headed for the door.

When she stepped outside, she squinted into the glaring daylight. She swung around the corner toward the statue.

Ron stood near the church tower, his task completed and his trunk loaded with items being moved to the shop in Oberammergau. He lifted his face to the sunshine and grinned. He hoped the hour alone had been good for Lucy and eased her tension. He was anxious for them to be on their way.

As Lucy rose in his mind, Henri's face followed. What was it about the man that bothered him? Ron couldn't put his finger on it. Was it the inappropriate sense of ownership? Maybe that's what it was. Henri barely knew Lucy, and yet he'd taken her over as he'd done her grandmother.

Shame riffled through his mind. Did he think the man was like one of those con artists who preyed on lonely and elderly women? This was Germany, not back home. And the man had done nothing that he'd seen. He'd probably heard too many television commentaries about people duped by swindlers.

Still, he wondered how Frau Stein had met Henri Wolfe. Lucy hadn't said, and Ron questioned whether she knew. He'd ask her. . .but not today, at least not now.

Movement flashed in his peripheral vision, and he turned his head. Lucy hurried toward him looking calm and refreshed. He stepped to meet her. "Where you been?"

"In the church." She gestured to the entrance around the corner. "Ever been inside?"

He nodded before he caught himself, then tried to cover. "It's a tourist attraction. Most everyone, even unbelievers, wanders into old church buildings."

Her face sank with his comment. His deception was getting out of hand, and he was sorry. "It's quiet and peaceful inside," he said, hoping to make amends for his thoughtless comment.

She tilted her head, searching his face. "You really think so?"

"Sure." He caught her arm and guided her across the street. "Are you ready?"

"For what?" she asked. "Are we heading home so soon?"

"Yes, but the long way. I thought you'd like to see a couple of sights."

"I would. I hate to go back home and tell everyone all I saw was Oma's house."

He chuckled.

When they reached the car, he opened the door, letting her slip inside, then circled to the driver's side and climbed in. "Okay, we'll see some new scenery."

Instead of heading north toward Garmisch, he turned the car west toward Füssen. Pine trees lined the roads and edged up the craggy mountains where, at the top, rugged rocks jutted up toward the heavens.

Lucy gaped out the window awed, as he was, at the beauty of the countryside. Yet surrounded by the lush grandeur, sitting beside Lucy captured him even more. She'd relaxed since earlier in the morning. He had sensed it immediately when she approached him by the statue. Her smile was natural and bright as the day, and she'd taken his hand without thinking.

He prepared her for the next stop by filling her in on a little history of the area and, especially, on King Ludwig the Second, known for his extravagant castles. Nearing the town, Ron slowed, waiting for the grand sight to rise above the landscape. When he heard Lucy gasp, he followed her gaze, knowing what she had seen.

"Look, Ron. It's that famous castle." She rolled down the window and leaned out, pointing to the magnificent white and gold building with its lean, pointed towers rising toward the clouds.

"Neuschwanstein," he said. "It's one of King Ludwig's masterpieces. Would you like to go inside?"

Her eyes widened a mile. "Really?" she whispered.

His heart swelled, seeing her excitement, and he followed the road to the tour parking lots. With a carriage taking them partway, they walked the rest, both panting from exertion at the steep climb. Inside the building, they gawked at the opulence of the rooms and the amazing wealth found there.

As natural as a sunset, Lucy slid her hand into his as they followed the English-speaking guide, explaining the gold leaf, Austrian crystal, velvet drapings, and magnificent murals that filled the halls and rooms.

The comfortable feeling of her soft flesh against his palm took him back. Why hadn't he listened to her back then? He'd been a cocky college boy, thinking he knew everything. But he'd been wrong. He'd known little.

Finally, they wound their way outside and without her resisting, Ron slid his arm around Lucy's waist as they followed the trail back down to the bottom. The experience was perfect, except for the nagging concern Ron had about Henri Wolfe.

He didn't broach the subject again until they had grabbed a bratwurst and stopped to view the gardens of the Linderhof. After climbing the stairs to admire the magnificent mazed hedges and flowers, he sorted his words, praying he'd initiate the conversation without creating stress.

Beneath the shade trees, they sat on a bench beside the pool, waiting for the hourly fountain display.

"I'm sorry about the way I acted this morning."

She looked at him curiously. "What do you mean?"

"About Henri. I don't know why I acted like I did. Maybe I'm jealous at all the attention he gives you and your grandmother." What he said was true, but he felt something stronger.

"It's okay. I acted silly myself. What difference does it make if you like him or not? I'll be gone in a couple more weeks and. . ." She faltered.

"What is it?" Ron asked.

"I hate to think about leaving," she said. "I'll miss. . . everything. The mountains, the quaint town, Oma, and you."

And you. The words tumbled through his veins and sent his pulse racing. "Don't think about it, Lucy. You're here now, so let's enjoy this time together. . .and you know, I'm not staying here forever."

"I know," she whispered.

He hated to drag the conversation back, but he had to. "How did your grandmother meet Henri?"

She stared at the ground, then pulled her head upward. "I don't know," she said, dragging the words out thoughtfully. "I never thought to ask."

"It's not important. I just wondered."

She smiled. "Now I'm curious. I'll have to ask her."

Enough. He'd accomplished what he set out to. Once he had the answer, maybe he'd feel better. He saw no need in worrying Lucy unless his fears were grounded in fact. And now for his second question. He swallowed, trying to find a way to move into the topic.

"You mentioned you'd be going home soon, and I know you came to see the play. When are you going?"

"Next week. Wednesday."

"Wednesday," he repeated. "I'm sure you'll love it. Everyone does."

That curious scowl shuffled across her face, but the ornate, gold-leaf fountain came to life, gushing at least one hundred feet in the air and interrupting her rising question.

His heart raced, knowing that on that day Lucy would realize he'd become a Christian. His surprise was turning into a monster, and the day couldn't come too soon. With a relieved sigh, he leaned back against the slats and gazed at Lucy's lovely profile as she gaped at the towering geyser. Another week and his wonderful news would be out.

Chapter 6

In the small café across from the woodcarver shop, Lucy sat at a table with Ron and studied him. She needed to talk. . .but sensibly, not getting him riled as he'd done the day he and Henri had met.

"You're quiet," Ron said.

"Just thinking." She ran her finger over the grain of the wooden table, wondering if she should admit her concern.

"About going home? I know the time's flying."

She shook her head. "No, it's just. . .well, I'm—"

"What? Just tell me." He scrunched his neck into his shoulders to look into her downcast face. "Did I do something?"

"It's not you. Promise." She didn't know exactly what she wanted to tell him. What was it that gnawed at her during the night, leaving her tired in the morning?

"I'm not sure what I'm thinking, Ron," she said finally. "It's Henri."

"Henri?" Ron straightened his back like a ramrod. "What did he do to you?"

"Nothing. It's not anything he did to me. . .and I'm not sure he did anything at all."

Ron crammed his palm against the table. "Lucy, you're not making sense."

"I know." She ran her hand along her aching neck, then caught the ends of her hair in her fingers. "He's just hanging around a lot, and I wonder if he has a job. Then I think he must, because he brings me. . .us. . .gifts, like flowers and boxes of Mozart chocolates. Those aren't cheap."

"What do you think?" Ron asked. "Are you worried he's doing something wrong? Something illegal?"

"Oh, no. . .well, not really." She drew in a deep ragged breath. "I'm surprised he's around so much. It's almost like he's guarding my grandmother. I figured with me there visiting with her that he'd take a break. He's a handyman, not her nursemaid."

"You're right," Ron said. "Did you ask your grandmother how she met him?"

Lucy nodded. That information had given her comfort, but only for a while. "Through a friend. A lady friend gave him a good reference. I felt better when I heard that."

Ron shrugged. "Sure, that makes you more confident that he's on the up-and-up." He slid his hand across the tabletop and caught hers. "So why are you worried?"

She swallowed, wondering if she should tell him. It was really her grandmother's business and not hers. And especially not Ron's concern. But she had to tell someone. "Oma gave him a big check the other day. I overheard them talking about roof repairs, and I was concerned. Slate roofs are expensive."

"What kind of repairs?" Ron's eyes narrowed, and trancelike, he dragged his thumb back and forth across the back of her hand as if in deep thought.

"I don't know exactly. A big job, I'd guess. She wrote a

check for a large amount and told me not to worry."

"Which roofing company? Maybe I can ask around and find out something about them."

Lucy felt herself sinking into the chair cushion. She had to tell him the truth. "That's what bothers me. She wrote it out to Henri and said—"

Ron snatched his hand from hers, tightening it into a fist. "Wrote it out to Henri? You mean in *his* name? I don't like that."

"But when I said something, Oma got defensive. She said he'd been good to Helga before she died and that she trusted Helga and Henri."

Ron's jaw tightened. "Who's Helga?" Concern riffled across his face, the same way she'd reacted when she heard.

"The friend who gave my grandmother the reference."

Ron caved against the chair back. "She's dead?"

"Died not long ago. She'd been sick, Ron. I don't think that Henri did—"

He caught her hand again. "No, I'm not saying he *killed* her. But some men hang around women. . .especially ones who are sick or frail. . .and they take advantage of them."

"You mean like steal from them? Charm them into giving large sums of money for—?"

"Exactly. For roofs that don't need repair or plumbing that needs a washer and the handyman diagnoses a major sewer problem."

Lucy's stomach knotted, wondering how many other repair jobs Henri had found to extract money from her grandmother. Still, she faltered. Maybe he wasn't a thief. Being a Christian, Lucy knew she wasn't to judge others without knowing the facts.

"I suppose we shouldn't condemn Henri without knowing the truth," Ron said.

Like hearing an echo, Lucy's mouth gaped. "I was thinking that myself. What can we do? How can we check?"

Ron rested his chin against his fingers and stared out the window.

Watching him sit in silence with his eyes closed, Lucy could almost hear the gears turning in his mind.

Finally, he turned back to her. "Let me think about this. I'll come up with something." His silence continued, then from nowhere, he changed the subject. "Are you going to the play tomorrow?"

"Yes, but you're not going to—"

He grinned for the first time since she'd mentioned Henri. "No, I'm not going to do anything. I'll talk with you first. So, tomorrow your dream comes true."

She nodded. "Yes, tomorrow." But if she told Ron the truth, her dream had come true the day she walked into the carving shop and saw him. She'd faced the truth herself. Hidden in the depths of her fantasy, every phantom suitor that she'd created had Ron's face and shining eyes.

The waitress delivered their open-faced sandwiches, and as she ate, she recalled why her heartstrings remained wound around Ron's. Though he needled others and her sometimes about their Christian beliefs, he'd always displayed the attributes that God's children should have. Always kind and thoughtful, he showed compassion and had a ready wit, a warm, caring way to help her pull herself up from sorrow and look for the good in things.

Somewhere, mixed in with his goodness, Lucy sensed that God had planted a seed of the Spirit and she had watered it with her own faith, hoping to see it grow. Sadness pressed against her chest, knowing that her attempts had failed. Still, God works miracles. Maybe, just maybe.

"Good sandwich," Ron said, interrupting her musing, "but I still miss my two slices of bread."

Not as much as she'd miss him when she returned home. Though Lucy laughed, her reflection was far from humorous. When she returned to Michigan, she'd leave him and her grandmother behind. That fact had not set well since she sensed the time flying away from her. Lucy pushed away the sadness. "Will I see you tomorrow night?" she asked.

"You can bet on it."

An expression flickered over his face that unsettled her. "Ron, you promised you wouldn't do anything about Henri until—"

"I'm not, Red. But don't let that hair get you fired up. I see smoke curling out of your ears. I only said I'd see you tomorrow for sure."

He leaned back, sending her a smile that filled her heart.

Ron passed three donkeys, their muzzles buried in the pile of oats. Though it was a cool morning, the sky was clear and he hoped the play would proceed without rain. He worked his way back to the dressing rooms, anxiety coursing through him.

Today was the day. He would tell the whole story to Lucy, how her faith had nudged him into reading the Bible and how God's Word had changed his life. Following the all-day performance, he'd seek her out. He prayed Lucy would notice him in the vast crowd scene outside "Jerusalem" at the foot of the three crosses.

A slithering concern wrestled into his reflections. He'd pushed it away so often. Once he announced he'd been a Christian for the past five years, somehow, he had to face up to the years that came before.

Lucy's faith had kept her pure, saving herself for her husband. Ron's lack of faith had led him in the opposite direction. He'd given in to sin, looking for someone like Lucy who filled his mind, but he'd failed. The flesh was not the answer, but the heart and soul was. And his heart had been tied to Lucy's. Since he'd given his soul to Jesus, he'd remained pure. He prayed Lucy would understand. But first, he had to find the courage to confess.

Sinful behavior brought Henri into his mind. He'd tossed plans back and forth in his mind—confrontation, subtle questioning, ambush, but Ron stopped his anxious mind, deciding he first needed to know the truth. Was Henri actually guilty of swindling Lucy's grandmother? Tomorrow, he had time to drop by Frau Stein's and take the necessary first step.

Lucy followed the crowd into the huge outdoor passion play theater. She felt blessed getting tickets to the popular, sold-out event. Another blessing was her grandmother's improved health. Yesterday when she accompanied her grandmother to the doctor's office for her test results, she had received a good report. No lasting damage from her stroke and a clear enough warning to encourage the older woman to use preventative medications.

The morning air in the mountain town hovered around her in a chilling dampness, and when she found her seat, she was relieved to find heaters below the seats that warmed her lower extremities.

Lucy focused ahead of her. The massive stage built into the mountainside provided an awesome setting for the story of Christ's passion. Everything was perfect except for one thing. Lucy wished that Ron were at her side.

Thinking of Ron, questions bumped through her brain like dodgem cars. Would he ever come to know God as she did? Did he still care about her. . .really? What had he decided to do about Henri Wolfe?

That eerie situation sent fear shivering down her spine and added new questions. Was Henri really a con artist? If so, what would he do when he realized Lucy and Ron were suspicious? Was he dangerous? She hardly thought so, but—

Lucy halted her soaring imagination. She had to be patient and see what Ron had in mind. He wouldn't do anything foolish. At least, she didn't think so.

Nervous energy sizzled along her limbs, and sorry that she'd allowed the concern to rise in her head, she turned her attention to the performance area. The sun rose in the vibrant blue sky, spread its light along the mountainside, and spilled downward to the stage floor.

Finally, the time arrived, and with anticipation, she pulled her grandmother's opera glasses from her shoulder bag. While an awesome hush fell over the crowd of nearly five thousand, the drama began.

Lucy riveted her attention to the play, and late in the afternoon as the passion unfolded, a massive crowd gathered around the three crosses raised on Golgotha. The hairs on Lucy's neck prickled. In the huddled crowd gathering around the crosses she pinpointed one person who looked familiar. With the hood of his cloak fallen back, now draped around his broad shoulders, the man's blond, wavy hair caught Lucy's attention. How could it be that in this mob of people she saw someone who resembled Ron?

She lifted the opera glasses from her lap and studied the figure. Her heart leaped. The more she studied the man, the more she was nailed to her seat in amazement. Like the day she saw Ron in the woodcarving shop, filled with disbelief, today was even more astounding. Out of hundreds of people, her focus had fallen on Ron. . .or a look-alike. If it was him, what could it mean? And how could it be? He was an unbeliever and a foreigner in Oberammergau.

Chapter 7

Unable to move, Lucy stared at the bare stage, awed by the performance. Her dream of seeing the passion play had in no way equaled the powerful experience. Wiping tears from her cheeks, she rose and made her way toward the theater exit. She longed to find her way back to the cast dressing area to see if she could spot Ron. . .more likely, the person who looked like Ron. But with hundreds in the cast, the task seemed impossible. Yet, wondering addled her.

Stepping away from the theater's covering, the warm sunlight spread across her uncovered arms. Earlier in the afternoon, she'd slipped off her sweater. Now, she tied it around her waist and made her way back toward the center of town.

The drama had filled her—had made every one of her earthly problems seem minuscule compared to God's sacrifice. She drew in a full breath of the fresh air and her stomach growled, reminding her of the small lunch she'd eaten.

Too soon for dinner, a pastry sounded good. Maybe an almond horn. She'd found nothing in the world as wonderful as the cakes and pastries she'd eaten at the local bakery shops. But before turning away from the theater, she scanned the exit again. Could the blond-haired man have been Ron? Her heart skipped with the question.

Blocking the entry of more foolish ideas, she turned her musings toward the rest of the day. Slowing as she approached a traffic light, a shadow appearing from the side of the building fell across her feet. Faltering from the sudden motion, she caught her breath. *Ron.*

He stepped beside her, a smile spreading on his lips. "I figured you'd come this way."

She searched his face, looking for an answer to the question that pounded in her head. With a trembling hand, she turned in the direction of the theater and pointed. "Was that. . .you?"

Without responding, he held her captive with his gaze, his smiling eyes toying with her.

"In the crowd," Lucy added. "Was that you in the passion play?"

He caught her hand, her finger still pointing toward the theater. "I didn't know if you'd notice me in all that crowd."

A myriad of emotions tumbled through her. "Your hood slipped down. I recognized your hair."

"That's what I hoped," he said, drawing her to his side. "What did you think?"

"I thought you had a look-alike. I couldn't think at all. Confused is what I was." She felt the same way still. Confused. Addled. Unsure what it all meant.

"I wanted it to be a surprise. It was the best way I could show you that I joined the ranks."

Befuddled totally, she gaped. "What ranks?"

"The ranks of believers. I should have told you before,

Lucy, but when I heard you were coming to the play, it seemed so right. I'd replaced Hans in the crowd scenes a couple weeks earlier, you know, the fellow who broke his leg. I couldn't resist telling you this way."

He raised his hand and caressed her hair, then brushed strands from her cheek. "But I'm sorry that I let you think I was the same old Ron who needled you for your beliefs."

"But. . .when?" Lucy asked, her heartbeat thundering in her temple. "What happened? What made the difference?"

He gazed at her in silence, cupping her chin in his hand and running his finger along the edge of her gaping mouth. "It was you, Red. You made the difference."

Unmindful of her surroundings, as reality settled in, Lucy wrapped her arms around his neck and buried her face in his chest. Tears of joy spilled downward, wetting his shirt and forming rivulets on her cheeks.

When she gained control, Ron wiped her tears with his handkerchief and, catching his arm around her waist, led her across the street.

As he walked her back to the town center, Lucy listened while he told her the story of how her faith and witness had eventually changed his life.

When they wandered into a small café for a soda, Lucy caved onto the chair, filled with wonder.

"Today's been like a miracle," she said, "almost as if all my prayers have come true. I saw the passion play, I know that Oma is in good health, and now, this."

Ron lifted her hand to his mouth and kissed each of her fingers. His gentle lips pressing against her hand sent her heart floating higher than the peaks that surrounded the village.

"I knew you'd be happy, Red. I don't know if I ever stopped loving you, and I'd hoped to find you again, once I returned to the States and had my business in order. I guess God moved the timetable up a little."

Holding back her tears, Lucy nodded, knowing that everything was in God's time, except she didn't always have the patience to wait.

Now, they had so much to discuss and Lucy's careening mind felt on overload. "I suppose we need to talk. I mean, *really* talk."

He nodded, her hand still caught in his grasp.

"Are you working tonight?" she asked. "Maybe, we—"

"I'm free," he said. "I'd planned to come over anyway because I want to check the roof before we decide anything about Henri."

"The roof?"

"The roof Henri said needed repairs. I know good roofing when I see it. We need to check it before accusing Henri of stealing from your grandmother."

"But how—"

He pressed his index finger against her lips. "I'm in charge, remember? You let me handle this. Then we'll talk about what to do afterward, okay?"

She nodded, feeling loved and protected. . .but also concerned.

With the summer sun still bright in the sky, Ron headed to Lucy's after dinner. As he pushed open the gate, he studied the slate roof of the tall house. From a distance, the tiles looked secure and unbroken, but he couldn't judge from so many feet below. He wondered if Lucy's grandmother owned a ladder.

His spirit had lifted since he talked to Lucy after the performance. Keeping his Christianity a secret had been difficult and probably stupid. He and Lucy had been struggling already with their feelings, and his additional charade had stirred up some unpleasant and unnecessary emotions. Today they could begin fresh, knowing where each stood and opening their hearts to what might be.

Lucy appeared at the door as he approached. Her face glowed, and for the first time he read a look in her eyes that he hoped was love. Longing skittered through him, wishing she had more time in Germany now that they'd talked. Correction, *he'd* talked. Tonight he hoped to hear the same from Lucy.

"Grandma's next door seeing the neighbor's new baby," Lucy said, stepping aside for him to enter.

"Then we're alone." Ron moved out of her way so she could close the door.

She nodded, her expression appearing shy and anxious.

"Let's take advantage of the situation," he said, sliding his arm around her waist and drawing her closer.

Her eyes appeared weighted and dreamy, shifting Ron's pulse into passing gear. The muscles tightened in his chest as he lowered his mouth to hers. With no resistance, Lucy raised herself on tiptoes to meet him.

Tenderly, lips to lips, Ron savored the feeling of Lucy's body in his arms and perceived the pounding of her heart against his. Lingering, he tasted cinnamon or some fragrant spice that warmed him and cloaked him with a comfortable feeling.

Lucy wobbled in his arms, her ankles seeming to give way to her tiptoe stance. He released his hold as she lowered to her heels. Then gliding his hand along her shoulder and up her neck, he caressed her flushed, contented face. Shyly, she leaned her cheek against his chest and nestled into his eager arms.

Ron whispered a silent prayer, thanking God for moving the timetable forward, for bringing Lucy to Germany and to the carving shop. God's hand had surely planned their meeting.

With a sound from the kitchen, Ron's comfort faded.

"Oma's back," Lucy said, stepping away and moving into the living room.

Knowing he had to talk fast, Ron caught Lucy's hand. "Do you think your grandmother has a ladder?"

Lucy shrugged. "For the roof?"

He nodded.

"I don't think she has one, but if I ask, she'll want to know why."

"Don't bother asking her then," he said. "Let me think of something."

"Are you sure?"

He nodded again, and Lucy left the room, heading toward the kitchen.

Pondering what to do, he struggled with his need to investigate the roofing tiles. If Henri was up to something, Ron needed to find out now. He closed his eyes, envisioning the shape of the three-story house and the upper dormers. His solution. Maybe.

He turned toward the kitchen as Lucy came through the doorway. "Oma wants to know if you'd like some coffee and sweets."

"Sure," he said, narrowing the distance between them and continuing in a muted voice. "But before we do, is there a way to get up to the top floor?"

"Top floor? The stairway in the entrance. But people live up there." She frowned, folding her arms over her chest. "We can't go into their apartment."

"But the upper-story windows are dormers. I can climb out to the roof that way."

"Maybe you could, but you can't. I won't let you."

"Red, listen to reason. I have to check." He ran his fingers through his hair. "Are all the upper windows inside the apartment? Is there a hallway?"

Her face relaxed. "There's one at the top of the stairs. I ran a rent receipt up there for Oma last week."

"That's all I needed to hear."

He threw his arm around her shoulder and kissed the top of her head. "You go tell Oma I'd love coffee, and I'll run upstairs."

Before she could protest, he turned away and hurried out to the enclosed vestibule. He took the stairs two at a time, passing the first landing, then reached the top floor. As Lucy said, he found one dormer in the hallway. He tackled the window, investigating the unusual hinge system. He pulled the window pins, and to his surprise the whole window swung open like a doorway.

He leaned outside and caught his breath at the steep incline of the roof and the slick appearance of the slate. At the base of the window, the roof lay flat. Grateful, he stepped outside and edged his way around the dormer. Beyond, the roof headed dramatically upward, but he couldn't stop now. He needed to see all the tiles.

He scanned the ones nearby, seeing no cracks or breaks. Then, Ron took a deep breath and lifted his weight upward, digging his fingers into the crevices of the slates for leverage. The speculation of looking down sent his stomach reeling. He aimed his eyes forward, moving slowly but surely to the peak.

"Ron!"

Lucy's voice reverberated behind him, but he couldn't turn around.

"Hold on," he called.

"Please, come back. This is foolish."

But Ron had neared the top and wasn't stopping now. A sense of relief washed over him when he straddled the peak, scooted along the top edge, and gazed down the other side of tiles. They looked perfect. No chips. No cracks that he could see. Nothing that indicated a whole new roof. The price Frau Stein had been quoted for repairs sounded like a full roof to Ron.

With the needed data, he swung around and his heart rose in his throat. Climbing up had been difficult. Climbing down seemed impossible.

Lucy stood outside the window on the flatter surface, clinging to the dormer, panic growing on her face. "You're going to fall," she yelled. "Why did you do this?"

He leaned as far back as he could, edging on the seat of his pants while clinging to the minute crevices between the slate tiles. He didn't try to answer Lucy, needing every ounce of breath and energy to work his way to the dormer window.

Lucy extended her hand toward him, and he kept his focus on her, praying that God would get him back to solid ground. When success seemed to be his, a gruff voice bellowed from down below.

Lucy swung around, teetered, then grabbed at the dormer eave. "It's Henri," she said, panic in her voice.

"Wave," Ron said. "Just wave like you're having fun."

"Fun?"

But instead of arguing, she gave Henri a silly wave and worked her way back to the window.

With Henri's booming voice no longer roaring from the ground, Ron knew the man was hotfooting it up the stairs. He'd tried not to lie since he'd become a Christian, but his mind flew, concocting a logical reason why he'd be crawling around on the roof—any reason except the truth.

Lucy's gasp sounded from inside the house as Ron's feet hit the flat area, and he swung into the room through the dormer window. From the top of the stairs, Henri glared at them.

His first words tumbled out in German until he caught himself. "What you are doing?" he asked, his voice wavering with anger.

Lucy released a bevy of sounds, none that made sense.

"A cat," Ron said, peering into the man's eyes. "Someone's cat was stranded up there."

"Then where is this cat?" Henri asked, staring at Ron's and Lucy's empty arms.

"He jumped," Ron said, turning back to fasten the window.

"What are you saying?"

Turning away from the window, Ron peered into Henri's glowering face. Instead of arguing, he shouldered past the angry man and headed down the stairs. "Cats have nine lives," he said over his shoulder. "He jumped."

As Ron tore down the steps, footsteps followed behind him, Lucy's quieter ones and the *clomp-clomp* of Henri's boots.

On the second landing, Henri caught up with him. "You are foolish to break your neck for a cat," Henri said. "You're foolish."

Ron nodded in agreement. "I know, but I didn't think about it before it was too late."

This time, Henri pushed past him and stomped to the ground floor.

"You lied," Lucy said, catching his arm. "Why did you do that?"

Ron pressed his mouth close to her ear. "Should I tell him the truth? We're on the roof seeing if you're trying to swindle Lucy's grandmother."

She dropped her hand from his sleeve. "Well, no. . .but."

"But what?"

"I hope God understands, that's all." She shook her head then lifted her curious eyes. "So does the roof need repair?"

Ron's heart sank with his answer. "Not in my opinion, but we should suggest that Oma get a second estimate."

Lucy's face shriveled. "She trusts him, Ron. I don't think she will."

Chapter 8

Lucy lay in bed and reviewed the past evening, realizing things didn't go at all the way she'd hoped. She'd expected Ron to sit with her and really talk about things that mattered. Instead, he'd nearly fallen off the roof, and they'd spent another half hour sipping coffee and watching Henri glower at them with comments to her grandmother about their foolishness. A disaster.

Ron made an early departure, and now Lucy had no idea what he planned to do about the roofing situation and whether or not she should say anything to her grandmother.

With a sigh, she pushed the huge feather comforter from her legs and sat up. Another couple weeks and she'd be home. The reality twisted inside her. The old saying, "Home is where the heart is," was no longer true for Lucy. Her heart was here with Ron.

While she dressed, her mind raced, deciding what she could say to her grandmother. As Lucy approached the kitchen, the aroma of fresh bread beckoned her. Engrossed in her needlework, Oma sat at the hardwood table with a crock of butter and the evidence of golden brown crumbs sprinkled in front of her.

"You baked," Lucy said, kissing the older woman on the cheek.

"Ja, ist gut," she said, reverting to her German.

Lucy plucked a warm *Brotchen* from the baking sheet, grabbed a plate, and slid onto the chair. "You must feel better, Oma."

Gretchen's face crinkled in a smile. "I do."

Lucy bent over her food, saying a blessing, then tearing the crusty roll and covering the piece with the creamy butter. But as she chewed, a knot rose in her chest, thinking of the conversation that she'd organized in her mind.

When she swallowed, the food formed a lump in her throat. "Oma?"

Her grandmother looked up from her stitch.

"What are you having done with the roof tiles?"

Gretchen shrugged. "Henri knows." She glanced down again, then inched her eyes upward. "Why you ask?"

Refraining from pressing her hand against her anxious heart, Lucy forged ahead. "Well, when we. . .when Ron was on the roof after the cat. . ." She saw her grandmother's jaw tense as if she questioned Lucy's explanation. "I looked around and didn't see any broken tiles. In my opinion, the roof looked in good condition."

"You are a roofer?"

Lucy sighed and shook her head. "No, Oma, but I have eyes. I think you should get another estimate, just to make sure. You're spending too much money on the roof."

"Ach, not you should worry, child. Henri is knowing what he does. Not to trouble your pretty head, ja?"

The delicious Brotchen sank like a rock. Lucy buttoned her lips. No sense in riling Oma. After watching her grandmother's face, Lucy was sure she suspected her of having a specific reason to ask, but her grandmother had great faith in Henri and wasn't willing to question his advice. What could she do to sway Oma's thinking?

First, Lucy realized she needed to talk with Ron. Maybe he'd come up with some grand idea to solve the problem. The way Henri growled and glowered when he found them on the roof made her certain he was guilty. All they needed was a way to prove it to her grandmother.

Sitting at the carver's table, Ron's thoughts wavered from Lucy to her grandmother's roof. Nothing had gone well. He'd wanted to get things out in the open with Lucy—talk about their relationship and tell her about his tarnished past. He needed to get that off his chest. For his own self-assurance, he longed to hear Lucy admit she cared as much about him as he did her.

But it didn't happen. Instead, he'd squirmed under Henri's glare, hoping that Frau Stein wouldn't quiz them too much about their presence on the roof. He hadn't figured that Henri might come along and find him up there.

One thing he knew for certain, the roof looked fine. He wondered how many "fix up" jobs Henri had suggested to Frau Stein. How much money had she given him to make repairs that weren't needed or purchases he made that were half the price she paid him? Ron's blood curdled at the thought of swindlers conning individuals out of their income.

Ron's fondness had grown for Lucy's grandmother. Despite her recent illness, she was an agile lady with a kindly smile, a generous heart, and loads of love for Lucy. He'd never had a sense of deep family ties with his own parents. Certainly, he cared about their welfare, but that was it. Maybe loving God made familial love grow more deeply. With the assurance of heaven, a lasting and binding relationship was promised. Love in Christ nourished family love with healthier roots.

Henri. The man's piercing eyes rose again in his mind. What could Ron do? After nearly a year in Germany, he was liked and trusted. Taking advantage of the situation, he'd casually asked coworkers and other townspeople about Henri Wolfe. No one seemed to know of him. Nothing good or bad. Nothing at all.

Pulling himself from his brooding, Ron eyed his surroundings. The afternoon had been quiet. Most tourists were at the play, and the shop would grow busier later in the day. One customer, though, had caught Ron's attention.

For some time, the attractive, middle-aged woman had been talking with the store clerk. He'd watched the stranger's gaze drift toward him, then back to the shopkeeper. He pushed a pleasant expression to his face, figuring the woman was about to come over and watch him carve. Then he'd have to struggle with his minimal German to answer her questions.

She stepped forward, and Ron knew he was correct, but instead of coming alone, the shopkeeper followed her.

"Ron," the clerk said, "this woman is Frau Oelster. She was telling me something about her mother that might interest you."

With his curiosity aroused, Ron dropped his carving tool and rose, introducing himself to the woman. "You spoke of your mother?" he said, wondering what this had to do with him.

The clerk spoke first. "You asked awhile ago about a certain handyman, and Frau Oelster was telling me about one her mother employed until she died."

Until she died. His interest piqued. Yet, he reined in his hopeful thoughts, not wanting to be disappointed. "Your mother died recently. I'm sorry," he said.

She spoke to him in clear, polished English. "My mother was Helga Rahm."

He flinched hearing the name. This was the coincidence he'd considered impossible. "I've heard of your mother from her friend, Frau Stein."

"Yes, the saleslady told me," she said, motioning to the clerk who had stepped away to help a customer.

"I live away from Oberammergau, and a couple of years ago, my mother reported how happy she was to find such a helpful handyman. He cleaned the flowerbeds, washed windows, and soon assisted inside and out with repairs. Little by little, he became what I would call her advisor. She trusted him."

Filled with anxiety, Ron nodded, hearing the familiar story.

"The sad thing was. . .so did we," the woman said. "I met him once, and he brought me a lovely bouquet of flowers. I was terribly flattered."

"I understand," Ron said, releasing a ragged sigh. "I believe I know this man."

"You think he is the same?" Her eyes widened.

"Yes, he works for Frau Stein. Your mother gave him a good recommendation."

The woman raised her hand and drew her fingers along her neck to her hairline. Tension pressed on her concerned face. "We have learned he is named as an heir in my mother's will. We had no idea."

"Her will? So that's it." Ron's pulse coursed through

him. Not only was Henri extracting money for invented repair jobs, but he was worming his way into the wills of unknowing individuals. "I hadn't realized it went that far."

"I have hired someone to investigate this man," Frau Oelster said. "Could you provide information?"

Ron eagerly agreed and quickly told the woman some of his concerns regarding Henri and Frau Stein. "I'll be happy to do what I can," he told her. "I need to talk this over first with Frau Stein's granddaughter."

"I understand," she said, shaking his hand before parting. "And I do appreciate your help."

His limbs twitched with anticipation of the pursuit.

Chapter 9

Heading into the woodcarving shop, Lucy grinned, thinking of her ingenuity. She couldn't wait to tell Ron. She'd considered surprising him later that evening, but she hadn't been able to contain herself.

The shopkeeper greeted her, but she hurried past, explaining she had stopped by only to see Ron. Stepping through the archway, she hesitated, seeing him surrounded by tourists who watched while he worked at his carving. She edged closer, amazed at the intricate work he held in his hand.

Lifting his eyes to the admiring crowd, Ron spotted her, then sent his greeting with a private nod. Waiting on the fringe, she listened to the people's questions and grinned when she heard him struggle to answer in German. Most often, he admitted defeat and spoke English. Tourists visiting from the States were amazed at his ability to speak their language so well. Lucy covered her laughter.

Some observers left and others appeared, and frustration needled Lucy. Why couldn't they all fade away and give her privacy to talk with Ron? She scolded herself for her impatience. She was the intruder. Part of Ron's education was demonstrating his work to tourists.

She wandered off down the rows of art pieces, admiring the gifts and selecting a couple of small, less expensive items to take back home. *Home.* The word sent her heart on a downward spiral. She missed her family, but she'd miss Ron even more.

"Hello, Red."

Ron spoke so near that his breath tickled her neck and lifted the hairs on her arms. She pivoted toward him.

"You scared me."

"Sorry," he said. "I'm finished. Did you come to walk me home?" He slid his arm around her waist.

"Not really, but I couldn't wait to tell you what happened."

His eyebrow arched. "Don't tell me. You're not meddling in anything, are you?"

She turned her nose into the air. "No. How could you say that? I'm getting information."

He loosened his embrace and shook his head. "What information?"

Lucy eyed the customers, thinking her tale needed confidentiality. "Let's go. I'll tell you outside."

"Looking for spies?" he whispered into her ear.

Though she knew Ron had fought it, a wry smile skidded to his lips.

"Hush," she said, hightailing it ahead of him. She paid for her purchases, dropped them in her shoulder bag, and left the shop.

The sun had slipped behind a cloud, sending a cooler breeze across her bare arms. Lucy shivered.

Ron's face sank to concern. "You're shaking, Red. Are you scared about something?"

"I'm just chilly," she said.

Answering her need, he slipped his arm around her shoulders, and they headed away from the shops.

"So what did you do?" he asked.

Lucy drew in a lengthy breath. "Well, the one thing Frau Oelster wanted to know was where Henri lives."

Ron skidded to a halt. "Don't tell me you followed him?"

"No, but I think I figured out how we can learn his address."

Filled with exasperation, Ron eyed Lucy's glowing face and shook his head. If he were a violent man, he would shake the story out of her. "Lucy, just tell me what you did."

Her face sank like a disciplined child. "I thought you'd be pleased."

"I would be if you'd get on with it."

Finally motivated, she lifted her shoulders in a deep gasp of excitement. "Today, a truck pulled into Oma's driveway. And guess what it said on the. . ." She looked up at him and grimaced. "Never mind. I couldn't really read it, but from the picture, I figured it was a roofing company. So I wandered outside and asked the man if he could speak English."

"And?" Ron said, amazed at how she still dragged out a story.

"He couldn't," she said, "but his partner could. . .at least a little."

"Great." Harnessing his impatience, Ron halted his heel tapping and guided Lucy along the sidewalk as she talked. If they stood there, the sun might set before she finished her story.

"I asked the man if they were replacing the complete roof. He said they were there to do an estimate."

"An estimate? I thought—"

"Right. Henri had already gotten a check from Oma. And do you know what else. . .well, anyway, I waited for him to look at the roof, and he said they would only be doing something I couldn't understand."

Controlling his laughter, Ron looked at her out of the corner of his eye. Lucy was a bright, capable woman, but today her detective work had turned her into an excited, blathering child.

"But he showed me a large can and demonstrated how they would patch. And then he showed me a trowel and some other goop. . . . " She turned her face toward his. "So you see, Henri was lying."

"But we knew that already." With all her enthusiasm, he had been confident that she'd really found something new—something more useful than the information about the estimate. He struggled to hide his disappointment.

"Yes, but now we know for sure. I had them give me a copy of their order form, too. I thought maybe you could call the company and somehow get Henri's address. They must have it there for billing."

He skidded to a stop, this time out of pure glee. His sinking heart rose like a missile. "Now, *that's* good thinking," Ron said, giving her hair a decisive kiss. "That's what we need to know."

"Right. That's why I was so excited."

Ron wanted to hug her until he ached. His life hadn't been so filled with fun and total joy since he'd allowed Lucy to walk away from him years earlier. How could he have lived without her?

Aware of her closeness, he relished the experience and kept quiet, thinking about the information she'd given him and, even more, remembering that she would leave him in a week. He had two more months of training before he could return home. Two long, lonely months until they'd be together. Then, never again would they be apart. He would see to that.

When they reached his apartment, he invited her inside. Though she'd been there before, he felt uncomfortable having her see the small studio-type room that he'd lived in for nearly a year. He wondered if she understood his career back home could be very successful. That is, if God was willing.

Grabbing some fresh clothes, he hurried into the bathroom, showered with haste, and dressed. When he returned to the living area, Lucy lay curled up on the sofa, staring at the telephone in her lap.

"Call," she said, handing him the phone and the roofing company order form.

Looking at his watch, he guessed the office was closed, but how could he ignore Lucy's exuberance? He read the sheet and punched in the numbers. As he expected, an answering machine announced the hours and offered that he could leave a message. He didn't.

"Tomorrow, Red. They're closed."

Disappointment weighted her usual smile. She uncurled her body and placed her feet on the floor. "So now what?" she asked.

"I'm hungry. How about you?"

She agreed.

They left the apartment and headed toward a small eatery. Inside, they grabbed a fast meal of schnitzel with spaetzle. Since the evening following the passion play, Lucy had changed—warmed and drawn closer to him as if time and space had never separated them. As they ate, they talked about family and events that filled their lives during their years apart. Nothing of deep consequence. That, he hoped, would come later.

After he paid the bill, Ron grasped her hand, and they walked through a quieting town toward the rising mountains. When they came to a park, they headed into its depths and, settling on the sun-warmed grass, propped their backs against a large oak.

Without speaking, Lucy studied Ron's thoughtful face. Tonight, she knew it was her turn to share her feelings as he had done many days earlier. Ron slipped his hand through hers, nestling it between them, and they sat in silence, watching the sun spread its colors across the mountaintops like a watercolor wash of orange, yellow, and lilac running together and spilling down the mountainside.

A deep sigh rattled from her, and Ron's head swiveled. "Something wrong?" he asked.

"No. Things are wonderful. . .except the inevitable. I leave in another week."

"I know," he said. "I have been trying not to think about it."

Releasing her fingers, he shifted his body and slid his hand around her shoulders, drawing her closer to him. The fading sun spread its golden glow across Ron's face, and though it withdrew its warmth, Ron's arm sent a new flame running through her veins, warming her body and heart.

Thinking back to the rainy day that seemed so long ago, Lucy basked in God's guidance. He'd led her to Ron as surely as He'd given her life.

"Why so quiet?" Ron asked, resting his cheek against her hair.

"Thinking about that first day I saw you. I nearly backed up and ran away. But I couldn't. The feelings I'd pushed away sprung at me like a rattler. I was bitten."

"I hope it wasn't a bad bite," he said, joining her silliness.

"No, but emotions flooded over me like a diamond-back's poison, only the feeling was sweet as honey—at least for a while."

"Only awhile?"

She looked into his toying eyes. "You know why I walked away when we were in college. You had a vagabond spirit that I didn't understand, and I had a God you didn't understand. It made a lasting relationship impossible."

"I know, and you were right. I might never have found salvation if you hadn't left." He took his free hand and rubbed the cooling flesh of her arm.

"And there you were that day," she continued, "and I ran toward you even as I wondered if I should head in the opposite direction. Then when I left the shop, I realized I had no choice. It was much better to see you again than never to have seen you at all."

He caught her chin between his thumb and finger and eased her face toward his. "For years, you were mine only in dreams. It's so much better to see you in person."

As his lips lowered to hers, Lucy closed her eyes. She breathed in the scent of summer grass, the aroma of rich dark loam, and the fragrance of Ron's musky, beguiling aftershave. She inched open her lids and gazed at his golden lowered lashes, his eyes hidden.

Releasing the kiss, Ron eased back, caressing her

face with his gaze. "I love you, Lucy. Always have and always will."

She nodded. "I've waited for you, too. I pushed my feelings so deep inside and yet they rose stronger than I could have imagined. I'm glad I waited."

Sadness washed across his face, and she faltered, wanting to ask him what was wrong. Yet, maybe she knew. They'd wasted so many years. "I guess our time apart served a good purpose. Like you said."

He nodded. "I'd have stuck to my stubborn denial, Lucy. It took loneliness and searching to make me understand that it's the love God placed in my heart that makes me whole. . .and you'll make me complete."

Tears pooled along her lashes and escaped in faint rivulets down her cheeks. She loved him, and God had known it all along.

Chapter 10

Lucy tucked her trembling hands into her jeans pockets and headed for the kitchen. The time had come to help her grandmother face reality about Henri Wolfe. She couldn't sit back any longer and pretend that the man was honest and good. He was like the wolf at Oma's door, stealing her security and her trust in people.

Stepping through the doorway, she avoided her grandmother's eyes and poured her morning coffee. When she swung around, her grandmother had placed her needlework on the table. Though her eyes focused on the cloth, Lucy sensed she was in thought.

Lucy set her cup on the table and slid into the chair. "Is something wrong, Oma?"

The older woman lifted her head, her eyes glazed with lack of sleep. "Nothing an old woman cannot make right."

Confused by her grandmother's words, Lucy leaned forward on her elbow and rested her palm on her grandmother's still hand. "Are you feeling ill?"

Gretchen lifted her fist and pressed it against her chest. "Not my body, Liebchen. Only my heart."

Struggling with her grandmother's meaning, Lucy drew back, guilt needling her. Had her grandmother learned they'd been investigating Henri? Fearing she'd hurt her grandmother's pride, Lucy knew she had to be honest. "Oma, are you upset about Henri?"

Her grandmother's head shot upward. "What?"

"You must have realized that Ron and I began to doubt Henri's honesty. I'm sorry, Oma, but it was necessary. I'm afraid you've been paying good money for nothing."

Gretchen nodded her head. "Ja, I know this, Lucy."

"You know? I don't understand. If you knew, then why did you—"

"You and Ron did not trust Henri. I think, maybe for good reasons. I look again at checks I wrote and make telephone calls. Herr Wolfe is not honest man. . .and I am a fool." Her voice faded as she lowered her head.

"No, Oma, you are not a fool." Lucy leaped from the chair and wrapped her arms around her grandmother's shoulders. "We all do foolish things at times. Christians tend to trust people. How do you know that Henri is dishonest?"

"Worse," her grandmother said. "The Bible says 'the love of money is the root of all evil.' Herr Wolfe is evil."

Lucy didn't know what to say, recalling her own foolishness. "You weren't alone, Oma. Remember how he flattered me with flowers and gifts? I was as deceived as you were."

Lucy rested her cheek against her grandmother's head, her own sorrow pooling in her eyes. "So what will you do now?" she asked finally.

"I must tell the police, I think. Ja?"

With her spirit lifting, Lucy slid back into her chair and told her grandmother all she'd learned about Henri. She explained how Ron had gotten Henri's address yesterday and turned it over to Frau Oelster, whose lawyer would proceed with a lawsuit.

"I hope you can get some of your money back," Lucy said. "I wish we'd realized earlier."

This time, Gretchen reached across to her grand-daughter and patted her arm. "No worry, Liebchen. When I saw Henri's anger with Ron on the roof, I think he is too angry. Later, I tell him I would not do repairs now. He returned the money. . .except for some. He said it was payment for canceling."

Lucy's heart lifted. "You knew then, Oma? See, you're no fool! You're a wise woman."

"Ja," Gretchen said, a faint grin curving her pale lips. "I am no dummy. . .is that how you say?"

Lucy laughed. "That's exactly how we say it, Oma."

A new sense of well-being tumbled through Ron's body. So many things had happened that made his life right and good. He'd heard from Frau Oelster, and she'd reported that they had enough evidence to take Henri Wolfe to court. When he'd learned that Frau Stein had realized Henri's con game before Lucy told her, he was doubly pleased. Now Lucy could return to the States feeling confident that her grandmother would be all right.

And topping his list, Lucy loved him. He knew they needed time. He wouldn't rush things. When he returned home, they would wait awhile. . .but not too long, he prayed, to get married.

He patted his shirt pocket to make sure he had Lucy's gift. Reviewing the elaborate plans, he shook his head at his presumptuousness. He'd not ask her to marry him yet. But he would. . .and he prayed she'd accept.

A dark reality shrouded his happiness. Before proceeding any further, he had to tell her about his past. He prayed she would forgive him. Still, her words flew into his mind like a neon sign on a black night. *I'm glad I waited.* Knowing Lucy, he was certain she was chaste. He lowered his head, wishing he'd "waited" as she had done. After he became a Christian, he followed the Bible's command about chastity, but before. . . His sin covered him in shame.

As he approached the three-story house, he looked upward toward the roof and grinned, picturing himself perched precariously on the rooftop. He thanked God that he and Lucy had meddled in her grandmother's business, presuming it had hastened Frau Stein's awareness of Henri's dishonesty.

Swinging through the gate, he dashed up the steps and punched the bell. Lucy's voice sailed through the closed door. Without waiting, he pulled it open. Inside the foyer, she waited for him.

Her welcoming smile filled him with happiness. He opened his arms, and without hesitation, she flew into his embrace, her lips seeking his. When they eased back, she beckoned him into the living room and drew him to the sofa.

Plopping at his side, she nestled into the crook of his arm. "Will you miss me?" she asked.

His heart slammed into his shoes. Tomorrow she would leave Germany. "You know I will." His mission rose in his mind, and Ron listened for the sounds of her grandmother. Hearing nothing, he asked, "Where's Oma?"

"Next door, visiting. She had me buy a gift for the baby's christening at the church."

Drawing in a ragged breath, Ron straightened and turned toward her. He had to tell her now while they were alone, but the words caught in his throat.

With her expression shifting to confusion, Lucy pulled herself forward and caught his arm. "What's wrong?"

"We need to talk while your grandmother's gone," was all he could choke out.

"What is it?"

Her lovely face twisted with apprehension, and Ron chastised himself for his lack of faith. "You know I love you, Red, but I need to confess something."

She didn't speak. Her gaze riveted to his.

"When you said that you waited for me, I think you were saying that you've been chaste. . .that you haven't—"

"Yes," she said, stopping his faltering words, "but you know, I wasn't just waiting for you, Ron. I was waiting for the right man, the man that the Lord directed me to love and marry. You were always there, hovering in my mind. . . but when I said I waited—"

"But I didn't wait, Lucy." The words raced to his tongue and he sent them out before he swallowed them for the second time. "I wish I had, but I can't lie to you."

Her face fell.

"It happened before I accepted Jesus, but I still feel sinful."

She clasped her hands around his knotted fists, and her look penetrated to his soul. "When you became a Christian, you were already forgiven, Ron."

He lowered his gaze, struggling with the sadness that washed over him.

"Please, look at me," Lucy said. "We all do sinful, foolish things. You aren't alone. But we trust that in our repentance, God forgives us."

He lifted his head. "But what about *your* forgiveness?"

A sweet smile rose to her lips. "There's nothing to forgive. That's the past, and we can't live there. We live in the present. . .and in *my* present, I love you no matter what."

Healing warmth traveled through him, and he wrapped her in his arms, holding her to his chest and feeling her heart thunder against his own. "I love you, Lucy Blake," he whispered into her hair, "and I want you to be my wife."

Be my wife. He hadn't meant to ask her yet. Not right after his confession. She eased her head back, and he looked into her loving, tender face. They needed time to get to know each other again, but God had brought them together and he knew she trusted the Lord.

"I accept your offer. . .with all my heart."

His distress faded, and a glow warmed his face. Without a word, he dug into his shirt pocket and pulled out a piece of tissue paper. With the other hand, he opened her fingers and dropped the paper into her palm.

She lifted the wrapping, unfolding the edges, and drew out a tiny hand-carved angel.

"It's beautiful. Did you—"

He nodded before she could finish.

"So delicate and fragile," she said, admiring the intricate details and muted colors.

"It's your guardian angel, Red. Something to keep with you when you're home and I'm still here."

"It's so beautiful. You know I'll cherish it." She brushed his lips with hers. "God will keep us both safe. I know He will."

Epilogue

Lucy's knees trembled as she struggled to concentrate on the final prayer. She asked God to forgive her. All brides are nervous and preoccupied on their wedding day.

Her hand clutched Ron's strong arm, and she felt his muscles twitch, revealing his own anxiety. Like a jittery bird, her heart rose and dipped in her chest each time she thought of all that had happened so many months ago.

Meeting Ron in Germany, waiting for him to return home, courting her as he began his new business, too much to keep straight in her addled mind. Today, earlier, as she waited to march down the aisle, her gaze had traveled to her handsome groom. With admiration, her heart delighted in his tall stature, his broad shoulders ready to protect her from harm, and his tender gaze caressing her with the deepest love.

His face glowed as she approached, and she could almost read his mind. She felt beautiful in her satin and lacy gown like a fairy-tale princess who had met her prince in a storybook land. In her hand, along with her lavish bouquet, she clutched a small satin bag, the gift sent from Oma.

The prayer's "amen" tugged her back to the present,

and she focused in time to hear the clergy's introduction of "Mr. and Mrs. Woodson." Ron leaned down with a fleeting kiss as the guests' applause rose in her ears.

They turned to face the congregation, and Lucy tucked her arm in Ron's, his fingers wrapped lovingly around her hand, and they returned down the aisle, ready to begin their new life together.

In the receiving line, while they waited for the ushers to guide the guests forward, Lucy slid open the strings of her satin bag and drew out its contents.

Ron looked at her hand and smiled. "Nice touch," he said, gazing at the tiny angel in her palm that he'd carved for her months earlier.

"If you remember, an angel brought us together. I figured this one ought to be at our wedding."

Ron's heart lifted like the music that filled the church rafters. He'd asked himself so often how God could take a sinner and turn him around, then shower him with blessings.

His finite brain couldn't comprehend, but he knew it was true. He'd been stubborn like a wandering sheep, and the Good Shepherd had brought him to the fold. "I know My own and My own know Me." God's message sounded in his head.

He gazed down at his petite, redheaded wife, thanking God for so many things, but today, he praised the Lord for his beautiful, cherished bride.

GAIL GAYMER MARTIN

Gail loves nothing more than to write, talk, and sing—especially if it's about her Lord. Beginning her career as a freelance writer, she has hundreds of articles and stories in religious periodicals, many anthology devotionals, and numerous church resource books, but since 1998, she has been blessed as a multi-published romance author with nearly ten contracted novels. "If God blessed me with a 'bestseller,' I'd continue writing worship materials. It's a direct way I can share my faith with worshiping Christians." Gail has two **Heartsong Presents** novels and two novellas published with Barbour fiction. She is also a contributing editor and columnist for *The Christian Communicator*.

Besides being active in her home church, Gail is an adjunct English instructor for Davenport University, Warren campus, and maintains her professional counselor license in the state of Michigan. She is involved in a number of professional organizations and especially enjoys public speaking and presenting workshops to help new writers. Gail loves traveling, as well as singing with the Detroit Lutheran Singers. She lives in Lathrup Village with her husband Bob Martin who proofreads all her work. "I praise God for Bob and my gift of writing."

A Letter to Our Readers

Dear Readers:

In order that we might better contribute to your reading enjoyment, we would appreciate you taking a few minutes to respond to the following questions. When completed, please return to the following: Fiction Editor, Barbour Publishing, Inc., P.O. Box 719, Uhrichsville, OH 44683.

1. Did you enjoy reading *Fairy-Tale Brides*?
   ❑ Very much. I would like to see more books like this.
   ❑ Moderately—I would have enjoyed it more if _____
   _____
   _____

2. What influenced your decision to purchase this book?
   (Check those that apply.)
   ❑ Cover   ❑ Back cover copy   ❑ Title   ❑ Price
   ❑ Friends   ❑ Publicity   ❑ Other

3. Which story was your favorite?
   ❑ *A Rose for Beauty*   ❑ *Lily's Plight*
   ❑ *The Shoemaker's Daughter*   ❑ *Better to See You*

4. Please check your age range:
   ❑ Under 18   ❑ 18–24   ❑ 25–34
   ❑ 35–45   ❑ 46–55   ❑ Over 55

5. How many hours per week do you read? _____

Name _____

Occupation _____

Address _____

City _____ State _____ Zip _____

If you enjoyed

Fairy-Tale Brides

then read:

COLORADO *Wings*

*Four Inspirational Love Stories
with a Dash of Intrigue by Tracie Peterson*

*A Wing and a Prayer
Wings Like Eagles
Wings of the Dawn
A Gift of Wings*

If you enjoyed

Fairy-Tale Brides

then read:

Montana

A Legacy of Faith and Love
in Four Complete Novels by Ann Bell

Autumn Love
Contagious Love
Inspired Love
Distant Love

If you enjoyed

Fairy-Tale Brides

then read:

❧

Heart's
PROMISE

four decisions to make
a change inspire romance

Remaking Meredith by Carol Cox
Beginnings by Peggy Darty
Never Say Never by Yvonne Lehman
Letters to Timothy by Pamela Kaye Tracy

If you enjoyed

Fairy-Tale Brides

then read:

❧❧❧❧

Only You

Four Romances St. Valentine
Would Have Applauded

Interrupted Melody by Sally Laity
Reluctant Valentine by Loree A. Lough
Castaways by Debra White Smith
Masquerade by Kathleen Yapp

$\mathcal{H}$EARTSONG ❤ PRESENTS

Love Stories Are Rated G!

That's for godly, gratifying, and of course, great! If you love a thrilling love story, but don't appreciate the sordidness of some popular paperback romances, **Heartsong Presents** is for you. In fact, **Heartsong Presents** is the only inspirational romance book club, the only one featuring love stories where Christian faith is the primary ingredient in a marriage relationship.

Sign up today to receive your first set of four, never-before-published Christian romances. Send no money now; you will receive a bill with the first shipment. You may cancel at any time without obligation, and if you aren't completely satisfied with any selection, you may return the books for an immediate refund!

Imagine. . .four new romances every four weeks—two historical, two contemporary—with men and women like you who long to meet the one God has chosen as the love of their lives. . .all for the low price of $10.99 postpaid.

To join, simply complete the coupon below and mail to the address provided. **Heartsong Presents** romances are rated G for another reason: They'll arrive Godspeed!

YES! Sign me up for Hearts❤ng!

NEW MEMBERSHIPS WILL BE SHIPPED IMMEDIATELY!
Send no money now. We'll bill you only $10.99 postpaid with your first shipment of four books. Or for faster action, call toll free 1-800-847-8270.

NAME _____

ADDRESS _____

CITY _____ STATE_____ ZIP_____

MAIL TO: HEARTSONG PRESENTS, P.O. Box 719, Uhrichsville, Ohio 44683